Fated to the Dark

A Shade Dimension Novel

Haven Fox

Hope you enjoy ♡ Haven Fox xoxo

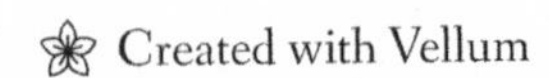
Created with Vellum

Content Warnings

Mental health is important. Please note this book contains scenes that may not be appropriate for readers under the age of 18. These themes are woven throughout the book. Please use your discretion.

- Cursing and foul language
- Violence (torture, death, descriptions of violence)
- Graphic sexual content
- Human trafficking

Chapter One

If someone had told Eva that a year ago, aliens would land on Earth and offer to move people to other planets, she would have said that they needed the psych ward, Jesus, drugs (or maybe all three). Eva could still remember the news channels reporting about messages received from alien lifeforms. She had hunched over the screen of her roommate's phone, the light flickering as it played reels from a faraway spaceship. Supposedly. They had collapsed in a fit of giggles against the back of the couch, sides heaving. Who was going to believe that? The guy looked like he was on the set of Saturday Night Live, not some kind of actual spacecraft. At least make it believable. The chair looked like a toddler's chair and the back screen was way too bright and colorful.

. . .

Also, who the hell was going to come here? Earth was tired. Water was scarce, empty lots with cracked pavement sweltered in unnatural heat and then flooded, fires raged during the summers in the west. If it were her, she'd advise the aliens to turn right around and pick some place else.

After a few months, more messages appeared on social media and news channels. The guy from the spaceship was back more often than not, but they showed others that were supposedly part of some kind of space council. Inter-Galactic something or other. Eva could honestly say that she didn't give it too much thought. Sometimes they changed out the backgrounds, a painted desert scene, an ocean scene. Daisy said they got them off sites like Pinterest or Shutterstock. That they were actually other planets. Eva couldn't disagree. The whole thing was pretty unbelievable. You got mixed responses about the topic if you talked to the average Oregonian. Aliens? Sure. Aliens? Nah, it won't happen.

But it did.

On the initial landing day, Eva and Daisy had watched with all the others gathered in the street, packed like sardines in tiny cans of oil. Her heart raced, sweat dripped down her back, and the condensation made her cocktail glass slippery. When the ship came into view, her throat had dried up, and gooseflesh sprang up along her rib cage. The excitement in the crowd died at that moment. The atmosphere, somber. (Except for Dwayne who apparently was too stupid to realize that he should be scared.) Eva knew then as the huge ships showed up in the skies that life, as she knew it, was irrevocably going to be different.

Except, it wasn't different. Overall, the last year had been pretty much the same. Eva knew it wouldn't stay that way. Call it instinct, call it a gut feeling, call it being connected to a higher power... she knew something big was going to happen.

For some reason, the end of the world meant boosted sales at work. Their bakery was filled with the smell of vanilla and sugar as Eva and Daisy took rack after rack of cookies out of the oven, they often ran out early. *End of the world* was dramatic, but people stress eating in these situations wasn't a big surprise. Prior to the landing, Eva and her best friend, Daisy, had worked at a cute little bakery together. It was the longest either of them had worked anywhere if truth be told.

. . .

When the aliens landed and offered to take Earthlings to other planets, the owner decided she'd expand her bakery into outer space and had left for a brighter future. Though lots of people had bought into the idea of leaving Earth for a different life, Eva still hadn't decided if it was a load of bullshit or not. It seemed a little too good to be true. She and Daisy would stay put on Earth until they made up their minds. They would miss the original owner, Patsy, but maybe one day they'd see her again.

The world had gone to shit. It had been headed that way for decades. If anyone said differently, they were a total liar. The surprise of the century was the fact that they were not alone in the universe. Like, *really* not alone. There were planets upon planets full of races and civilizations beyond the Milky Way. Other life forms had always been suspected, but the reality of the landing was something else entirely.

People of Earth had gotten used to a limited idea of space travel. That idea of space travel had been thrown around since billionaires first suggested that they could do a better job than NASA. Certainly, there were successes and triumphs. Earthlings had gotten off the surface of the planet and started exploring the Milky Way.

Rovers had been sent out to other planets. However, once aliens arrived from other galaxies and other areas of the universe, the concept of space expanded and the realization that we hadn't even explored our galaxy properly had set in. That said, the Milky Way was just a raindrop in the ocean now that they had a better understanding of how vast the universe actually was. We had just been traversing in a very tiny portion.

Our knowledge of life and everything that came with it (including technological advancements) was limited to just one planet and one species. Whether or not people admitted it—it was a limitation.

Earth was probably not winning any space wars, that was for sure. Not from what she and Daisy had seen so far, anyway. The spaceships that had come down had been incredible. If they were out zipping around the universe, Earth was way behind. Eva snorted to herself, just thinking about it.

The landing had been very civilized, too. Communications —video messages, an envoy, and news that were sent and verified before the ships arrived. In the end, aliens landed, and people accepted it the way they accepted the way people accept the inevitable.

People moved on. They went back to trying to scrape a living from a planet on the brink of imploding itself.

Eva and Daisy weren't exceptions. They found a catering kitchen to do what they did best—bake. So, they'd been hustling, baking, and then delivering orders in the Pearl District. So far, they'd made ends meet, but things were getting a little tight as people began realizing that the borders of their world weren't really borders at all. They were suggestions; they were the beginning. Whole worlds were out there. Even Eva, if the truth were told, thought these things. She was starting to contemplate if something bigger was out there for her.

Eva dumped her ingredients into a bowl, creaming her sugars together, the whir of the mixer blades humming while she let her brain wander.

She wondered if aliens had mixers. She hoped so. Everyone should have the pleasure of watching the process of butter whipping. Maybe she was weird.

Okay, let's be honest—she was definitely weird. It also made her wonder what sorts of sweet treats people enjoyed on other planets. What constituted desert in those far other galaxies?

"Hey." Daisy popped her head through the doorway from the storeroom, holding up a container of raisins. "You know what I'm thinking right now?" She waggled her eyebrows in that way of hers that always made Eva laugh.

"Oatmeal cookies? Pina coladas?" Eva guessed randomly and then laughed when Daisy frowned with furrowed eyebrows so close, they nearly smooshed her eyeballs. She had that expression down pat. She held up her other hand, revealing canned coconut and pineapple.

"Try again. Can you give me a better guess now?"

"Ohhhh," Eva said with a wink. "Carrot cake muffins? Hummingbird muffins?"

"Now you're on the right track. Geez, Pina coladas. I wish," Daisy said with a laugh. "Pina Coladas and Maui are what I wish for every day." She sighed.

"And the beach." Daisy gave her head a shake. Maui was as far away as Pluto if they were being honest. Resources were scarce on Earth for the last years. Flights to places like Maui and the thoughts of beach vacations had never been something they indulged in.

"Anyway, we have just enough ingredients left from that last batch, I think... and time to finish the batter and pop them in the oven." Eva gave a thumbs up, so Daisy went back to the storeroom to fetch ingredients. They had been baking since before the sun came up and were almost finished. Customers expected fresh inventory when they delivered, and Eva and Daisy didn't like to disappoint. Their makeshift bakery had to be rented by the hour since it was a catering kitchen, so they really had to make the best use of their time. Glancing at the windows, Eva realized the metal roller shades were still down, so barely any light filtered around the edges through the glass.

They bustled around the kitchen to make the last few batches of goodies. The sweet, sugary aromas filled their noses as they worked. Eva mixed a large batch of cookie dough while Daisy puttered around with a bowl of cake batter. Every now and then, one would stop to check on the ovens, making sure that everything was baking evenly, and nothing was getting too brown.

Eva set out the last row of cookies in the case onto cooling racks. Death By Chocolate—chocolate cookies with chocolate chips on top. Add in dried sour cherries—delicious. They were her absolute favorites. Even now, Eva struggled not to plop one in her mouth while they were fresh and warm.

"Did you save me one?" Daisy asked as she pulled the muffin pans out. She sent Eva a narrow-eyed glance.

"Bitch, please." Eva gave her long chestnut ponytail a toss and then gave Daisy a swat on the ass with her dish towel for good measure as she walked by. "I saved you two."

Eva took care of her bestie. No way would she risk her wrath if she didn't set aside a few of the best cookies. They rarely had all the necessary ingredients for the recipe, and they were the first cookies to go when customers found out they'd made them. Ingredients weren't cheap either. They never took shortcuts with their food or each other. No reason to live life with half-measures. Supply chain difficulties were a huge issue for everyone, especially when someone was trying to keep a booming business. They did the best they could, sourcing a lot of their ingredients locally. But with more and more people going off-planet, it was getting harder.

Daisy and Eva spent the next twenty minutes grating carrots and mixing up muffin batter. Once Eva finished with the carrots, she went to get spices from the cupboard, fondling the cinnamon.

“Look, Daisy,” Eva said with a jaunty smile as she held up the plastic industrial spice bottle.

“Don’t sniff the cinnamon, Eva.” Daisy scowled at her, but there was total laughter in her voice. Eva had a well-known “enthusiasm” for cinnamon. She had been caught more than once hovering over the cinnamon bottle.

Eva moaned as she removed the lid. “I’m not.”

“Stop making sex sounds.” Daisy gave an exaggerated eye roll as she snatched the bottle from her. “You’re not to be trusted with this,” she gave her a smile. "Last time, Mrs. Wilson said you put so much in them you burned her tongue."

"Whatever. They were good." Eva's laugh sparkled around the shop. Daisy side-eyed her. Eva was magic. There was no denying it, cinnamon problem or not. Some people were just at the front of the line when God handed out blessings. Daisy didn't hold any grudges though. Eva was the total package, beautiful, talented, and kind. You couldn't help but love her—although she was a little quirky.

"SUUURREEE... it was too much, girlie. Here, stir and get those in the oven. I'm going to box orders." Daisy handed her the bowl. It was a sad, small batch of mix—but they'd have no problem selling them. Eva took the bowl and immediately hunted around for the cinnamon.

"Looking for this?" Daisy was at the back counter getting their boxes, holding the cinnamon triumphantly in one hand. "I know you too well," she said and waggled a finger at her friend. "That mix has plenty of cinnamon. It's fine. Pour!" she directed.

. . .

Eva grumped a little but had to admire how her friend outmaneuvered her. The two worked efficiently to load their homemade creations onto the cart and wrap them securely in plastic bags before packing them into boxes or containers according to customer orders. She had just gotten the muffins out of the oven as Daisy boxed up the first few preorders. They had a lot of standing orders. Some were small, like Mrs. Wilson at the vintage shop, with one dozen cookies twice a week. Some were a little bigger, like the cafe a few blocks over that wanted several dozen muffins every day. They couldn't keep them in stock. On the days when they had extra, they sold to the landing ships at the outpost. For some reason, their new visitors were crazy about baked goods, but then again, who didn't love baked goods?

Eva had been raised by her grandfather. She didn't remember her parents, and her grandfather never spoke of them. They moved from place to place with no stable home until he died unexpectedly when she was fourteen. She'd scraped by for a long time until she'd gotten the job with Patsy at the bakery when she finally landed in Portland. Patsy had really helped her develop a sense of self. She hadn't been proud of anything until she learned to bake. When she met Daisy a few years ago, it had been natural to circle her into the life she'd built for herself at the bakery. They needed help in the kitchen, and Eva needed a friend. Now that Patsy had moved off-planet, Eva was extra glad she had Daisy, or she would be all alone.

It wasn't long before Eva and Daisy had their orders completely boxed and ready to go. They took a lot of pride in their products and learned a lot about packaging. They loaded their goods into the back of their delivery van, which they had charged up the previous night. Bless Patsy for leaving it for them. The electric van was an absolute must these days. It made it so they could continue their deliveries and pay their rent. But lately, charging station space had become a larger expense.

Mrs. Wilson was just around the corner. It was Daisy's turn to drive. They took turns since driving and hanging in the van was a bit of a drag. It was a lot more fun to go in and chat with the customers. Although Eva kind of enjoyed people-watching, she wasn't too sad when it was her turn to drive.

Mrs. Wilson's shop was one of Eva's favorites in a lot of ways. She was a careful curator and recycler of all things. Mainly, she focused on clothing and jewelry, finding unique pieces, pairing them together, and up-selling them. Granted, the new move off-planet gave her an extra opportunity since most folks couldn't take all their things with them. There was a strict cap on luggage.

The shop smelled distinctly of incense and Patchouli. There were richly decorated scarfs, sunlight gleaming off carved frames on the walls filled with random paintings and prints. Eva never knew where to look first, but there was always something new to see. Mrs. Wilson was busy at the counter with a customer, so Eva waited patiently, letting her eyes rest on a new display with a bird cage surrounded by raven feathers and a broken doll's head. It was perfectly creepy, and Eva loved it.

"I have no intention of leaving," Mrs. Wilson told her customer as she bagged up a pair of jeans. The customer scoffed, which Mrs. Wilson obviously interpreted correctly because she continued. "Really. These people are being jettisoned off to God only knows where. Could be anywhere in space." Mrs. Wilson then addressed Eva. "You aren't thinking of going, are you? Not buying into the nonsense, right?"

Eva slid Mrs. Wilson's order onto the far corner of the counter, away from any clothes. "I don't think so, Mrs. Wilson. Daisy and I are still feeling things out." Her face was blank, and she kept her smile in place. She really liked Mrs. Wilson, but she had learned the hard way that Mrs. Wilson wasn't a big fan of the aliens or the landing. She had a big sign in the window that said they weren't allowed. Eva wasn't sure of a few of the finer points, but she was thought that was discriminatory. She was pretty sure Mrs. Wilson couldn't do much about it if they wanted to come in the shop, not that Eva ever saw any of the aliens out and about now that she thought about it.

"Glad to hear you are being cautious," Mrs. Wilson said with a sage nod. She opened her register, took out the exact amount for her order, and handed it to Eva. Eva gave her a wave as she left, tossing a smile at the customer. "Have a good day." Eva stopped in her tracks. She felt the oddest presence hovering on the edges. The shape of a man formed and unformed there on the sidewalk.

"Hello?" He gave no indication that he heard, but his eyes were on her, searching. He was gorgeous—straight out of her naughtiest fantasies. Shoulder-length dark hair, eyes that were the color of warmed honey, tall and muscular. There was something other-worldly about his energy, dark and powerful. Small shadows danced along at his feet, the smokey and sinuous ribbons wrapped up his calves. They were hard to see properly, but they were there. Instead of being afraid, Eva wanted to step closer. She locked eyes on the form as he seemed to fade in and out. Eva wasn't sure what kind of aliens there were. Maybe he was one of them? She felt inexplicably drawn to this mysterious figure, Eva couldn't quite explain why or how, but something inside her strangely recognized him.

"Where are you, Fated?" The voice was dark and silky— she had unknowingly taken a step forward. She felt the bolt of fear, but she didn't mistake the attraction that slithered down her spine and straight to her core.

He scowled a little at her and then ... evaporated. Particles vanished into the air like a dream. Like he hadn't even been there.

Eva stood for a moment, wondering if it *had* been a dream. But then, a faint whisper in the air told her otherwise. It felt like an invisible force had pulled her somewhere else for the tiniest moment.

Somewhere far beyond the boundaries of space and time.

. . .

A darkness. A pool?

Eva swiveled her head around the sidewalk for a second and then moved her feet towards the van. She walked past Daisy on the sidewalk without a word, ignoring the fact that Daisy's mouth was open in surprise. Even before she fully settled into the seat, she pressed a button, so the air conditioner was blasting away. The van seemed to sag beneath her. The vinyl seats felt sticky against her thighs. She didn't want to think about how hot it would be on a summer day, trapped in this rolling tin can. She stopped a moment, trying to take a breath—think about what had just happened.

"Eva! What the hell? Did I just see a dude, maybe?" Daisy's voice was quick as she slid into the van, her palm smacked the steering wheel. "I'm officially losing it. Asking you if I saw an *invisible* guy."

"Yeah." Eva took a deep breath and shook her head to clear it. Daisy had put the boxes in the back of the van and then slid into the driver's seat after tossing the keys to the cupholder.

. . .

"What or who was that?" Daisy asked, pulling back onto the road. It wasn't an actual question. Not really. Daisy processed out loud. It was one of the things that Eva loved about her.

"I don't know." Eva shook her head again. "I don't think he could hear me."

"You spoke to it, him." Daisy turned to stare at her friend. "Shit, he looked like a sexy wet dream."

Eva groaned, "God, I know, I couldn't breathe. I literally couldn't breathe." She shook her head. She looked back at where the man had been, or where he was or possibly was. She had no idea. It was a weird encounter.

"*Alien maybe*?"

"Yeah, I think so. But there was this... pull. I felt like..." She shook her head. "Shit, that sounds stupid. I don't know. Let's get going. I'm sure it was my imagination. We have deliveries." She waved Daisy forward, chewing the edge of a finger. Daisy side-eyed her. They both saw him. It wasn't her imagination.

. . .

They had seen aliens over the last few months, but interactions weren't common. They'd always seen them from afar. She'd also never had any experience like that one. Still, that was the only explanation. Or maybe she finally had gone crazy.

Most aliens were here strictly for work or transportation of Earthlings off-planet. For these reasons, they mainly stayed at the airport where the outposts had been set up. That's where the action happened.

All communication about the aliens said there was a regulating government that kept things locked tight. Eva was sure she wasn't the only one curious about how everything worked out here with all the extra politics. It seemed way more civilized than she thought it would be.

Eva thought about the incident with the person on the sidewalk (alien?) throughout their morning deliveries and into the next few days. She hadn't mistaken her feeling of desire mixed in with the fear. Or that sense of something more—that darkness.

. . .

It wasn't until the month's end that she found out their *runner* to the outpost had been short-changing them, so she volunteered to take the baked goods herself. Only then did she acknowledge she hoped to have a chance to look around. Maybe it would enlighten her a little. Perhaps she'd see *him* again. Perhaps she'd learn a little more about the people who had come down from the stars.

Chapter Two

Callan Adiim gazed over Tiebus, the three green moons rising in the distance. Flowers bloomed across the verdant planet, their petals brightly colored in shades of vermilion, apricot, and violet. Plants twined around trees and grew in bushy clumps—their sweet scent filled the air.

Callan leaned against the balcony rail and sighed as he watched the beautiful display below him. He loved Tiebus and all its lush greenery. It was one of his favorite planets and a welcome respite from his time spent in the pools of Fate. He breathed in the fresh air, allowing a sense of peace and tranquility to wash over him.

. . .

The flowers soft perfume mingled with the fragrant herbs growing around the palace, and he smiled, closing his eyes. Everything seemed so perfect, but it was not. He was frustrated beyond reason. Days ago, he had glimpsed his Fated for the first time.

Against the cliffs near the pools of Fate, you could see just the edges of opaque clouds. It was beautiful here—almost as beautiful as the woman's eyes —his Fated. You could see many things in the pools, but he was sure that she was the one. He knew it, if only he could pinpoint her exact location. Until now his forays into the pools had only allowed him glimpses of her. He hadn't been able to narrow down an exact home world. He clenched his fists.

A sense of frustration filled him. He had tried again and again, but had been unsuccessful at seeing her again.

He sighed, listening to the soft trills of forest animals in the distance. He'd return to the palace in a moment since he had a million things to do. Callan heard the scuff of a footfall on stone behind him and the scent of his friend, technically a member of his court. He turned, waiting.

. . .

“My king.” Serix came to his side, his tone deferential, but just. Callan raised an eyebrow.

“How goes the search for your Fated?” Serix asked. Callan turned away and continued to gaze out over the beauty of Tiebus. She was out there somewhere, waiting for him to find her. He was determined to do just that.

"I've been looking for days to find her from among the stars, but I can barely see her from such a distance." He needed to change the subject. "What's this I hear about an IGC job?" He quirked an eyebrow at his friend.

He had heard that the Inter-Galactic Council would send a team to look for traffickers on one of the newly discovered planets. They'd need some help. Maybe he needed a distraction, or...

If he couldn't find her while on his home planet, he had to look elsewhere.

He also had to decide about his role with the council anyway. The council was tiresome and hiding his identity had gotten tedious. Whether to get the Shade Dimension and Tiebus involved, either officially or not needed to be decided. He had used a cover before—gone in and observed the IGC and their dealings as an anonymous mercenary for hire. Perhaps that was how he would continue. For a while.

The IGC occasionally tried to tamp down on the trafficking. As more and more species were discovered, exploitation was always a possibility. The smaller worlds became targets. The IGC just wanted to control things the way they wished to. Callan had no illusions that the Inter-Galactic Council always kept their hands clean. Trafficking was as big as ever, with no end in sight. Of course, that might beg the question .... Why would Callan wish to involve himself? Well, killing things was always up his alley. Especially if it meant killing scum like the Pavo.

Callan had no desire to get involved in intergalactic politics. The backstabbing and plotting were a waste of time.

"The IGC job is the slavers on Earth." Serix said, his voice steady. Callan knew though how Serix felt about planets with lifeforms that were fragile.

. . .

Callan nodded. "I'm going to take that IGC job. My brain could use a break I think." His gaze darted from flower to flower to tree. Even though he loved Tiebus and all its lush life, he needed to find his Fated. The soft scent of Tiebus tickled his nose.

"You're restless." Serix's voice eased away some of Callan's tension. Serix, for all his rough edges, had a way about him.

Callan flicked his wrist at Serix in acknowledgment of his words. "How can I not be? She's out there somewhere. But I don't know where. I've been using the pools, but they are difficult to navigate." His eyes scanned the distance.

"I was thinking, and..." Callan paused and glared pointedly at him, "... enjoying the quiet." He said it without heat though and sent a wave of his power to let his true form flicker over him, expanding and then settling. As King of the Shade Dimension, Callan could hold many forms, but this form— considered by his court as his true form – was perhaps his oldest.

Serix sighed with relief. "That other form freaks me out."

. . .

"Whatever." Serix was rather new to his court, as court members went. He wasn't quite as ready for some missions as a few of the others.

"I asked Sapphrius to put me on another mission," Serix said unnecessarily. Callan watched him through hooded eyes.

Serix didn't flinch away. As he stood now, the king was massive, shadowed, a true warrior of the dark, with massive horns curling from the sides of his face. Bare-chested with low slung pants, he looked at Serix with a bored expression.

"I'm aware," Callan replied easily. His second hadn't informed him that Serix wasn't coming to Earth with them on the Inter-Galactic mission, but he knew about it, anyway. This would be Callan's last mission for the IGC. It wasn't a good idea for Serix to come on the mission. Typically, they would shapeshift to the form of the population and Serix didn't like to do that. Callan didn't "hide" exactly when he did things with the council, but he didn't advertise that he was from the Shade, let alone that he was the king. They called him "The Hunter" when he worked for them—he used a muted form of his powers, weaker, and shifted into a more humanoid form. Now, he let his power curl out, settling in ebony pools around him. It felt like a release, an exhale.

"That's a good job for you there with the Jurox," Callan agreed. They didn't need a full team for the Earth job anyway.

The Earth job. He could just send one of the others —Brilius, maybe. But he had an idea that the woman he saw was an Earthling. There was a moment in the pool when her face seemed to solidify for him, along with her scent. He had only met a few Earthlings, but there was something ... Either way. He could continue to visit the pools and search at the same time. At least if he went on the IGC Earth mission, it wouldn't be a waste of time if she wasn't there. He'd eradicate a Pavo cell, stop some traffickers and get to kill something (or many somethings). All pluses in his book.

"I'm going to find her somewhere else. That's the only way." He bit the inside of his cheek. He would have his answers soon.

. . .

Callan huffed and shook his head. He supposed he'd go ahead and complete the IGC search first. Maybe he'd get lucky, and they'd find her on one of the planets they were searching.

"You'll take up the other mission for the IGC on Jurox. That's what I hear. Correct?" Callan moved to the small table and picked up a glass of Dimea. The liquor swirled in the glass, a peacock blue. Callan sipped carefully, the burn exquisite.

"Yes, exactly." Serix poured himself a drink and sat in one of the chairs.

Callan didn't mind. It was a good place for him. Jurox was a shifter planet and uniquely suited Serix. Honestly, if Serix hadn't chosen it for himself, Callan would have moved him over there anyway. Serix preferred planets that allowed less *delicate* work. Earth needed more care with its life-forms and Serix was not known for his finesse.

"What about your hunt for the Pavo?" Serix asked.

. . .

The Pavo Arcturus was their quarry in their hunt. They were slavers that often-targeted planet populations that were being moved.

Callan grinned. "I think we have a pretty good idea of where to start." He shot the rest of the drink and allowed his power to push a more Earth-like form back over him, tightening, shrinking, pulling his shadows back.

"Ugh," Serix grunted and got to his feet. "The Earthling form is so..." He waved a hand over Callan. "Delicate." He wrinkled his nose.

Callan couldn't help but laugh. Serix was from Ghetea and was anything but delicate. He wasn't gigantic, but he was basically indestructible. He also was invaluable because of his ability to shift into multiple forms. A brutal and a skilled warrior, also made him a perfect candidate for the Jurox job.

"I'm off then. I'm sure I'll see you soon. I hope you rip out their spleens." He tossed the last comment over his shoulder as he went. He actually wasn't joking, Callan thought as he walked away.

. . .

There was a commotion in the back of the ballroom as Serix moved through. Callan saw him laughing with Brilius and Paron as they passed near the arched waterfalls. Callan was happy that Serix had found his place here in the Shade. He had been worried there for a while that he wouldn't.

"So," Brilius said with a quirk to his lips as he approached the balcony's edge. "Sulking around still?" Callan knew he was only half joking.

"No," Callan grumbled. They both laughed. Brilius and Paron, like Serix, were members of his court—such as it was. The Shade was a dimension that operated like its name—in the shadows. Most planets in the dimension were uninhabitable, filled with fearsome demons and nightmares. The other handful of planets in the Shade—perfect planets—were idyllic and lovely, like Tiebus. Those planets were brooded over and guarded by his court. This is not to say that Callan didn't find all planets in the Shade special and unique. As king, his powers gave him certain rights—some he earned the hard way, with blood, violence, and nightmares of his own.

Outwardly the Shade and the IGC had an uneasy truce—for the most part. The Shade was not a dimension that accepted trade, visitors or encouraged travel. The residents of the Shade weren't prisoners. On the contrary, most of the beings that lived in the Shade fell into their own categories. Some never left out of choice, some were perhaps hiding, and some were too dangerous to leave. The Shade, overall, was not kind to outsiders. It was best that outsiders stayed away.

After a moment of silence, Brilius asked. "Are we going on this mission? To Earth?"

"Yes," Callan murmured. "After the Pavo." He felt desperate to see Earth and had long ago learned to trust his senses.

Paron slumped into a chair next to him, his lanky body nearly the color of the moons in the sky. "You're worried about finding your Fated?"

"Yes." Callan didn't want to look at Paron, though he knew that the demon's sharp, intelligent eyes were on him. He was young, compared to Callan at least, but that didn't mean he didn't know how to look at a problem from different angles. "I've waited a long time."

. . .

Paron didn't really believe in the Fated, or at least not the way the rest of the court did. There was no reason to fight with him over it. Callan believed—that was enough. Paron would follow and help him no matter what.

Callan stared at the glass in his hand. "And I should have . . . gotten over the worry and found my focus." He confessed the feeling he'd been having—this concern that he wouldn't find her.

"I wouldn't say that." Paron said.

"A distraction?" Callan looked at his friend. He shrugged. He supposed he wasn't wrong.

Paron tilted his head. "You've done it before. Joined missions for the IGC and left court. You always return, but you haven't been on planet consistently in centuries. Your people miss you." He smiled gently this time.

"I know," Callan said, but didn't add anything else. He didn't have a reply to Paron's words. He was lonely on the planet. The Shade was a beautiful place. But he was lonely. He ached for his Fated.

. . .

"How long will we be gone?" Brilius asked.

"I do not know," Callan said honestly. He had joined IGC missions before but knew they could go on for years. He had to be sure that the Pavo discovered on Earth were eliminated. The planet could not be left vulnerable.

Paron's eyes narrowed. "There are thousands of planets just like it. You know that."

"Yes," Callan said again. Paron wasn't wrong. He also wasn't wrong that there were thousands just like it. The IGC loved to intervene and manipulate its own agenda.

"You're right. However, it isn't wrong to help protect people either."

"No. It's not wrong." Paron conceded. "It's just not the Shade's job though."

. . .

"What if you go to Earth and find your Fated?" Brilius asked.

"Then I would bring her back," Callan said. His eyes narrowed at Brilius, who was grinning broadly. Brilius was the most supportive of the bunch but the biggest jokester. He never knew when he was being serious.

"What . . .?"

"The IGC doesn't like the Shade. They only accept our help for their missions. If they knew *who* was helping." Brilius barked out a laugh. "You aren't going to Earth for the IGC." He stopped his grin then and leaned forward. "You are going to find your Fated."

"I have to kill this Pavo cell first," Callan said. But he really was planning to look—to see if his gut was wrong.

"Do you know where we will start?" Brilius asked.

. . .

"I don't know." Callan sighed. "I just need to get there. The council says that the cells are on Earth. Perhaps..."

Paron and Brilius looked at him. "Perhaps Earth?" Paron asked. "You're only going to check it out as part of the mission?" He looked at him with a raised brow. His smooth skin always looked unnaturally pale—like a moon.

"Yes." Callan sighed.

"Earthlings are so small, so soft," Brilius said quietly. "Would one be suited here?"

Callan grew silent for a moment. "If she is my Fated. She will be. I will help her to be."

"*We* will help her," Brilius assured.

Earthlings were not quite as hardy as those from the Shade. Earth was considered a planet undergoing a tremendous amount of change. Their technology was advancing, but not rapidly enough. It was making the planet a dangerous target. The

IGC was doing its best to keep them from being an issue for the rest of the galaxy.

"If we are going to look for the Pavo there ..." Paron began. "Then you really should take a look... with your powers." Paron's lipid eyes went to Callan's. Paron knew Callan disliked using his power to invade people's consciousness, to use the full scope of his gift, to break people. "So that we have a place to begin." Paron finished firmly.

"I know." Callan slung back the rest of his drink, rising from his seat, the pads of his fingers pressing into the cold iron of the table as he stood. "Give me a moment." Paron nodded. If anyone understood, it was him. Paron had powers that could break minds as well.

Callan drifted toward the edge of the balcony. He would go to the pools and would search through their dreams, through their intentions. It was the best way to accomplish his task. Even though he despised this part of his power, it was necessary. What they needed was information, confirmation about locations, movements regarding the Pavo cell on Earth specifically.

. . .

He stepped out of the garden and transitioned through time and space. Letting his power push him away from his home and dropping him into an IGC complex in the Aeris Quadrant. He slid into the mind of one of the IGC agents that had been assigned to the Earth evacuation. It was easy. They didn't even realize it had happened. It was like being in another reality altogether. The mind was an illusion.

Callan let his mind slide through the architecture and the complexes of the agents' minds, across labyrinths and hallways, until he found what he was looking for. A Pavo agent. His target.

He looked through the memories, slowly taking them apart until he had the needed information. When he was finished, the Pavo agent was dead, and he hadn't even blinked. Discarding the agent he moved forward, finding another one and then another.

Callan moved through all their minds and memories, sliding past the points that prisoners had been taken, searching for as much detail as he could. Finally, he found an agent that had been in charge of the sale of incoming merchandise, parsing species out to various star systems based on need.

The Pavo used a variety of planet populations in their flesh trades, but with the opening of Earth this new cell that was operating had found a new home base in one of the human cities. Callan's stomach curdled. Disgusting. There were always groups around the universe that were willing to participate in the buying and selling of others.

Callan spooled himself back toward Tiebus, back toward his court.

"I found them. I have a location," he said. Brilius just rolled his eyes and threw a Jielbius fruit at him, unimpressed.

"Fabulous. Did you hear that, Paron? Shit to kill." Brilius surged to his feet, his claws out.

"Excellent," Paron said, who shoved Brilius away with one hand. "We'll leave immediately. I can't wait to wear an Earthling suit." The last, he said sarcastically, eyeing his pale moon-green skin with sadness.

"I guess we have to take the ship too. Stupid IGC." Brilius grumbled.

. . .

This last part was no small discomfort. The IGC was unaware of Callan and his court's talent for teleportation across large interplanetary distances. They had agreed over the centuries that it was a talent best kept hidden. To date, very few know about it. It would have brought too much attention to them. Certainly, their technology was capable, but it was much more convenient to teleport where they wanted to go.

Brilius grumbled some more but conceded they needed to collect Sapphrius, the last member of their court, anyway.

"Have you informed Sapphrius?" Callan asked, hearing the grumble.

Callan felt the excitement that rippled through his friend. He sighed and turned toward Paron. "I'll be gone for some time."

Brilius' eyes flared and he retorted, "We're all going, idiot." Callan wasn't surprised. He had expected it, actually.

. . .

Callan couldn't help the eye roll. "Fine."

The group headed down the path to find Sapphrius. Immediately, they were met with a world of deep greens and vibrant colors that seemed endless as they moved farther and farther in. The air was thick with exotic aromas and Callan heard the faint sound of chirping birds as they made their way through the wilderness. The group quickly made their way through the dense forest, weaving in and out of trees until they suddenly stopped.

Sapphrius lounged in a shimmering pool of sapphire blue water that sparkled like diamonds in the sun, fed by a gentle stream from the nearby falls. A small waterfall cascaded into the pool from above, surrounded by lush foliage and vivid flowers of every color imaginable. Butterflies fluttered around while birds sang sweet melodies in the background, creating a symphony of nature's beauty.

Sapphrius grinned broadly as Callan approached. "Are you joining me?" Her deep voice was melodic but loud. Her skin was graced with intricate designs all over her body.

. . .

"No," Callan smiled. "We go to Earth. We will search out the Pavo cell there."

Sapphrius eyed Callan. "I see." Sapphrius nodded, seeing the frown on his face. " I'm always up for a little bit of traveling. A new form to try out." Sapphrius was from the Proloxius Galaxy. As such, their species couldn't utilize all five senses. Sapphrius loved to take on new forms when they traveled, not to mention she loved a good fight.

"Let's get going then."

He gave a last look to the skies of Tiebus before the ship left for Earth. He'd find his Fated. Callan was sure of it.

Chapter Three

Water was a precious commodity, so Eva rinsed her face quickly from the basin and braided her hair. She made a note to ask Daisy to give her hair a trim. It was way too long. She didn't like to waste too much time on her appearance and long hair was bothersome. Eva didn't need to impress anyone these days —let's be real. She finished getting ready and hustled to the already too-hot kitchen in the small Portland apartment she shared with Daisy for the last three years.

Daisy was an early riser and had been up since before the sun, since it was an early bake day. She had checked over their delivery that Eva had insisted on making today herself. Daisy knew it was necessary, even if she didn't like it. Costs were too high to let someone scam them out of such a significant amount of cash. Daisy looked up at Eva as she came into the room and put on a forced smile.

"Hey, you. Did you sleep alright?" Daisy passed Eva some eggs. "You need to eat and don't give me attitude." Daisy's tone was joking, but she had taken into consideration all the facial expressions Eva was pulling at the moment. Eva always skipped eating when she was in a hurry. She gave her a smile to show she appreciated the gesture. Food was their love language.

The heat in the small two-bedroom was approaching scorching. It was December in Portland, Oregon, but that didn't stop the heat from already rising in the small two-story complex to a near unbearable level. Electricity rationing in the city meant things like air conditioning weren't always allowed anymore (even if you were equipped for it). They had been making do as best they could. Eva hoped after today it wouldn't be so hot.

"Well, gift-horse and all that," Eva said and murmured appreciatively as she shoveled them into her mouth. They were warm and fluffy. Eva sighed around a mouthful as she looked at her friend framed by their kitchen window. "Delicious, Daisy, thanks."

Daisy shook her head at her. "You always appreciated your food." She gave her a small, satisfied smirk and then paused seriously. "Do you think this is a good idea?" Daisy glanced at Eva with a concerned look.

Honestly, she knew they needed the catering orders, but the idea of going to the outpost, either of them—seemed dangerous. They should just keep going through the runner. It wasn't much money, but it was enough. They were doing alright. Or maybe, she could convince Eva to get on the list. They could go off-planet. She knew Eva didn't want to – wasn't ready to. But this place was dying. If they were together, they could make it – they could do anything.

Eva finished her plate of eggs and turned toward the small kitchen to keep herself busy as she avoided her roommate's question. "Yeah," Eva nodded, acquiescing. "I have to. We need those orders to keep up with the rent for the catering kitchen. We're too close to the line. We don't have enough money to keep this up. We are barely keeping this roof over our heads."

. . .

Daisy didn't answer, wiping her hands off on a towel, but Eva saw how her face pinched. Daisy was her best friend (her only friend, really), and she was worried. Eva rubbed her slender hands over her face. Shit, *she* was worried. Not so much about going out to the outpost, but just generally stressed. Making ends meet, staying in the apartment, and day-to-day living was difficult. Keeping safe was getting harder and harder.

She and Daisy had been roommates for the last few years. They had met on the bus of all places. Eva almost sighed at the memory of riding buses. Ah, the nostalgia. She gave a mental chuckle. Honestly, being sentimental about riding the bus. Hilarious. Some asshole had tried to snatch Eva's backpack and Daisy tripped him as he ran off with it, making them fast friends. Daisy was unmistakably badass and Eva had known it then. Eva never really had a friend like her (or had stayed in a place long enough to have a friend). It wasn't an easy friendship at first. Both had a long history of not trusting the people in their lives. However, they had found things to talk about— books, book boyfriends, non-existent family, and unattainable dreams. They bonded over their messed-up childhoods—the parts they had been willing to share, anyway. Daisy had tales of her messed-up situations with her mother, who had bounced between boyfriends that tried to be a little too familiar with her. Eva suspected Daisy had a lot that she didn't share, but she respected that.

Eva shared stories of living on the road with her grandfather. There were parts tucked away that Eva still couldn't share--stories of the constant moves, the continuous hoping that things would be different in the next place or that maybe he'd stay. Then there were the social workers who wanted to know why she was alone, the homelessness, the hunger. Eva didn't tell many of those stories, but it seemed like Daisy understood and was more than familiar with them. Daisy was loyal in a way that Eva had never known before. Eva felt lucky to have her in her life.

They made quick work of packing the finished cookies. They were meticulous with their products, cooking based on what ingredients they could find. While money was tight, Eva wasn't willing to sacrifice their quality—their products would look good every time they were sent out. They were proud of the work they put into their small business. When they first heard that the IGC was accepting goods from the locals, it was only logical that they see if the outpost wanted some baked goods. It had only been by chance that they had found a contact to take them to the outpost. That had made it easier. They hadn't thought cookies would be something the guards there would purchase. Who knew that the aliens would have such a love for homemade cookies? Eva had gotten a great laugh out of that. Although who didn't like cookies? Especially theirs. Only absolute assholes didn't like cookies. Even if they are from outer space.

When Gary had offered to take the orders to the outpost to sell for them, Eva thought it was a perfect arrangement since he was going anyway. Eva had a hard time admitting that she was a little nervous about doing it herself.

The runner had told her he'd take a portion, but she hadn't known how big of a cut. She discovered by accident last week, when she checked the actual margin, that they were being cheated. However, knowing how much they lost, she was willing to take the risk. Money was scarce since the landing, and they couldn't let someone cheat them out of their hard work. Eva wouldn't allow it. She was also beyond pissed at herself. She really thought she was smarter than that—tougher than that. Her grandfather would be seriously disappointed.

. . .

Eva lifted her eyes to her friend. She couldn't let Daisy down either. Eva fiddled with a corner of one of the cookies, a shortbread one, flaking it with a fingernail. She knew why her friend was concerned, of course. There was serious cause for worry, and she was a little nervous, but it was important not to let Daisy know how scared she was. She didn't want her to insist on coming. They needed to divide and conquer. Daisy needed to get ingredients and Eva was pretty sure she'd secured a few hours at the kitchen too.

"I'll be totally fine," she said firmly, then glanced up at Daisy's brown eyes. She gave Daisy a confident nod too and forced herself to hold her friend's gaze until Daisy dropped hers. "I can do this. It's not a big deal at all." She softened her voice, gave a soft chuckle, and went in for a hug. "I'll be fine. That jerk face has been totally cheating us. Giving us less than half of the profits." She gave her friend a little prod as she pulled from the hug.

"Okay, I know you're right. Just be careful. Don't take chances. You heard about Mrs. Wilson?" Daisy darted a glance at her. Her eyebrows knitted together.

. . .

Plenty of people in the city were taking the aliens up on their offer of going off planet. The idea of a shiny new future in the stars was alluring, especially when things on Earth were getting harder and harder. However, people typically planned it out. They said goodbye, gave things away, and closed their shops like Patsy had.

Their long-standing customer, Mrs. Wilson—had up and vanished. The vintage shop remained shut, her standing bakery order left unfulfilled. While others around her shop suggested perhaps that she took a ship off-planet, Eva didn't think so. She couldn't help but think back to the conversation they'd just had a few weeks back.

"Yeah, I heard," Eva muttered.

"You don't think she went, do you?" Daisy asked, although Eva could tell by the look on her face that she knew the answer already.

"No." Eva's reply was sad. There were a few too many disappearances happening lately. People that tended to live on the fringe—loners without a lot of family. Eva didn't think that was an accident at all.

. . .

The news was vague on details but mentioned that the aliens resembled humans. Eva thought that was probably incorrect—or a narrow view. (Insert eye roll) Eva had thought aliens were little green men or scaly or something. Apparently, the news reports all said that wasn't the case. Eva wasn't sure what to think about any of it though. She had acute cynicism built into her from her childhood. The images from the news showed outposts that had popped up worldwide. It really was insane. Leave Earth? Honestly, it was crazy town.

There weren't a lot of closeups to be had of the actual IGC aliens either. But they looked just like people to Eva. Should they call them aliens? Beings from another universe? People were still confused, Eva among them. They had shown up with their overwhelming force, made camps, and essentially taken over Earth without a shot fired and no resistance from the ground to be seen.

Within the last year, they put out the message that they were there to relocate the people of Earth from their dying planet to other planets. So those that wished to could go. Eva still wasn't sure what to make of it. Plenty of people were believers and had signed up to leave. So many, in fact, the waiting lists were enormous (according to the news). Although, the streets were starting to be empty and the jobs that were previously full were now left undone. Logically it was true. People were leaving in droves. The Earth wasn't doing well (also not a lie). However, that didn't mean she was signing up to be jettisoned off to only God knows where. They didn't tell you where they were sending you either. Eva needed a little more to go on than a "Hey, we'll send you *somewhere*." That was a little too vague for her. They still hadn't received news from Patsy yet, either. It had been months—how long did it take to get to another solar system?

"Eva?" Daisy asked as she helped stack the boxes they had made.

Eva paused as she tied her pair of old, battered converse on her feet. They were honestly falling apart. "What?" Although she didn't need Daisy to answer—she knew what she was going to say. Daisy had thought for a while that maybe their chances were better if they got on that list to leave. Earth was just drying up like a husk of corn left out in the sun, wrinkling up, cracking and crumbling. Soon it would dry into dust, floating away into the stars.

. . .

"Maybe..." Daisy offered tentatively. "...it's so hard here. It's dangerous too." Daisy played with a strand of her curly hair. "I talked to a guy yesterday who said we could get on the list. He could get us moved up." Daisy had been thinking hard about how to get Eva to agree to go off planet. She still had some big concerns, but anywhere was better than here. It had been a shit show for a while now. They had stayed put long enough. The city was too dangerous to even be out on the streets, especially after dark. People were getting way too violent. How could it be any worse?

"Ok, I'll bite." Eva tucked her hands into the back pockets of her jean shorts and leaned against the counter. "What'd you hear?" They had heard these stories for a while, and it was harder and harder to dismiss. At first, many people did their best to ignore the idea that the landing had happened and shut the possibility off, like turning off a spigot. But gradually, the outposts were built, and people saw the transports come and go. Disbelief was no longer an option.

Those that went out for actual transport didn't actually return, so you couldn't ask them how it was. Eva hadn't heard of anyone saying that their loved ones or friends had been able to communicate with them. She just didn't have enough information to make a good decision. It was one of those things that she put aside to think about later. She had enough on her hands. They had rent coming up, and they were short. (One reason she was going.) They had other bills to pay too. She had been in worse situations, and she was capable and strong. A fighter if it came to it. She would not worry herself sick about going to the outpost by herself—it had to be done.

Daisy gave a small laugh, but Eva saw the uncertainty. Daisy leaned forward a little. "Get this, Eva." Light shone off her features as she said in a rush, "This guy, right... he said that the IGC... they set you up with jobs and everything. It's a legit deal. We could have a future. We both know we can't do this forever." It was this that resonated with Eva. They had talked it over before—the idea of wanting something bigger than a small apartment that offered no opportunity. Once upon a time, they both had dreamt of adventure and travel, of love—of a future.

"That sounds nice," Eva admitted, albeit grudgingly. "Let's really talk about it tonight. Let's consider it. I'll have a much better idea after seeing it for myself when I go to the outpost. Okay?" She wanted to promise to think it over. She would, she told herself—later. Right now... right now, she needed to put her game face on, get to the outpost, and then get their money.

"How long *do* you think we can keep this up?" Daisy said as she zipped the bag shut. The question wasn't a question at all. They had gone round and round on this topic. The answer was always the same. They would keep it up as long as they could (probably longer). After Patsy had left, they'd been on borrowed time anyway. She'd begged them to go with her, but Eva hadn't been ready to leave.

"Probably not long." Eva was honest to a fault. "But we'll be together." Eva gave her a smile. "You're not getting rid of me."

"Other way around, bitch." Daisy scuffed the linoleum with her bare toes, painted a bright fuchsia today. Eva barely bit back a laugh. Daisy always did things like paint her nails, even in the middle of an invasion. How she bought the nail polish, Eva didn't want to know. Maybe she stole it.

Eva rolled her eyes and gave Daisy a smack on the ass and a tackle hug. "Come here." She squeezed her bestie tight. "I love you. You're amazing."

. . .

"I love you–only a little," Daisy said with a teasing lilt and a squeeze.

"Okay. Gary does this every week. How hard could it be? He comes back alive every time—like a fucking cockroach." She shrugged and gave Daisy a saucy wink.

"Are you sure you want to wear that?" Daisy gave her outfit a look that spoke volumes. Daisy insisted Eva was much too pretty for her own good and seemed constantly oblivious, making her more appealing than ever to every man who seemed to see her.

Eva laughed as she looked down at her worn jean shorts, converse, and t-shirt that at one time might or might not have been a Goonies shirt from Target. She had French braided her hair down the sides and rubber banded the ends. She looked a little rough, but she wasn't dressing up to go to an alien outpost.

Unless... Eva envisioned her hunky alien from the other day. Her belly gave an answering tug. It must have shown on her face.

. . .

"You're thinking of that guy?" Daisy asked. "That ... man? The alien? Dude?" She waved her hand in the air.

"Maybe," Eva answered. She tried to keep it light, but she was puzzled by her body's continued reaction to the tall, dark, and mysterious alien that had materialized in front of her the other day. She'd had her share of sexy times and there were some good-looking guys in her past. At nearly thirty, she'd not found Mr. Right, but she'd found Mr. Okay a few times. She scoffed a little at herself. Who was she kidding? Whoever, whatever, that guy in that apparition or whatever it was ... particles? he was WAY more than Mr. Okay.

"Alright, well, maybe you'll see an eyeful out there." Daisy gave her a blinding smile and tugged the end of one of Eva's braids.

"Hopefully, I'll get our money. Seeing someone is just a bonus," Eva teased her.

"Help me carry these down, will you?" Eva popped some of the bakery boxes on a hip. The elevator was broken so it would take a few trips up and down the stairs. They had a cart to use once she got to the outpost.

"Sure, babe." Daisy grabbed a stack and followed Eva to the van she'd parked earlier as near the apartment as she could. It didn't take them too long to get everything stacked up and loaded.

Daisy had cautioned her that Gary wasn't one to be trifled with. Thanks to how she was raised, Eva was well-acquainted with people like Gary. That said--Gary was nothing if not consistent. He always did his deliveries on Wednesday to the outpost. Today was Tuesday, so Eva was confident she could go to the outpost and skip Gary altogether. Would he be pissed? Probably, but it would be too late, and he had other customers. How mad would he be, anyway? He had been cheating them. She'd keep her mouth shut and he could keep his other customers. Eva wasn't dumb, so she wouldn't take his other business away. It'd be fine.

The day was suspiciously bright, in her opinion. Once upon a time, this time of year would have brought rain daily to Oregon. The skies would have been grey and full of heavy clouds. Now, the blistering sun baked the pavement, and everywhere Eva looked, she saw the signs that Earth was indeed struggling to keep up. Even the scant weeds that attempted to come through the pavement here and there were withering in the heat.

Her route was straightforward. The outpost had been positioned at what was once the Portland International Airport. Plane travel had been restricted for years to only emergencies or military purposes. Jet fuel had become too scarce and too expensive. Eva barely remembered a time in her distant childhood when planes took off from airports regularly. She had only flown a few times, but she remembered that feeling when you were pressed into your seat, your head against the upholstery as the plane struggled to heave itself into the sky. Eva had always loved it. When she was little, she had thought it was magic.

She focused on her route as she drove. The stench of the city was getting worse. Services like garbage collection were cut down to just once a month if that. Luckily Oregon had always been progressive in the years leading up to the landing, requiring recycling and composting so people had already been doing that. Before the landing, there was plenty of homelessness in the city. But now keeping a roof over your head was imperative—just much more difficult. The streets and the sidewalks were filled with people that looked at her with barely concealed envy and hunger. Eva knew that feeling well. As businesses shuttered in the city, it created a strange vacuum. The desperation and scarcity of resources before the landing were amplified.

Those with no resources were split into two camps. Those willing to take a transport and make a go of their life elsewhere. Then those entrenched in the idea that nobody could tell them anything, let alone someone who wasn't from their home planet. Those with resources, of course, were like they always were—they'd make a deal that was most comfortable for them.

Eva sighed and concentrated on where she was going.

Chapter Four

Callan steepled his fingers as he looked over the screens that made up the faces of the members of the Inter-Galactic Council. The universe, of course, had multiple complex governing bodies. Not only because of the sheer number of planetary systems but also their wealth. One might argue that one followed the other. The IGC, by default, had managed mundane tasks in most of the universe for longer than Callan had been alive, frankly (which was quite a long time). Meetings such as this were an evil necessity among the council. A council the Shade wasn't a part of, but he had considered whether he should change that. At of the moment, though, he was here in an Earthen form as their hired *Hunter*. He had played the role before—it was occasionally amusing, and it had helped him figure out the type of individuals that made up the council.

The video conference allowed members to take part no matter where they were. Which was very convenient for Callan since he didn't want the IGC to know his location. Luckily for him, he was always on the move anyway, so the fact that he was on his ship wasn't unusual. Callan leaned back in his seat. He always kept his mouth closed and listened, even if he was bored with the petty politics surrounding their courts, governments, personal armies, and star systems. But you never knew what you might pick up. While it was good to keep himself aware of what was happening, it was equally critical to not involve himself or his team unless necessary. He was having difficulty paying attention. All the information seemed unimportant if he was being honest. The droning incessant.

"The planet is new to us." The governor of Nordrok spoke up. "We will need to be cautious. The possibility of outside factors taking possession could be a factor."

Stukkned of the Nordrok was a greedy man and Callan gave him an icy glare through the screens. He wasn't wrong though. Earth was vulnerable at the moment. “Hunter?” Callan was startled when Paron kicked up under the table.

“Yes,” Callan had done his best to look attentive. The Governor gave him a disgruntled look. Apparently, Callan wasn’t doing a very good job, not that Callan gave a shit (let’s be honest).

“You are on your way to take care of the problem with them? The group that has been stealing Earthlings?”

“I well understand my responsibilities to the council, Governor. I am proceeding as we outlined.” Callan drawled. The Nordrok had been notoriously vocal about asking for the resettlement of Earthlings to their planet. It was a decent fit for the people of Earth since the atmosphere there was conducive to sustaining life. However, there were some definite things to consider as an Earthling if you choose Nordrok. Callan tapped his fingers impatiently on the table in front of him. He wanted this meeting over.

“I’ve made myself clear, we are happy to have settlers. The Nordrok planet is well-placed at this time to host,” the Governor said again. His jowls swung heavily as he spoke. Callan was happy that this wasn't an in-person meeting, firstly because the communication screens instantly translated for him, which was convenient, and secondly because he didn't have to put up with the spit that flew whenever Governor Stukkned spoke. Callan had been unlucky enough to know first-hand that you didn't want to be within six feet of Stukkned.

"Good that you are so welcoming." Governor Faneh's voice was cool through the connection of the link. She was from the neighboring planet of Baseon, but her tone was heavy with sarcasm. Baseon wasn't one to take settlers.

Nordrok had suffered heavy population losses in recent years due to not being involved with the Inter-Galactic Council. People left to find jobs elsewhere. It had also fallen victim to heavy raiding from roving space pirates before petitioning the IGC for help and membership. Lucky for them, they had mines that interested the council, which made them an attractive member. Now that they were under the council's umbrella, they wanted to increase their population again. They had also increased trade routes and funding, so they were back to being a viable planet for refugees.

. . .

Callan hated being here. Hated the game that all the governors played.

"However," she sent a look toward Callan, "Stukkned is correct. We cannot afford a repetition of the past..." she allowed for a pause full of meaning, and the hint of accusation was unmistakable. It surprised Callan that she dared. His fist clenched as he held his temper, barely. She was lucky they weren't on the same planet right now. He didn't need anyone to remind him. Callan met her gaze with his molten gold, bright and fierce. Governor Faneh blinked and swallowed.

He let some of his power seep into the gaze. Faneh and her petty games and manipulations. She was a beautiful creature, nothing humanoid in her features whatsoever. Her outer skin was inky blue and satiny. Callan knew for a fact that her skin exuded poison if she chose. Personally, he thought she'd be a dangerous bedfellow. She certainly mirrored her planet, unpredictable, beautiful, and dangerous, and she was no fool. She also knew better than to tangle too closely with the IGC Hunter. Callan wanted to be upset, but he was used to the council's innuendo and jabs. He had had to answer for his actions for a long time now.

. . .

She was the perfect example of the politics of the universe. Callan knew she was hoping to gain some leverage against Stukkned by pushing his buttons with Callan. He was not going to let her use him in this game.

"We are working on a solution to the raiding issues," he said calmly and firmly, shooting an icy glare at Faneh that told her he would not be used by her.

"Yes, we are well aware of your efforts," she answered quickly, avoiding his gaze now. "But I think we need additional reinforcements to fully protect our borders and trade routes. We cannot afford any mistakes or delays here..." she trailed off as if expecting something from him but also conscious of how far she had pushed already.

"Of course," he dipped his chin, but his eyes burned. "Certainly, it pays to be wary. I will be cautious moving forward." He knew exactly what the female's intention was. The rest of the meeting passed by with no more talk of Earth. The Governor from Holnir requested an additional trade route, which the council immediately shut down and the meeting moved forward. There was some disquieted talk regarding an attack on some vessels outside of the Ettore Dimension. Callan perked up at this. There was often talk surrounding this area—space pirates flourished there. While Callan had completed a profitable contract that led him through that dimension not long ago, pursuing a murderer (who didn't make it). Ah, good times. There was a branch of the IGC that dealt with the criminal element of the galaxies. They never could stop the rampant theft and piracy that carried on through the galaxies no matter how hard they tried. It was as tiresome as it was frustrating. Callan knew the IGC was a constant balance of systemic bribery for goods and services that went on behind the scenes and politics that weren't his business.

"Can you give us any updates on your search, Hunter?" Faneh kept her tone respectful this time and her gaze lowered. Even through the display of the video link, Callan could see that she'd lowered her secondary eyelid and clasped a set of hands on the table. She was faking her demure pose, of course, but she tried. It appeased him slightly.

"Of course." He ground out—reluctantly. "The Pavo Arcturus has been active in one particular location. My team and I are on the hunt. They are farming the populace. We have spotted signs. I'll find the cell in short order and destroy them as requested."

. . .

The Pavo Arcturus was notorious in star systems everywhere. Brutal in every way—they were traffickers that swooped in on planets being cleared by the IGC. They packed up civilians and sold them to planets based on supply and demand. It was a big reason Callan had such little respect for the council. He suspected the Pavo on some planets were sanctioned. But for the moment, it was inconsequential. They weren't sanctioned on Earth—so that was all that mattered at the moment.

"As you say, Hunter." Faneh smiled at him coldly, then inclined her head toward Stukkned before disconnecting from the link.

Eventually, Callan disconnected, taking care that his location was masked and his link preserved.

Callan leaned back and sighed. Overall, he supposed he shouldn't be surprised that members of the council were still reminding him about past deeds. While it was years ago, he knew they were not forgotten by any stretch. Although, he thought with fierce pleasure, he inspired quite a bit of fear, which he didn't mind. They should be afraid.

. . .

Callan made his last notes and had his AI, Amura, save them. Only then did he begin to go over his files, the transcripts and anything that would help him. The last thing Callan wanted was to be unprepared. He wanted this job over with. The most important task was finding the little Earth female he had bumped into or who had bumped into him.

Earth was a dying planet. The species there had been doing their best to kill the poor planet over the past several centuries. Overpopulation, overuse of its resources... certainly a tired story and one Callan had seen repeatedly. Other planets, worlds, galaxies, dimensions, and species weren't any different.

One of the things that the Inter-Galactic Council did was redistribute populations from dying planets. They claimed benevolence; however, Callan knew that wasn't entirely true. The Council was founded upon the nature of their parasitic relationship with other planetary populations and the redistribution of them. Granted, it was a mutually beneficial situation. Planets like Earth were dying. Species on such planets were given choices on where they wanted to go and resources to make new lives, jobs, homes, and comforts.

. . .

Nordrok wanted people from Earth, mainly for miners or sex workers. Certainly, honorable lives, but Holnir was a much more diverse planet lifestyle better suited if those weren't things one was interested in. If the Pavo got them, that was a totally different story.

The one thing Callan felt sure about was that the IGC gave people options. Plenty of planets and groups out there didn't view these planets the same way or have the same goals. They saw them as an opportunity. Some wanted to utilize these populations for other nefarious purposes.

Ultimately, that wasn't Callan's job in this scenario. Callan and his team were contracted by the council for criminals they couldn't find through normal channels. Callan had special talents that the IGC coveted, and Callan liked the work. It broke up the monotony. Lately, he had been saying 'no' more often than 'yes', though. He supposed he should return to his throne and kingdom rather than galloping about. In this case, Earth was calling to him on a much deeper level—one that he was sure would lead him to his Fated.

Chapter Five

As soon as Callan stepped onto the dock on Earth at the Portland Outpost, the gathered Inter-Galactic Council warriors bowed in reverence. The Hunter, they whispered, not daring to look his way. It was no secret that the Council's Hunter had strange and powerful abilities and was not someone to cross.

The rest of his court had already teleported to scouting locations within the city. Callan had to make the best use of their time. Have them investigate and return with the information as quickly as possible.

He didn't bother giving the warrior an answer, as an answer was not expected. He gave a curt nod, but the young man dropped his eyes quickly. Callan was already hot, annoyed, and a little tired. The heat was oppressive on the planet. It tasted dry, like hot sand.

He wanted to shield his eyes against the harsh light. Callan had heard that the Earth had once been beautiful, full of green fields, waterfalls, and flowers, but now it didn't seem very pleasant. The air held not a drop of moisture and there was not a speck of greenery to be seen. He could breathe; that was a win. Why anyone would want to stay here, he couldn't even fathom. What a cesspit. Of course, it could be worse, he reminded himself of that one planet where you sank up to your ankles in that vile muck every 30 seconds and the air was poisonous.

The warrior remembered the hushed conversations he had heard in the barracks only the previous month, tales of Hunter Adiim and the devastating destruction he had wreaked on a distant outpost. He shuddered, now all too aware of who he was facing. Some other recruit said that their father knew of him. The warrior couldn't believe he was standing next to the actual Hunter of the IGC. He kept his eyes on the dirt to avoid bringing the Hunter's attention to him. As much as he wished he had the courage to speak, it wasn't worth it.

. . .

Commander Talon Azer stepped forward to intercept him as he descended the ramp. Azer was the assigned commander of the dusty Portland outpost. Callan respected him; however, the situation there wasn't tolerable by any stretch. If Callan could have landed outside the city, he would have.

"Hunter," Azar gave a small head bow. "I was wondering if I could have a moment of your time?" Callan couldn't help but sigh.

Callan's feet pounded the ground, the earth reverberating beneath his heavy frame, an evenly paced staccato, in time with Azar's heavy strides. Callan's mouth pressed together in a grim line; his eyes roved the surrounding area.

Azer's jaw was tight, but he didn't say anything, so he kept his mouth shut too. He wasn't sure what this was about, but he wanted to meet with his team, not get waylaid by the Commander.

He also wanted to look around this Earthen city and see if anything looked familiar from seeing his Fated. There had been that one time in the pools of

Fate where he almost had a clear look. He had sworn he had seen an outline in the background ... Callan reluctantly pulled himself back to the matter at hand.

The outpost looked far less stable than it should, as far as outposts went. It wasn't set up with enough warriors. There weren't the proper number of buildings or barracks. A strong wind could blow it over, let alone a good assault. It could be taken over by a hundred determined individuals easily. Typically, there was always resistance on planets that the IGC set up outposts on. Reception was generally positive; however, there were always dissenters.

Guards were at every entrance and exit but weren't as plentiful as they should be. He had also noted there weren't transports leaving the landing pad. There should be more activity. Callan's teeth ground with impatience. He had things to do. If the man wanted to speak about the outpost, he should go up the chain of command, not speak with him. That wasn't his role in the IGC. Callan clenched his fingers in frustration, his power pulsing slightly. Azer stutter-stepped next to him. The Commander still had said nothing, and he wondered if the poor man was going to, but perhaps he wanted privacy. Everything was tidy, but Callan viewed it critically, cataloging it all against his previous experiences. He knew the numbers, and something wasn't right here. As Azer ushered Callan into what served as his office, Callan took a position in a chair and gestured magnanimously for Azer to sit down.

"Get to it then. What can I do for you?" Callan's eyes took everything in as he spoke. The office was neat as a pin, typical of a field office building, sterile without a lot of the personal effects one would have at a home office. The buildings were functional enough with all the items required for the job, including the articles, technology, and functionality. However, there was still a staleness in the air. It looked like these were facilities previously used for aircraft the Earthlings had. Primitive but serviceable. Sometimes they weren't so lucky and had to do with much less.

Azer liked the Hunter. He had served with him a few times, although he doubted he remembered him. He had the impression of him as a fair individual. He didn't seem to be someone who acted without purpose, intent, or honor. However, it didn't mean Azer wasn't nervous about speaking to him. It was also said that the Hunter had high standards and a wicked temper. But Azer was taking his career into his hands and risking everything. He was betting that he was an honest man and not on the take. Azer needed him. He hoped he was right.

"We are having issues," Azer began. Callan saw a flush begin at his collar of his IGC uniform. Callan had limited interactions with Azer at a few outposts he'd frequented. But Callan hadn't ever had a conversation with him. He had taken the time to read his file. Commander Talon Azer came up through the ranks, not the academy path that an IGC warrior would typically take to become a commander. Callan appreciated hard work and the guts it took to get through unaccompanied by sponsors or big names. Those that were only academy didn't understand what it was to work their way up from the bottom, to starve, to struggle and suffer. He could respect that.

Callan waved a hand, "Continue." His voice was low, his face hard.

"Of course." Azer handed him a file. "These are my notes." Callan tilted his head at him. "I know I could have sent these up the chain, but I felt it best for you to have them. I know you are here about the Pavo cell...." The Hunter eyed, him, picking apart his words and recasting them.

. . .

Callan took the file and flipped through it, noting the information he knew already. Azer was meticulous in his notations, the graphs, and the statistics that he included. Callan came to a conclusion as he met Azer's gaze.

"You think there is someone on the inside, then? That's what you suggest." Callan rose to his feet and paced the little office as he read. He could see Azer's face had paled as he steeled himself for Callan's judgment. Mists and shadows curled around the Hunter's feet, licking up his boots. Azer swallowed audibly.

Azer dipped his head and waited for the metaphorical axe to fall one way or the other. He would either have an ally or this would be the end for him. Perhaps he had gambled wrong, the Hunter was difficult to read after all. His face seemed almost impassive. Talon wasn't sure who he was angry at. Talon reflected on his time at the outpost. He had kept quiet when he first suspected that they had someone on the inside, manipulating things, shorting their supply. He had *tried* to work the issue himself then he got shut down time after time. However, he had remembered what he had heard about what the Hunter had faced on Janus. He had wondered and speculated, made some leaps. Fates, he hoped he wasn't incorrect in jumping over the chains of command. Azer was betting more than his own life on him. He hoped he had done the right thing in skipping the report to his direct supervisor and the Inter-Galactic Council.

"Yes," Azer went ahead and confirmed. "Someone is intercepting some of our transports from the Portland camp. People are going missing, not just from the city. Last week we had three transports vanish outside of Aeris Quadrant." Azer cleared his throat as Callan leafed through the file. He gave a significant pause and met Callan's gaze with a determined look in his eye.

"We've seen a few suspicious incidents that make me believe someone here is on the take. Supplies have been disappearing, equipment has been misappropriated, and I've heard whispers of corruption and bribery. We can't afford this. Not if we're going to keep this outpost secure and functional."

Azer was a hardened member of the IGC force. He was no new officer. Callan knew he was nearing thirty-six and had seen more than his share of battle, both on and off planet. He was a capable warrior and tactician. He had close-cropped dark-brown hair and significant tattooing, as was favored by foot warriors of the IGC. He was originally from Jurox and had limited shifting capabilities on his home planet.

Callan finished reading and tapped the documents on his thigh, waiting. He narrowed his eyes and waited. A new lieutenant colonel had been assigned to the Pacific outposts that Commander Azer reported to, who should have been notified first of any issues. Callan was quite pleased that Azer had brought this to him. It reeked of corruption; if he could sniff it out and stamp it out, he would.

Azer winced at the look on the Hunter's face, then said, "From the start, when the outpost was set up, we've been shorted. I requested through regular channels more provisions, more warriors, more buildings for housing warriors, and more transports too to make quicker work of things. We have always had a long list of Earthlings who wished to be moved off-planet. However, at every turn, I've met resistance or refusal. Requests are partially filled but still short. The outpost runs, but barely. I've been able to get things going here over the past 8 months, but we have been behind at every step." Azer gestured again to the reports in Callan's hands. "I've tried to work through the Lieutenant Colonel," Azer said cautiously.

"So, they have shorted you here. Less than your allocations of staff, provisions, housing. You don't have the same transport schedule to offload the population. Most of the numbers I've seen show that we are behind in this sector. Is that right?" Callan leaned back in the chair as he focused on Azer. He was trying to put the picture together, tapping his fingers on Azer's file. "Now, you are having transports taken, all from this outpost. People stolen. What's intriguing about that is that I haven't been alerted at all. Not a peep—except from you. I find that fascinating." Callan turned his gaze to Azer and let a little more of his power leak out.

Azer didn't know whether or not the Hunter was accusing him. His hand clenched on his thigh under the desk and he forced himself to meet the amber eyes as honestly as he could.

"You came to me? Why?" Callan found that especially interesting. He had seen this pattern before long, long ago, and he honestly wasn't surprised to find it again. The Pavo loved to work within the IGC systems. They were insidious that way. "You could have taken the credits, you know." Callan saw the moment that Azer understood his meaning and he stiffened his spine.

Azer's voice was icy. "I'm not for sale, ever." Azer's eyes were hard and black as night. He had straightened in his chair, his bulky shoulders squared as if preparing for a fight if Callan was in on this.

Callan wouldn't be surprised if multiple people on the outpost were selling information. For that matter—in the IGC. Taking credits in exchange for information wasn't a new tactic. Perhaps even going further than that, assisting in the treachery. To find out Azer wasn't part of it—well, that would be helpful.

"Really?" Callan's grin was wolfish. Anyone watching might have been concerned by the calculating look he gave Azer. "Very well, then," Callan said in a bored tone.

Azer realized that was the answer and response required to move to the next step. It had been a test. He gave him a tight nod.

. . .

Callan stood again and paced; hands clasped behind his back as he spoke. "Long ago, during a similar resettlement...." Callan remembered the treachery and the death. He shook himself and forced himself to focus. "Janus." He made himself turn his gaze to Azer. People didn't speak of Janus, a topic that was off-limits, taboo. People didn't speak of it to him. Of course, there were rumors that always caused people to look at Callan with speculation and fear. Rumors that were warranted. However, those rumors were only half the story. Azer was focused and still. Callan couldn't help but appreciate it.

Azer held his breath. This was what he had suspected and gambled on. He wanted the Hunter's help but was half afraid of what he would hear next. However, if what he suspected was true, he would need to push past that because there were people that needed his help. Not to mention that his career depended on him solving the issue, but that was of small importance.

"Janus was very similar to Earth. The people there were just going about their lives. The time clock for resettlement and transportation also wasn't short, but it wasn't long either. They had two years to move most of the population off-planet to other solar systems and other sectors. There were choices for destinations. The council had contracted with someone to provide backup. To support them as they moved the population. By the time I was contacted, the Pavo had taken thousands upon thousands." Callan's voice was bleak. "I'm still not sure how many were involved, but I know it was an inside job. Transports got hit. We would lose them mid-way." Callan turned to look at Azer, who gazed at the shadows clawing the floor. "Sound familiar?"

"Sure does." Azer nodded cautiously. "I had heard some of what happened there." Azer's words were carefully bland, noncommittal. Callan respected the lack of judgment in the comment and nodded, clenching a fist at his side. The memories flooded in.

"Yes, I'm sure you did," he agreed as he paused and then forced himself to continue. "I suspected some individuals were working with a rogue trafficking group in league with Pavo Arcturus." Azer's face had gone pale. "It took me weeks to track them," Callan admitted. He didn't like how long it had gone on right under his nose. It made him feel ashamed about the transport that escaped him and what had happened to those lost men, women, and children.

. . .

The Pavo Arcturus was notorious in star systems everywhere. Brutal in every way and so insidious that they had been on most governments' lists for elimination from the Shade Dimension to Talogath. They still sank their claws in and found footholds. They were feared everywhere but often difficult to find. They worked in the shadows in coordinated attacks, often in illicit trades like trafficking, sex trades, and mercenaries for hire. The Pavo Arcturus were not individuals to cross. They had long memories and secret hit lists you did not want to be on. Those working for them didn't outwardly let it slip who they were doing a job for. The contracts were under other names, bribes were made, and the job was done without connecting them to the Pavo. The cells couldn't be connected properly, and a new rogue cell popped up as soon as one was stomped out.

Every government faction throughout every star system either was trying to eradicate the Pavo or working with them and buying their merchandise. That was essentially the issue. They worked well within systems and hid their spreading evil within shadows, slippery and hard to grasp at the best of times.

. . .

"I was able to find the mole at Janus." A muscle ticked in Callan's jaw. "A sergeant. He talked, eventually." Callan looked off into the distance, remembering the lengths he went to get the needed information. Some might have called it a smile, but it was nothing resembling a smile, more akin to a grimace.

If anyone had asked Azer, he would have said it was chilling what he saw there. Death. Azer had enough sense to be frightened of what he saw in the Hunter's face. Azer had wondered before about the Hunter, about who he really was. He knew he was long-lived but very little about him or where he came from.

"I tracked the rest of the cell to an off-planet sector. We killed them all for what they had done there." Callan swallowed once. "They had women, the ones they had taken from the transports. I recognized one of them... at least, I thought I did. It was difficult to tell. They had them in cages." Callan paced and then turned. "We killed all the Pavo we found." He met Azer's eyes, deliberate in his next words. "We didn't kill them quickly either." He knew this was part of the rumors about him. The death, the slaughter, the destruction that had occurred with the Pavo. He wasn't sorry about it. As he held Azer's gaze, he let that bleed into his eyes. He wanted the other man to understand the lengths he went to and the depths of darkness he was willing to go to again. He was typically careful about giving his powers free rein, but he held nothing back that day.

Azer had heard that the Hunter had gone rogue that day. He had killed in a haze of blood and gore. Of mist and blood. Until utter destruction was left in his wake.

Azer was quiet for a moment, but he was sure, and steady as he spoke. "As you should have." He held the Hunter's gaze, understanding flashing between them. Azer knew then that while the rumors about what had happened on Janus were warranted, the killing that had been done there had been deserved. What had driven the Hunter to kill the people who had held the people of Janus in cages like animals and whether the killing had been slow, he couldn't fault the Hunter for it. If anything, he was more confident now in his choice. These transports that were missing, fates only knew what had happened to those people, what was happening to them, even now.

Azer said, "You can find this person then? If we have another mole? You think this is another situation like what happened there? That they are taking people from the transports?" Azer had known something was happening, something that needed to be stopped, but had never once considered that the Pavo was involved or had even considered this level of evil if he was honest. He had grown up as a child with evil and had not known kindness, but this—what the Hunter described—was another level that perhaps he was unprepared for.

Callan only nodded. "It seems likely. The missing transports. Someone on the outpost. Or more than one person, for that matter. Someone who is feeding information to them to allow them access to coordinates. They work best with bribery, concrete information, and stealth. The outpost at Janus had also been understaffed and under-provisioned. I always thought the Pavo had potentially bigger plans than the transports they took, but I interrupted that. It had been a rogue operation though. Maybe they are trying again?" Callan studied Azar. He was probably thinking of the potential implications of this. It was bad enough that transports had been going missing, bad enough if this was another Janus-like situation involving the Pavo. But if Callan was onto something, it was bigger than that. The implications were bad, with a capital B.

. . .

"As far as what they are doing with the rest of the transport passengers. I would think that they are selling them. The Pavo are traffickers. They go with the market demands. I hadn't realized the depravity until I saw with my own eyes." Callan felt the shudder go through his body but held his body still, gritting his teeth. "Flesh peddlers have a market for all types, unfortunately."

Azer nodded at him and took a deep breath as he stood. "Well, I'm in, whatever it is, to put a stop to it. Whatever it takes and whatever it costs." Azer let the intent of that show on his face. He would make sure to show it in his actions as well. He would not be content to sit on the sidelines and let people be trafficked. They were his responsibility.

"I'm due to meet with my team now that that infernal meeting with the council is finished." Callan didn't bother to hide the disgust in his voice.

"Anything you need from me... you have it. I'll have my team continue to do what they can of course," Azer replied, rising from his desk. "We have an interesting amount of Earth offerings for food if you need refreshments." He gave Callan a wry smile. "Most of it comes from the locals. We get all our provisions that way." Azer grimaced. "It's good and bad, really. Some of our men are partial to their products. We try to limit their access though. Deliveries and such only on certain days." Azer gave a cough. "You wouldn't believe how much these warriors love some of these deliveries. Sometimes I think it's the only thing that keeps them obeying orders."

The outposts always allowed trading and bartering for credits when landings occurred. Once things settled and the populations weren't hostile, that is. Typically, trading for credits allowed for a couple of things. Primarily it permitted the people of the planet to trade with them and see that they wanted to help. It gave them a way to gain currency, which was also good. It also provided outposts a wide variety of goods they would never see otherwise, so sometimes that was entertaining. Variety when you were stuck on-planet typically helped morale.

Those under Inter-Galactic Council orders and conducting official business could leave the outposts, but warriors weren't just allowed to gallivant about planets. Callan and his team were a special case.

Callan gave a small laugh. Occasionally they got interesting things, although he had known it to go terribly wrong. However, sometimes the small luxuries were the only thing that kept warriors sane. Nobody would ever say that any military gave their warriors perfect provisions—even the IGC. Most advanced life forms didn't need food to survive in the traditional sense like the people of Earth, but it made life more pleasant. The IGC military and other off-planet systems had long ago developed nutrition cubes to take the burden of food and water production off their planet systems. Earth was so far behind. No wonder it had failed, Callan thought as he left the building with Azer.

"Where are you meeting your team then?" Azer ventured. He had heard of Adiim's team, although what was spoken about was mostly rumor and supposition. He had only known Adiim to travel with Sapphrius, a female from the Proloxius Galaxy that he'd never want to cross.

Callan sent him an inscrutable look. "By the gate." Azer nodded at him, and Callan didn't have the heart to deny him when he offered to walk with him. He'd just planned to port there, but he'd humor the commander.

The outpost was an odd mishmash of interconnected buildings that wove through the defunct airport terminals. Callan saw signs everywhere for airport gates, baggage claims, elevators, etc. After an interminable walk and a brutally hot stretch across asphalt where Callan was irritated again to be out in the Earth's sun and not in the cool of his home dimension, they finally neared the improvised outpost barrier.

Obviously, deliveries were occurring, and Earthlings were entering for processing and transports. The gate was busy. As they neared, voices rose from the gate, which he recognized. He couldn't help but be pleased.

Chapter Six

Eva's mouth had turned to sawdust as she approached the outpost. She had heard some information about it, but she wasn't much of a believer in things she didn't experience herself. But what she saw outside the airport was unbelievable. The tarmacs were swarmed with airships, from small and nimble to mammoth and menacing. She swore some of the ships could transport entire semi-trailer loads of cargo. As she got closer, she saw this operation wasn't anything like she had thought. She had been around a few military outposts before in her travels—driven by them, she supposed. But this... takeover of the airport was insane. The airships–spaceships that she could see on the tarmacs in the distance ranged from sleek to colossal, with enormous wings and engines that hummed like a chorus of bees.

. . .

Eva wasn't sure what she had expected, but the hive of activity at the airport was not it. There were signs, buses, and shuttles. Then, there was military personnel. This was her first up-close look at the aliens' military force. *Impressive.* They were imposing and professional in their uniforms. Eva was super interested to note that some of them obviously sported traits that weren't human. It was subtle, but Eva was sure she saw differences.

Of course, it was the airport, parking was a nightmare. What else did she expect? Thankfully, the signage was good and since she was making a delivery, she could park near her destination. Still, it was a chore to pop out the cart and load her bakery boxes up. She double-checked for breakage to make sure everything traveled okay. It was hotter than hell, and her t-shirt was stuck to her back by the time she hit *lock* on the van key and started rolling her cart toward the gate entrance.

In the distance, people made their way toward processing lines. An enormous variety of people queued up, every sex, age, and race. Most people had a small bag or backpack, but that was all. Eva briefly wondered how it would feel to leave everything behind and go somewhere totally new. Eva couldn't help but feel a little envious of this brave group of individuals embarking on such an incredible journey in search of a better life for themselves and those dear to them. These people had left behind loved ones and routines to start a new life in an alien world. As she watched them go by, Eva was filled with emotion.

Another sign nearer to the gate read, *Supply Deliveries Only*. Eva was relieved. This was where she needed to be. She wheeled her cart closer to the gate and took a deep breath as she approached. The outpost gate was made of sturdy metal fencing, thick and imposing.

The IGC military stood on duty. She had had all these expectations, running alien movies on a loop through her head. In Eva's opinion, they were all good-looking, but looked a lot like humans. Eva nearly kicked herself. Geez, why wouldn't they be good-looking. All of them looked tall with gigantic frames dressed in black leather uniforms. Eva had expected crazy weapons, green aliens, face masks, armor. She gave a little laugh. She was almost a little disappointed, maybe. Although the eye candy was a plus. She better not mention that to Daisy. She would be out here in a heartbeat as a volunteer. Maybe there was something freaky about them, although that wouldn't dissuade Daisy either.

. . .

She got behind a man that probably hadn't bathed in the last two weeks by the stench rolling off him. It wasn't uncommon. Water was getting scarcer by the day. Using it to wash regularly was foolhardy. Sometimes the cost was just too high. His long hair had some mats that a brush probably couldn't help at this point. He had a small wagon packed with e-cooler bags, which surprised her. The bags were valuable. Eva wondered idly what was in them. She was curious but was not stupid enough to ask. These days people were volatile and not to be trusted. It was always better to keep to yourself. Safer that way.

She eased the cart forward, double-checking that the bakery boxes were stable. Eva kept at least arm's length from the man in front and made sure that she kept her eyes to herself. She used her time to study the outpost so she could see the gate.

As Eva neared the front, she noted with some trepidation the guard had a tablet he was checking. She also saw the gate guard looking at her more than once. There were guards at the perimeter fencing that also kept shooting glances her way. The man in front of her shuffled to the front, pulling his wagon. He gave the girl behind him a quick look. People these days couldn't be trusted to be sane. Especially women. They were crazy. The man wiped his nose with the back of one hand, ignoring the disgusted look the IGC guard was giving him.

"Name?" The guard eyed the Earthling with barely concealed disgust. Honestly, he wasn't sure how this planet had made it this long. Their hygiene certainly was lacking, and the smell was horrific. He kept his nose from wrinkling, but barely. All the warriors had been briefed on Earth prior to landing; however, many found it difficult still. Why did the life forms here not clean themselves? The air around the camp was hot, and he was glad that his uniform allowed for an even temperature.

Outpost guards in the IGC forces were typically only recruited from planets with life forms capable of some form of camouflage. In this fashion, it made whatever populations much more comfortable with their presence when they first arrived. It was protocol to attempt to fit in with the form of the population present.

Eva was surprised at how normal everything looked. There was a gate guard, a list of sorts (although the tablet thing looked pretty fancy), and the whole gate. All of it seemed on par with what one might find on a military base.

The man gave his name to the guard on duty in a muffled voice. The guard nodded at him after looking at the tablet. "You've been here before. You know where to go then?" The one guard sounded bored as he moved to open the gate. Eva's heart pounded a little. She hadn't expected this. Maybe their business wasn't on the list?

"Yeah, I've been here. Kitchen for delivery and then to Building 5 for my pay. I know how it works." The man nodded as he shuffled his feet and got ready to move his wagon forward. Eva gulped as the guard swung the gate open. The man moved on through the gate, the wheels on his wagon squeaking and a little evaporative moisture dripping. Eva gathered herself as she wheeled her cart up into that last space.

"Can I help you?" The guard said, eyeing her with skepticism. Eva felt suddenly beyond cranky. Even though her hair was in braids, she felt the pieces that had escaped clinging to the nape of her neck and the sides of her face. Beads of sweat dripped from her neck, making her feel gross.

. . .

"Yes, I've got a delivery order." She pointed to the carefully stacked bakery boxes. "Sweet Treats Bakery," she said firmly and set her shoulders back, trying to ignore the fact that she wore a crappy nine-dollar t-shirt and jean cut-off shorts. The entire scene was a B-rated movie waiting to happen. Jesus. Selling cookies at the edge of an alien outpost, like a fucking Girl Scout. Eva almost rolled her eyes right there. When in the actual fuck had her life gone so far off the rails? What a joke. Nobody could have written such a dumb story. She tried to focus on the situation at hand, but still giggled a little. The guard glared, probably not sure what the crazy lady was laughing at, which made the hysteria bubble up a little more. She covered her mouth and coughed. "Throat is dry." She raised a shoulder half-heartedly. "Sorry," she mumbled.

The guard eyed his tablet for a moment, but Eva knew that a lot of it was for show. He eyed her with a bit of disdain and no small amount of incredulity. Eva was used to this. As a woman (and a small one that often was mistaken for far younger than her 26 years), she was used to not being taken seriously. His tone was dismissive. "A male named Gary is our contact and the man we deal with for this product. Sorry." Eva narrowed her eyes. Seriously? He didn't sound sorry at all. A "male"? Eva took a beat on that. Interesting.

. . .

Guards had gotten some Earthlings that had shown up at the gate in the past without clearance; however, there were strict rules. It was hard to ignore that this woman was lovely. The warrior, glanced at the small female. He could tell she was already getting angry. It was his job to make her go away. It was too bad really. He peered over at the product she was bringing in. He had tried one of the products she was bringing to the outpost. They were quite good. He hated to let them leave. However, rules were rules. He had no desire to draw any attention to himself.

"No, that doesn't work for me." The warrior looked surprised, and to be honest, it surprised Eva. She had turned off that nervous part of her. She didn't have that luxury right now, and she didn't know when she stopped being scared and became more weirded out by the whole insanity of the situation than anything else. "Gary has been selling *my* product. Mine. I'm the business owner." Eva's skin flushed with some of the anger (and no small amount of embarrassment). She was on the fair side with dark brown hair. When she got flushed, it was obvious. The heat made it even worse.

"I'm sorry. Gary is the contact. Tomorrow is his day. It's best for you to go through him." The guard said, not unkindly, but his tone was firm. "If you need to make contract adjustments, those can be done through your embassy liaison in building eight." He pointed toward the other terminal buildings.

Stephen tried to adjust his weapon his belt and tapped the tablet even though he didn't need to. He certainly didn't sneak another look at the pretty little Earth female. like his instructor had taught them at the Academy. When she yelled at him, he was completely unprepared.

The guard had his eyes on the ground, his back straight, and his shoulders back. "Are you serious right now?" His head popped up, and he stared at her with wide eyes.

"What?" Eva goggled at him. "I brought everything with me and it's my business. It's fresh *today*. That guy has been cheating me. It's not his contract; it's mine. Why can't *I* bring it?" She was loud but couldn't stop herself.

She tightened her grip on the handle of the cart and stared at the expanse of the tarmac, the outpost beyond, the fence. Trying to process. Okay, she could go to the embassy liaison, she supposed, and come back again. The thought was like sawdust. They needed the money. All this product would just go to waste. The thought of turning it over to Gary to bring tomorrow to sponge off them again was awful. Just as she opened her mouth to speak, a pair of men emerged from a building. One man turned to her, and she froze as she met his gaze. Her thoughts washed away like foam on an ocean tide.

She was sure it was the hot alien she'd seen last week, the vision in particles of light on the sidewalk. Here in the flesh, he was even *more*. Eva felt embarrassed and flushed. He looked just as delicious as she remembered. He didn't blend in with all the others in their military garb. Eva realized she was staring and quickly looked away as he approached her and the guard.

The guard turned to take note of her gaze and groaned. He came to attention as the two men moved toward the gate. Eva's mind was blank, and her body had trouble getting with the program. Her eyes darted back to his without meaning to. He took her in as he walked forward. Pinned in place, she saw every plane and shadow of his jaw, every eyelash. She felt the attraction humming along her body, tightening her nipples. It pissed her off. The man was gorgeous in a way that was totally unfair to everyone on any kind of planet. Suddenly she wished she wasn't some nobody in dirty sneakers and sweaty clothes.

The guard couldn't even believe it. The female had raised just enough of a fuss to draw attention to herself–and him, for that matter. He had heard that the Hunter was visiting, but he hadn't really thought it was true. Shit.

"Commander," the guard nodded respectfully to his direct superior, came to attention, and drew his shoulders back. "Hunter an honor." He was proud of himself that he kept his face blank as he spoke to the man who had caught Eva's attention, his head and chin back as his eyes went to the ground.

Eva's breath sucked in. These two men weren't just grunt soldiers or something. Then she stopped herself. *Who cared anyway?* She didn't give two shits. She needed to get this done and get back. She didn't care about their outpost or who the hell they were.

The two men eyed Eva along with her cart and boxes. This Hunter guy, with his unfairly gorgeous face, watched her with interest. It was already late afternoon, and Eva noted that no others had gotten in line behind her. She had been the last one, which was good because she felt somewhat humiliated. However, she wasn't leaving without making her point. She steeled herself to deal with more assholes.

Eva eyed the men with frustration. The guard handed the commander his tablet and snuck a look at Eva. The gorgeous guy whipped his gaze to the guard for just a fraction of a moment, his eyes narrowing. Then the guard dropped his eyes again to the cement and gulped.

"So, what appears to be the issue? Report?" the commander asked the guard.

Eva was off balance. The delicious man was eyeing her with predatory interest. The gate didn't seem as imposing compared to him. She raised an eyebrow at him and saw his lips twitch.

"Sir," the guard started, but Eva had been quiet long enough. She was practically choking on her irritation from the ride, the heat, and the indignation that she had been cheated already once and now might be again. She was thirsty and more than tired of the bureaucratic shenanigans to sell what was rightfully hers. This was fucking stupid.

"I'll tell you what the issue is. Tweedle Dum here doesn't have me on the list. *That's* the problem. The cookies are my product. *My* bakery is contracted for them, by the way." She paused and used air quotes, "Just because *Gary* is listed instead shouldn't matter. That guy is a prick." Eva said in a rush, the last word coming out fiercely.

The guard didn't know what a 'Tweedle Dum' was, but he felt insulted. The looked to the Commander in affront and raised an eyebrow. The Commander just shrugged. Apparently, it was an Earthly thing. However, it was the Hunter who answered the female.

"Cookies?" The delicious one said with a look that could only be disbelief. It only annoyed her. "Is this an Earth thing, then?" He let out a small chuckle. He looked to the commander who was shorter than him but still quite impressive.

Eva wrinkled her nose at him. "I don't know what you do here, but he's in charge, right?" Eva extended a hand toward the commander. To the delicious one, she said in an off-handed fashion, "I'll give you a sample later."

His eyes flashed at her. "A sample, little Earthling? That's a deal." Eva suddenly realized that perhaps she'd misinterpreted the situation. The commander and the guard paled, and the guard looked like he might pass out.

"I believe that..." the commander began, but the other man waved a hand, his eyes still fixed on Eva.

"Well, I have things to do. Help the little Earthling settle her affairs, commander. I have faith in you." He acknowledged Eva with a small nod. "Until later, little Earthling. I'll be back, for my—how did you say... sample." His grin was wicked.

"But—" He vanished into misty shadows of nothing. Eva didn't even know where to begin. "Did he just?" Eva waved a hand at the empty spot.

"He ... teleported," the guard said. "I think." His tone was somber and quiet. She could tell he was shaken. His eyes were glued to the spot where Hunter had been. Eva blinked and bit her lip.

. . .

"Is that even possible?" She watched as the guard continued to stare at the empty space. She cleared her throat and he looked at her. He blinked and rubbed his hand over his eyes. Eva's heart went out to the male.

The guard and commander exchanged a look. The guard nodded. The commander sighed and his shoulders sagged. "Yes," he said quietly. "It's possible."

"So ..." the commander drew her attention back to the matter at hand.

"Erm. Yes, cookies. The outpost has been purchasing the cookies that I've been selling. I've sent them through someone else, but he's been cheating me. So, I decided to come myself." Eva finished, twirling the end of a braid. The men watched her in avid fascination.

"Yes. We typically buy these from a person on-planet. A male named Gary. He comes tomorrow." The guard studied Eva carefully. "You make these?"

. . .

"Yes."

"They are quite good. The warriors fight over them," the commander answered, looking at the tablet he had taken from the guard. Eva was a quick study, and she was trying to catch up.

"Well, G-a-r-y is a prick." Eva dragged the name out. "He's a cheat and it's not his product."

The commander nodded, and it wasn't long before he instructed the guard to process her. Eva sagged with relief by the time the commander left.

Eva was hardly ever without her words though, and she wasn't sure exactly what had happened. "Well? Let's go, *guard*. Daylight burning and all that. What do we do next?"

The guard didn't look like he appreciated her humor or her company. Honestly, he should just appreciate that she was still holding her shit together. Life was hard. She had rent to pay and—

fuck, she was at the airport. It didn't get much worse.

"So, who was that?" Eva asked. The guard immediately looked concerned.

"Probably nobody you'll see again," he mumbled. "Don't worry about it."

"What's his name?" Eva asked, sticking a hand in her back pocket. She certainly hoped she'd see him again. "He was delicious."

The guard looked at her seriously. "He's the Hunter. If you're lucky, you won't see him. Nobody wants to see him." He bent back over the tablet. Eva realized she hadn't really gotten any answers.

Rude.

Chapter Seven

Callan ported to the energy signal of his second in command. His team lounged near the side of a building alongside a sluggish waterway.

He stopped to lean against the building, breathing in deeply. Fates, he thought. He could barely breathe. He closed his eyes, recalling the woman at the gate. As he stood there, questions swirled around in his head.

He shook himself out of his thoughts so he could meet up with his team. However, as he approached, it was just Sapphrius waiting.

. . .

"Where is everyone?" Callan asked as he walked around the corner. She sat with her back to the wall, her head resting on her knees.

Sapphrius rolled her eyes at him. "Well, Serix, as you know, is on Jurox. He says that is going well." They both knew Serix was being Serix, meaning he was a one-being wrecking crew (definitely not Earth material). It was disconcerting to see her in this Earthbound form. As his second, she was lead on keeping track of their motley crew because she was a great taskmaster. "Brilius and Paron are checking a location we got a tip on." She chewed on a thought for a moment.

"We'll see what they find, but we're close. It won't take long."

Callan gave her a grin. "I think I may have a lead at the outpost, too." His thoughts drifted back to the woman. He gave his second a grin.

"What's that?"

"What do you mean?" Callan was distracted by his thoughts, and her question took him off guard.

. . .

"Did you find her?" Sapphrius asked with a smile.

"Who?"

"Your fated," Sapphrius stated matter-of-factly.

Callan's head jerked toward the building across the street, but he only saw only the woman's face from the outpost.

"I-I," he stammered. His tongue tripped on a response. Then he stilled. "I think maybe I did."

"Don't worry. I won't say anything to the others." Sapphrius reassured him, her eyes dancing. "I can't say I'm not pleased you found her. We will take care of the Pavo cell in short order."

"You're right." Callan shook his head. "Of course."

Sapphrius' tone was sympathetic. "Maybe she is your fated, but if she is, it'll be clear soon enough."

. . .

"Right." Callan grinned. "Right."

While the Pavo thought they could operate without repercussions, that wasn't the case. Callan and his team would root them out—and then they'd die. Hopefully, he could get the saboteur at the base at the same time.

"Well, good. This planet is awful. Although," Sapphrius ran an appreciative hand down her blond tresses, "I quite like this form."

Callan gave his head a rueful shake. She always embraced each new form—in EVERY way. Often, she encouraged him to as well, although he wasn't quite interested at the moment. She was from the Proloxius Galaxy and many of the senses that life forms on other planets enjoyed were things the Proloxians never experienced. This was one reason Sapphrius lived exclusively to travel with the team. She said she felt more herself when she was someone else. Callan didn't understand that when she first said it, but the longer he lived, the more he understood.

. . .

"I'll check in with you again after you hear from Brilius and Paron then?"

She gave him an absent nod. "Sure, I'll give a shout." Which meant a literal shout telepathically. Callan had tried to coach her not to yell, but she was still a little too loud.

Callan ported back to the guard gate, startling the guard. He wasn't sorry and felt savage satisfaction since the asshole looked at the little Earthling with lustful eyes. He'd like to pluck them out.

"Has she been processed?" Callan asked the guard. He took her in now with a different perspective and an appraising glance. Fates, she was beautiful, and Callan couldn't wait to put his hands on her. He would too—of that he was certain. Did he feel such a draw because she was his Fated? He thought so.

The guard could almost not believe that the Hunter had returned to the gate.

"Processed? You make it sound like I'm a cow at an auction," the woman said with a disgruntled huff.

The Hunter looked at her, confused. She sounded angry as she glared at him. He didn't know what a cow was and was a little afraid to ask. He thought she might be more grateful for his intervention on her behalf since, without his help, she would more than likely have been turned away. However, he admired her spirit.

"Building five, you said? That way?" she asked the guard and then pointed toward the appropriate area.

"Yes, that's right. The paymaster will get you squared away. He'll also take your goods. I suppose you can speak with him about being the permanent contact person." The guard looked nervously at the Hunter. It was obvious his presence unsettled him.

"I'll show her. Thank you, Private." Callan said as he started walking with her. Obviously, she wanted to argue about his presence, but just bit her lip. Callan groaned, tortured, eyeing the white teeth on her pink lips. She kept pace with him, despite having to rush her steps a little.

"What's your name, little Earthling," he asked.

. . .

"Eva. What's yours?"

"Callan." He gave his name easily and without thought, giving her a small glance as he did so.

He didn't even bother to slow his pace as he continued toward their destination. The whole thing was a little intimidating, so she was glad that he had returned to be honest.

She wondered what he thought of her and of Earth. She wondered what types of things that he had seen. How many worlds that he had been to. Was Earth strange to him? Vaguely, she wondered about the fact that they all spoke English. Surely, they didn't have the same language.

Callan noticed her taking in the outpost the entire time with some trepidation. Neither said anything as he continued to lead her to their destination.

He neared the door to Building Five and went to move into the building. When she didn't follow, he looked back at her.

. . .

"Come on, then." He gentled his voice and held out a hand to her carefully. Eva eyed him warily. Callan braced himself as he felt the mating mark of the Shade flare to life. He inhaled sharply as she placed her hand in his. Callan felt it settling into his bones. The moment stretching as he took in the image of her, the faded white of her shoes in the red dirt, her tanned bare legs, faded shorts (he had never seen such a fashion, but he was a huge fan), and the shirt that had a few holes and some writing on it. Her eyes, like the color of storm clouds, settled on his, and he knew she felt it too.

A jolt hit her, not unlike static electricity, as she placed her hand in his. His eyes went wide as they met hers, flashing gold. Eva could hear his sharp intake of breath as he drew her close to the heat of his bond. She felt a brief sear across the hollow of her throat, but she was focused on the dark tendrils of shadow winding between them, binding them tightly. The ribbons of inky dark spilling from his fingers as they wound around hers. Eva supposed she should be scared, but as she tipped her face up and looked into his, he brought his other hand to cradle her neck and all she could feel was a sense of rightness.

"A sample then," he murmured and leaned down to anchor her mouth to his, dipping his tongue into her mouth, tasting once, and then retreating, dipping in again. Eva groaned and surrendered, and he plundered her mouth, pulling her tighter to him. When he pulled back, she whimpered. "So sweet," he said.

It should surprise Callan that his Fated was here, born amongst the Earthlings, but he was just grateful. He had waited centuries for her. He fought his nature to reel himself back in, spool his shadows back and not bleed the darkness, but it was difficult. He wanted to make love to her right there, in the dirt, sweep her up in his arms, and consume her.

Callan smoothed his hands down her face, tracing the delicate bones of her form. She was beautiful. His Fated. He must control himself. He took a breath and remembered himself. Patience—his Fated deserved patience.

His lips curled in a smile, and he tugged her hand and pulled her over the threshold into the cool air of the building. He liked that she didn't seem to have any fear of him. When she tried to pull her hand from his, he only gently tightened his grip on it as he ushered her farther into the building. It wasn't easy.

. . .

Eva couldn't pinpoint the feeling she had as she put her hand into his. The weird sense of rightness. She trusted him, and that was definitely against everything she stood for. Eva was well known for her caution with people, especially with men. She almost rolled her eyes, thinking about what Daisy would say if she could see her now. Her bestie would have a field day with her. She couldn't decide if Daisy would say, "go for it" or "Eva, what the hell."

A long counter almost directly in front of the door was filled with crates of goods to still be logged. Behind it was a seemingly endless array of shelves filled with a myriad of items, refrigeration units, locked cabinets, and a wonderland of products. Callan had always loved paymasters' offices. Each planet always had such interesting things to share. Although the IGC made sure outposts were self-sustaining, bartering credits provided a way to learn more about the population. It didn't hurt that sometimes the trade of items brought a lot of joy to the dry day-to-day life of the military. So many interesting foods, liquors, and other items. Some were intriguing, some were downright disgusting, and sometimes there were some concoctions that other races found useful.

. . .

"Hunter." The paymaster of the outpost, a craggy-looking corporal who looked as if it wasn't his first duty station, was already on his feet and at attention. "I-I heard ...you were here, how ... " he stumbled on his words, his face pale, hands slightly shaking at his sides. "How may I serve?" Callan knew what he had heard—all the rumors of the Hunter, the killing. He had a reputation as quite the unnatural butcher. Here with his Fated, he wondered what she would make of it. The stories from Janus told a tale of Callan going in for close kills, of him torturing for pleasure, the battle taking place with knives and the daggers he kept strapped across his back, of him not shying away from the blood and the darkness. The woman at his side looked at him in confusion and then back at the corporal. She obviously was trying to figure out the dynamic, the reason behind the fear she did not instinctually feel. The corporal suddenly seemed to notice the female that Callan had tucked to his side.

Eva wasn't sure what the guy's problem was. He was giving Callan some weird looks. Like he was afraid. Callan looked more like he was constipated than anything else. Eva was confused about the dynamic, but it wasn't really her business. Her feelings in her gut told her she had nothing to fear, so she didn't understand why the paymaster was acting the way he was.

. . .

"This is highly irregular," the corporal began. "The guard said she was coming through, but ..." the words seemed to die in his throat as he looked up at Callan again and lost his nerve. Whatever he had thought was irregular suddenly wasn't worth discussing. "Of course, an exception will be made." The corporal nodded and then hastened to pull his tablet from behind the desk. "Name?" he asked.

"Eva. Eva Madden." Her voice was sure and as she answered, she tugged her hand from his and gave him a dirty look. Callan chuckled at her efforts as she edged around him and closer to the counter. It was a little high for her and Callan found it somehow charming. His little Fated was amusing and he couldn't wait to get her alone. *Eva.* He rolled the name around in his head. She turned her head sharply at him, giving him a surprised jolt.

How did she know? Did she feel the bond? He would have to talk to her about that. He liked the idea of them being as close as they could be. This little Earthling was just as he had always imagined. She was her own person, fiery and strong. And perfect for him. Her eyes narrowed and Callan leaned in closer to her and breathed in her scent. It was delicious.

. . .

The corporal's gaze lingered on Callan as he tapped away at the tablet, fingers blurring in a stream of practiced movements. Eva unstacked the boxes and passed them to Callan to place on the counter. The small boxes were neatly wrapped and tied with string. She had said they were cookies. Cookies? The corporal counted the boxes. "We typically purchase this product regularly from someone else. My understanding is this will no longer be the case?"

"Correct. He won't bring it anymore. You'll deal with *me*."

Callan wondered about the nature of her relationship with this man. She certainly didn't seem to like him very much. Callan thought he'd very much like to visit with this G-A-R-Y, the prick she spoke of. Maybe he'd have more than a talk with him—the up close and deadly kind. Maybe he would kill him slowly. The idea gave Callan a wicked thrill.

The male had said something to her, and Callan wanted to know what it was. The corporal continued to bubble with nerves as he looked up at

Callan. Callan could see the cold sweat beading on his forehead. His eyes were like saucers and his hands shook at his sides.

"You'll still bring them, right?" the corporal asked. "Everyone really enjoys these. We always run out. They'd be disappointed if we didn't have these anymore. They fight over them." Eva's face broke into the first smile Callan had seen on her face and he was rocked. Her eyes had lit with pleasure at the compliment. Callan wished to make her smile like that all the time.

"Of course I will. I'm so happy to hear that they like them." She turned to Callan, grasped his hand, and squeezed it. "Did you hear that? They like them." Callan's heart stuttered as the mark on his wrist gave an answering pulse to his Fated's touch.

The corporal looked at him with horror, obviously confused by her familiarity with him—that she was touching him. The idea that this Earthly being would dare. There was also the issue that IGC females did not touch other males in this way. It was not done. However, Callan was so pleased—it was thrilling.

. . .

"I heard, Fated." He squeezed her hand gently, careful not to crush hers and with his other hand brushed a stray piece of hair from her face that had escaped the braids she had down her back.

The corporal fumbled a box of cookies, knocking a few over as his wide eyes locked on Callan's wrist where his sleeve had risen.

"H-Hunter?" the corporal stuttered in confusion.

His Fated snapped out of her fog and shook her head. She pinned the corporal with a stare. "Are you okay? You're going to pay me now, right? That's what we are arranging?" She then glared at Callan like she was irritated at him for interrupting her business transaction.

"Well, normally, yes." the corporal started, and Callan could have punched him for the hesitation. Or perhaps, let loose this Earthly form and wipe him off the face of this planet. He didn't want to upset her though. Callan had a pretty good idea the people of Earth didn't understand the concept of fated markings. He didn't want to explain right now.

. . .

"That's exactly what he's doing. He's *paying* you. Explain to her how it happens, Corporal." Callan used his coldest tone and leveled his gaze at him. It gratified him when the man paled, swallowed, and began to restack the treats.

"Certainly, certainly. Of course, sir." His eyes darted again to the Hunter's face when he finished counting. Then he retrieved a credit fob from the locked cabinet behind him and keyed it with the tablet. Callan looked at Eva, who was eyeing the whole transaction with suspicion. He wondered what she was thinking. She was biting her lip and Callan wished it were him doing the biting, but he would have to wait. He was getting hard just thinking about his little Fated. He could ease her nervousness though. He forced himself to concentrate on the matter at hand.

Eva needed to focus though. The little item the guard had pulled out looked like a flash drive or something. Eva wasn't totally sure what it was. It almost seemed like the soldier had been about to change his mind about paying her, but Eva wasn't sure why. She was a little confused about the whole thing.

. . .

"Did you have questions?" Callan prompted her. Her face went through a multitude of expressions that captivated him. Her eyebrows scrunched together as she looked at the fob and the tablet as if she hadn't seen one before. Then a faint redness lit her cheeks.

"This is how you normally do it? With these?" She pointed to the small metal fob the corporal worked with. Callan was perplexed. Surely this was common here? "Normally, Gary brought me cash. You know. Earth money." The corporal fiddled slightly with the fob and then laid it on the counter. He shifted his feet and cleared his throat. He looked to the Hunter and when he realized Callan wasn't going to bail him out, he picked up the small fob.

"Yes, this is how it is done." Callan willed himself to be still. It wasn't as if she would need the thing any longer; however, he didn't want to cause her any distress. Eva had lifted a hand up to touch the end of one of her braids. He watched her move her fingers up and down, stroking it, and had difficulty listening to the conversation.

"We load these. We call them credit fobs, with your balance of credits. In this case, we are paying 10

US dollars per item, so 2000 US dollars." Callan heard her inward gasp from where he stood.

"What?" Eva said in a small voice. "Really?" The corporal looked at her, confused. Callan wondered briefly if the amount was too little.

Eva felt her heart give a little jump in her chest. Two grand? What the actual fuck? That was so much. She almost couldn't contain the bolt of glee she felt. Then she realized that this whole time Gary had been getting all that money and her mood soured. It was ludicrous.

"Yes, that was our arrangement. You can take the fob and use it at any of the banks. They will exchange for your local currency. However, you can also continue to securely use it off-planet as well if you decide to move relocated." He shot a look at Callan. "It's one reason we use the fobs. Bring it back each time and we will reload it, add to it."

Callan could see her thinking the information over. He was now positive that she hadn't ever seen one of the credit fobs before, which surprised him. The IGC typically introduced them as currency in and around the outposts as soon as they landed—eight months ago. She should have already been exposed to them.

"I have a partner, my roommate. They need half of it," she paused, and her eyes darted to him. "Can you put half on another one?" Eva indicated the fob with a small wave of her hand. Typically, this wasn't something that the outposts bothered with. A contract for products and the details of splitting profits was beyond their interests. Many people that sold goods did so on behalf of others. How they divvied up those profits later was not the concern of IGC.

The corporal didn't even know where to start with this entire business. He had managed the paymaster's offices on many outposts, and he had never run into the Hunter, although he had heard everything about him. Certainly, he was respected and feared throughout galaxies for a good reason. The very idea of having an Earth female with him was strange; however, if he wasn't mistaken, he was seeing a fated marking on the Hunter's wrist. The corporal knew the female had just arrived at the gate. He wasn't sure what had occurred, but the very idea of a true fated marking—it was staggering. Let alone that it was with the Hunter. Poor girl.

. . .

"I'll need a name then," the corporal said carefully. At that moment, it hit Callan and he really thought about it. His Fated had an entire life he knew nothing about. What if this roommate was a male? His jaw clenched in fury and then decided—if so, the male was dead—along with the *prick*.

Eva had flicked a glance at him. The inky tendrils were back swirling about his feet. She laid an arm on his, squeezing it gently. The shadows receded and dissipated and she smiled at him.

"Daisy, Daisy Whitlock," Eva replied. The corporal returned to the tablet with another fob. Within moments he had keyed the details to the other fob and pushed both across to her. "Thank you so much." Eva's voice was full of relief and gratitude. It had been important to her. Callan's breath eased. Not a male then, a female, a friend.

They said their goodbyes to the corporal. Eva was excessively grateful, and Callan wanted to hurry his little Fated away so they could talk in private. He liked to see how she interacted with others, but they needed to speak.

. . .

She was the very first Earth female he had met, so there was no reference based on the representation of her people, but her emotions were written on her face for all to see. He had met many races the universe over but no one like her.

Within moments Callan was escorting her from the building. She tucked the fobs into a pocket in her shorts as they exited into the scorching desert sun. Callan was more than eager to get her alone so he could speak with her, learn more about her, and talk to her about the marking.

Chapter Eight

She had just turned to thank him when he looked at her, his gaze considering and filled with longing. It was a moment she would think about later.

A blast sounded from the back of the outpost. Eva heard the concussive sound and tried to register it, locate the direction. Was it a car backfiring? A gun? Then a giant fireball rose above the buildings, and flames licked the sky in tongues of fire. She froze and felt Callan grab her arms as he pulled her close to him. Another blast sounded near the transport area. Fiery eruptions hit the buildings nearest them, one after the other. Eva found herself flat in the dirt, his body against hers, hard and unyielding. She tried to turn herself so she could see, process, but it was an effort, her head pinned against his body. The ground shook with the force of the explosions. She realized the airport was getting hit.

Callan's terror was unparalleled. He had never felt this way in battle before. He had been in situations where bombs were going off, weapons firing, death around every corner and he hadn't felt this fear. The small female beneath him was his priority. As the heat surrounded them, his priority was to protect her. He felt it rising in his throat. The Fates made sure that the fated mark helped instill a sense of urgency, an overprotectiveness for your fated. Callan felt that now, choking him as he draped over her, trying to cover her body with his power as he let it rise within him, draping a shield of darkness, cocooning them.

"What's happening?" She could feel an impact against them, a groan. His palms were flat against the ground near her face, a trickle of blood down the back of his hand. She was frozen. Both her hands were trapped beneath her body, squashed, her face turned toward that male hand of his. His chest heaved, his body drawn tight against hers, a shield of flesh that had been placed between her and the carnage. Eva felt her throat closing, her body began to shake, and she tried to focus on her breathing, on being here, now, in the moment. The staccato beat of his heart she felt was calming, although she heard nothing but the pounding of blood in her head, her breathing and the chaotic chorus of screams of the dying and the injured. She watched as a rivulet of blood ran dark red onto the tarmac. She could feel him turn his head this way and that trying to assess what was happening. Tears pricked her eyes and she tried to calm herself. She was fine. It was going to be fine. She shut her eyes and tried to take a breath without inhaling.

"Callan." She pushed herself at him. "Callan!" she cried, panic rising knowing that something was very wrong.

“Okay, let’s move,” he said. Callan pulled her to her feet as she scrambled to find purchase. His hands pulled her up and against him. She tried to look around in the chaos of fire and didn’t know how to process was she was seeing. Where the building had been, there was a sea of fire, of smoke, of dirt and dust and pieces of mangled metal. The ground shook again with another blast, this one from behind them. The building they had just left, the paymaster’s building, was utterly destroyed. The roof was a mass of twisted metal. What was left was burning. Eva could make out parts of the counter, pieces of the products she had seen, a body, a leg. Her brain stuttered for a moment and then her body caught up, her feet moving, but Callan held her tight.

"We ... need to check," she began, indicating the building they had just left. His hand moved up to cradle the back of her head and tilted it to look at him.

"Look at me, Fated. I will keep you safe. He is dead. There is no need to check." His voice was sure, his strength palpable to her as he held her there. She nodded at him. "The corporal, he cannot be helped. He is gone." Eva watched as he looked over building five again briefly. Assessing. The explosions were going off in the distance, but they seemed to have subsided now. Eva heard what sounded like shouts, possibly gunfire.

Callan looked down at her. "I got you," he said, his voice a whisper.

"You okay? Are you hurt?" His face was so close, his eyes searching hers in the dim lighting, but there was a distant look to them like he was looking through her, to the ground behind her.

. . .

"What's happening?" she asked, her voice shaking.

"The outpost is under attack. Stay close to me and do exactly what I say," his voice serious.

All around her, the tendrils of shadows wrapped around them, swirling in inky haze and shrouds, lightening and darkening, covering and cloaking.

Callan steadied her. *The outpost is under attack.* He sent the message out to his team.

Sapphrius was quick to reply, but he could feel the press of Brilius and Paron against the link he'd sent.

Do you need help there? Her voice was fierce, protective.

Not yet. Stay on mission. Callan terminated the link.

Someone must have taken the opportunity to attack the outpost, as understaffed as it was. While he didn't have time to explain to Eva how he was getting his information, he knew a group was fighting on the edge of the outpost. He hoped he could get one of the attackers alive. He'd bet one of them could lead him down the trail they needed.

Callan took her hand, and as Eva felt hers enveloped in his large one, she again felt the sense of rightness settle over her. All she knew at that moment was that she trusted him to keep her safe. She believed him. Eva's heartbeat rose as something tingled again against her throat.

"Hold tight," Callan murmured and in a whip of blackness, they ported. Eva felt like everything was too tight for a moment, but it loosened almost immediately.

She realized with a start that they had teleported to another location. The world had disappeared in a flash of darkness and light. How strange to have such a power. As she glanced around, it seemed they had gotten closer to the fighting, not farther away.

That didn't seem like a great idea. She looked at him anxiously. He was blocking her with his body, angling so he was in front (which wasn't difficult, to be honest—he was huge). The mist and shadows moved from him to her, keeping her in a pocket of opaque black.

At the edge of the next building, Callan stood to his full height, eyed her and gave her a nod. "Stay out of sight." Eva peeked out and realized they had reached the area where the fighting was happening.

"Wait, if you give me a weapon. I could help." Eva grabbed his arm. He stopped his forward movement—looking at her patiently.

"I don't have weapons for you right now Fated. I'll be right back."

"Be careful—please." His mouth gave a little quirk.

Eva was suddenly cognizant that her heart felt irrationally concerned and invested. Her breath came in on a gasp as a hand touched her throat. Eva couldn't have predicted that this was how the day would go. That she would be here in this moment of death watching a man yielding two daggers going out into the heat of explosions. "Stay here," he ordered. "I'll be back."

. . .

The world around her was in chaos. The flashes of movement were so close. She could hear screaming, shouts of pain and shouts of anger. This was real. This was happening.

Behind the shell of a building, she guessed had been destroyed, Eva saw the commander and some guards crouched. She could make out that the commander was obviously wounded but shouting orders to another group behind another barricade. They were firing weapons at an opposing group of men near what she assumed was the transport ship.

They weren't IGC. Eva knew that much because they weren't in uniform. He had said to stay there, but she sure wished she had a weapon, just in case. She didn't know who these people were, but the corporal had been nice to her, and it wasn't fair that they had bombed the outpost when they weren't hurting anyone.

Little flashes of light marked the soldiers firing small, cylindrical objects. The red blasts left scorch marks wherever they hit. She guessed this was her first look at laser guns and almost had a surreal thought about Star Wars.

. . .

But the fighters weren't going down easily. They returned fire, blurs of movement and noise around the commander. Eva could tell that the attackers were using Earth weapons. The bullets pinged off the buildings. Callan sauntered forward into the open, twirling the daggers. Slowly, he spun to face the men, who charged again, closer this time. Her fingers splayed against the metal of the building, her anxiety increasing. She eyed the faces of the others. They looked as incredulous as she felt when they spotted him, but there was something else in their faces, awe and a mix of fear.

All the IGC were hunched behind a barricade and the assailants fired Earth weapons at them. Callan wasn't here to play youngling games with them. His Fated had been put in danger and he'd had to put her into the ground like an animal to protect her. His teeth ground together. Someone was going to die for that, and he didn't much care who.

On a side note, he only needed one or two alive. They'd lead him to the rest. He let another small drop of his power loose, reveling in it. Clouds of vapor rolled beneath his feet as he moved forward.

. . .

Eva swore he had grown in mass and that dark horns curled around his head, arcing up and back. Yet, when she looked again, it seemed like just a trick of the shadows. He looked otherworldly and deadly as he stalked forward.

The commander shouted something to Callan, but Eva was too far to hear it. Azer ducked as gunfire pinged wildly off the metal siding they were crouched behind. She could see that some of his hair was singed and blood coated one cheek. He didn't seem too bothered by the injuries, although the sight of Callan striding out into the open seemed to alarm him. Eva's heart was in her throat. She wanted to shout to the commander to not draw attention to him, but it was too late. As soon as he had stepped out of the shadow of the building, he was seen larger than life, with the daggers twirling in his hands and the shadows ebbing and flowing around them. He made no effort at subtlety. The men in the other group fired at him, but the bullets that made contact disintegrated into the mist that almost coated Callan. Eva filed it under "ask later."

Then, even as she thought she'd seen crazy shit, things got crazier. He did a running leap over the barricade the group had erected and jumped straight into their midst. It seemed he was almost suspended for a moment, daggers out, stretched in the air like an action hero she used to go watch at the I-MAX with Daisy. Eva's heart in her throat, she watched as he landed on the other side of the barricade. Then the fighting began in earnest. The close quarters meant they couldn't use the guns effectively. Of course, it meant that Callan's side couldn't continue using their *blasters* either.

Callan fought hand-to-hand with them, the daggers whirling so fast she couldn't keep track of them. To be honest, Eva never believed the other men had a chance. Blood arced from the blades as he moved in leaps from one person to the other. Eva was sure she saw a savage smile from him when one combatant landed a fist to his face. Seeming to gain courage from his actions (although he was crazy), some other warriors from the outpost joined him, including the commander. Within a few moments, bodies were scattered, dozens had surrendered, and Callan stood in savage triumph, blood dripping from the tips of the blades. The dark shadows now ebbing around his feet.

Callan didn't think it would surprise anyone, but fighting was oh-so-satisfying. A darkness within him craved it, finding solace in administering justice. He felt it was deserved for their callous disregard for life. Callan already knew the cost of life from the explosions was grave. Not to mention his Fated could have been injured. That was inexcusable. He had just found her.

Eva gazed over the tarmac, buildings blown apart, the bodies, the blood, and Callan. The sky was just turning orange as the sun was setting, flames chasing themselves over the edges of the buildings. Callan looked at her from the distance that separated them, seeming to know she was looking for him. He was bloody and dirty. He had slid his weapons away, but his face was grim. Streaks of blood covered his hands. She left the corner of the building she had been leaning against, the metal warm and solid. Her feet gained speed without her willing them to, running to him. She was vaguely aware of the startled warriors, either surprised by her appearance, or her actions, she didn't even care. She barely registered the turn of the commander's head, whose eyes might have widened in shock, or the captives that looked at her as if she was from off-planet.

"Are you alright?" she whispered and drew one hand up to his cheek. He wrapped her up in his arms and at that moment (although she couldn't have said how), she knew she was home. She had never really had one of those.

. . .

“Fated,” Callan murmured to her. “You were worried for me?” He softened his voice and his mouth quirked in a smile. Callan wrapped an arm around her waist and pulled her close, pressing a kiss to the top of her head. He then glared darkly at the bodies that littered the field and clutched her to him tightly. “I’m sorry if you were scared,” he said as if the whole incident was a personal affront to her and him.

“I wasn't,” she said in a hushed voice against the hollow of his throat (even though that wasn’t totally true), not letting herself be bothered by the blood, the gore, and the smell of battle. Eva pulled away from his grip, gently cupping his face in her hands.

"Who are they?” she whispered. Men were kneeling in the dirt and the bodies lying not too far from them. Eva tried to not look too hard at those.

“Pavo.” He ground the word out, although Eva wasn’t sure what that meant. The way he said it though, Eva was sure it wasn’t a good thing. The commander had come forward. He was bleeding from the cut on his forehead, and the leather uniform looked more than a little beat up. Eva had the powerful impression that she knew less than she should about these men and people. She had kept herself separate from the landing and opted to ignore it; however, that obviously would not work anymore. She was invested now, that couldn't be denied.

"Hunter? Are you injured?" The commander asked, almost hesitantly, as he came forward. Eva gave a laugh and then almost couldn't stop, sounding a little hysterical, even to her ears. The commander turned to her. "Miss? Are you injured?"

"I'm pretty sure *he's* fine. Actually," Eva waved her hand (the free one, the other was trapped), "He's F-I-N-E." She gave a laugh and then clapped the same hand over her mouth. Jesus, Mary, and Joseph, what was wrong with her. Granted, the man was good-looking, fine with a capital F, but what was wrong with her? Callan gave a chuckle and swung her up into his arms with ease. Eva gave a little squeak. "Callan, I can walk," she said indignantly, but without a lot of heat. She enjoyed being in his arms.

"We are both uninjured, Commander." In a low and steady voice meant just for Azer, he said, "Take the ones alive to the detention center. I'll be along shortly. We need to clean up." Callan indicated with a nod to Eva. Then Callan firmed his grip on her and ported.

Azer, for his part, wasn't sure how to process what was happening. He had seen the Hunter fighting before, but not like this. Just as the stories of him on Janus, and as the Hunter himself had described to him earlier, he was obviously more than willing to fight if necessary. He was a force to be reckoned with and if anyone was going to stop the Pavo, it was him. The woman though, what in the Fates? Did he see and hear correctly ... he wasn't sure how to catalog it in his thoughts. Azer shook his own head. Unbelievable.

"I can walk," Eva wiggled but wasn't sure how much effort to put in when she was being held so nicely against his chest and it had been a long day. She was thirsty and tired. Eva wasn't sure what a Pavo was or what was happening, but she would let him hold her, looking up at his face and thinking how fine he was with a capital F.

The transport ship lay in ruins, blackened, hollow. If there had been people in it, Eva knew without a doubt that they were all dead. It was chilling to think those people had been about to embark on an exciting new future, and a fiery explosion had put it to a terrible end. How sad and how unfair.

She saw bodies in the dirt, torn beyond repair, and warriors with vacant eyes. She dared a peek at Callan; she was sure he had seen and done these things before. Surprisingly, it didn't scare her. If anything, it reassured her. She believed him when he said that he would keep her safe. Believed him with everything she was.

Fated? What was that he was calling her? She would need to ask.

Chapter Nine

It had started with a rumble in the distance, then the earth shook violently beneath them as the explosions lit up the sky. The air was thick with the smell of smoke and destruction, and Brilius knew people were dead.

He turned to the group around him and asked quietly, "So, are we going to head over to the outpost now or what?"

He and Paron had been scouring every seedy Portland establishment around the city all day. They were fairly sure they had a meetup invite; however, Brilius was unnerved that so many things were happening at once. Normally, these cells were smaller and not so difficult to find.

. . .

"Wait." Sapphrius had her forehead scrunched, a sure sign that she was attempting to send Callan a message. If Brilius knew anything after all their time together, it was that Callan was down in the thick of the fighting, dealing damage and kicking ass.

"We head toward the outpost now. But we are stopping—" Sapphrius's breath stopped as she laid a hand on Paron's thigh, clenching tightly. Both men looked to their second. She was a fierce fighter, competent, and deadly in any form. Seeing her hesitate was interesting. She was intelligent and shrewd. Overreacting was not in her nature. As she met their eyes, they knew the news was big. She took another breath.

"We have an errand. A human girl." The look on her face was priceless. "The girl is important. That's all you need to know." Sapphrius's voice left no room for conversation. They looked at each other. This was not their world, and they had no right to question their king or his motives. "Callan will meet us at the outpost as soon as he can."

. . .

"Is she connected to the Pavo?" Brilius wasn't too impressed by the Earthlings, to be honest, although he was quite fond of their form. He gave Sapphrius's form a side glance. Their females were nice to look at but not much else. Her skin was soft and warm, and her smell was intoxicating. Why would the king ask that they make a stop for some wayward human girl? Brilius took a deep breath, looking out at the tired city, the lights sparkling like stars in the distance.

"No," Sapphrius said quietly. "Our king has found his Fated." Many emotions were floating for Paron to taste and he let his own power free for a moment. A touch of disbelief, doubt, and then the primary emotion shining through juicy and bright ... hope.

Implications settled over the three as they ported toward the Earthling their king asked them to locate. Theirs was a world steeped in war, blood-shed and death. Their females were rare in number, so they were precious. That their king had finally found his Fated was momentous to be sure.

They landed on the top of a high-rise building in a quiet part of the city. They stood still, concentrating on the feeling. Underneath them, the Earthling slept.

"Do you think she'll be awake now?" Paron asked in a hushed voice.

Daisy curled up on the threadbare, plaid couch, a yellowing paperback open in her hands. A trio of loud voices echoed through the small apartment as she made out shapes in the doorway. "Well, who the fuck are you? I'm busy." Daisy's default was always sass, and this was no exception. She didn't sense any malevolence from them, but they were in her apartment and that immediately made them enemies.

"We are from all over the universe, Earthling. It's complicated, really," Brilius began in an exaggerated voice. He loved to distract, and he loved to argue.

She pushed her hair from her eyes and lay her book on the side table, looking at them with interest. Aliens. Huh. They didn't really look any different. She was a little disappointed if she were being honest.

. . .

"Daisy. I'm Sapphrius, and this is Paron and Brilius." Sapphrius said with fake formality. "We are here to talk to you." Sapphrius's eyes glittered from under her lashes.

"Okay." Daisy was at a loss. I mean, what do you say to a group of people that appear in your living room out of thin air? "Well, I'm busy reading and don't need any more complications." The human's soft brown eyes told a different story, though.

Paron liked the way she looked, soft. He wouldn't mind a closer look, but he checked himself when Brilius sent him a warning glare.

"Paron." Sapphrius halted him from edging closer to the beautiful woman with pillowy breasts and skin the color of the sands of Talogath.

"Are you lost? Do you need help?" Daisy asked, a sardonic smile flickering on her lips.

Paron could taste her lack of sincerity, but also the beginnings of unease. "No, little human. We are here just to relay a message to you." Sapphrius took a moment to give a disgruntled snort.

. . .

"Your friend Eva is safe. She will be much later than expected, but you should not worry for her." The words had the opposite effect.

Daisy jumped up. The book dropped to the floor. She came toward them, eyes that had been calm were now filled with fury. Paron thought she was a vision, her chest heaving, her curls bouncing, and her eyes flashing.

"What are you talking about? Did you take her? People have been disappearing. Go get her! I don't believe she's okay. Go get her!" Her panic rose with every breath.

"Your friend is safe; she is just not where you expected her to be." He knew the girl before him would need explanations. "Eva is fated to be the king's." Both Sapphrius and Paron heard Brilius' voice in their heads, telling them to omit this part. They'd have time to explain the situation to her later.

"I don't care what the fuck you say, you demon fucker. You better not have touched her. I'll fucking end you." The words were barely out of her mouth before she was on him. He caught her hands before her nails got too close to his eyes.

Paron reached and laid a hand on her. She was as delicious as he had imagined. He sent his power forth, calming her.

"Dick. Stop it." Daisy's voice was sharp as she jerked away from his touch. "Don't touch people without their consent. I'm not sure what fucking planet you're from, but that's not acceptable here." Paron was stunned. He looked back at Sapphrius and Brilius who were no help at all. Paron hadn't ever come across anyone who had such an aversion to him. Most of the females were quite willing to allow him access. Granted, she wasn't wrong about what she'd said. He'd gone for easier—he shouldn't have done that.

"Don't try any weird alien hocus-pocus on me." She glared daggers at him. "Bring me Eva."

Paron help up his hands in a sign of surrender. "I won't do it again, human. My apologies. Our king sent us to notify you that your friend is safe." Paron was still confused, but Sapphrius looked at her with genuine admiration.

Light flared in Daisy's eyes. "Well, that's not good enough. She moved from the couch, ignoring the hot eyes of the 'dick', and addressed the female. "You tell me where she is."

"Eva and the king will see you in the morning. You can see for yourself then." Sapphrius had to admire the spunky Earthling. It was impressive but already tiresome.

A burst of light and the three of them were gone. Daisy sat with a huff. She didn't enjoy being out of the loop.

She'd feel better if she could see Eva herself and make sure she was unharmed.

Chapter Ten

Callan couldn't believe what had just happened, but he was sure that the Pavo was involved. That whole little act had been nothing but a minor skirmish played out with on-planet actors unless he was mistaken. He was fuming that it had taken place and could have potentially injured his Fated.

Eva gave a small huff in his arms and readjusted herself, looping an arm around his neck. He gave her a light squeeze.

"That was a little crazy," she commented.

. . .

When he responded, his voice was...strained. "That my Fated almost got injured in a firefight?" She heard the heartache in his voice and pulled him tighter.

"Well, you know what I mean." She made a dismissive gesture and tried to look unconcerned.

Eva's eyes were wide as the ship came into view. The landing ramp opened for them, heavy as it hit the tarmac with a small sigh, the dirt rising in a puff as the edge hit the ground. "Callan? We aren't ... leaving?"

Eva couldn't believe she was about to go on a spaceship. Wasn't that a riot and a half? She chuckled to herself. Although she was pretty sure Callan had work to do and they weren't going anywhere, she still felt like she had to ask.

"No, Fated." Understanding she was asking if he was taking her off-planet. He would never do that without a much longer conversation with her.

Although, he was planning to have that conversation with her and VERY soon. "We are going to clean up and get some clothes, refreshments, and then we will deal with these camp issues," he said candidly. His boots didn't slow as they hit the ramp, his pace steady as they entered the cavernous ship.

He felt his little Fated taking in the ship's interior, she was surprised, but he hoped she was impressed as well. His were an advanced people. They loved their creature comforts, and if they weren't going to port around, Sapphrius was especially finicky about her sleeping quarters. Of course, he could port anywhere he liked— anywhere in any world, star system, galaxy, or dimension in existence— and often did. But the IGC didn't know that he could do that. As King of the Shade Dimension, it was best to keep this power a secret. The IGC would be uneasy to think he could just pop in and out wherever, however, and with whoever he pleased. The ship was strictly to keep up this *hunter* persona in his travels. Sometimes he made one of the team members take it so he could port instead.

He lowered her to her feet, holding onto her briefly to check that she was steady. "Let's get some nutrition cubes first." Callan couldn't help but run his palm down her arm, enjoying the feel of her response as he did so.

"Get what?" Eva said, his words registering as he moved away from her to a small box in the wall. "Is that a microwave?" It was his turn to look at her, confused. The interior looked a lot like she had expected, with slick panels and fancy things she didn't know what they did. It was larger than she thought it would be.

"A what?" Callan gave a small laugh. "I suppose we'll do a lot of translating and explaining as we go. You can teach me."

Her clothes were dusty (probably from lying on the ground earlier) and it looked like she had scraped her shin. He frowned. He needed to do a better job taking care of her. "No, it's a refreshment mechanism. It provides nutrition cubes. I key them in here, what our requirements are, basic height and weight, type of life form—that sort of thing. Then the technology does the rest. They aren't very interesting, but they do the trick." Callan touched the front pad on the outside of the box. It lit up as Eva watched in astonishment. He began to type in a variety of items into the keypad.

. . .

Type of life form? Eva's mind stuttered a little. Granted, she hadn't ever thought they were A-L-O-N-E in the universe. But life form really sunk in for her that there were legit aliens. Then the hamster gears started rolling again with what Callan was saying. Nutrition cubes. Huh, okay, whatever. She could wait and see. The rest of the ship beckoned, and she was suddenly curious to see it all.

Callan noted her puzzlement and moved to explain. "Well, a lot of the planets we have encountered, like Earth, struggle to produce enough resources. It is one reason planets struggle to sustain life. Basic resources like enough food and water for their people." Eva moved farther into the ship, her footfalls tentative, fingers not quite touching but grazing the surfaces as she went. "Often, that is why we relocate populations; the planets cannot sustain life anymore." Callan finished keying in the final information. "These are just for when we travel though."

"So, it's food?" Eva asked. She crossed her arms and then uncrossed them. A frown crinkled her forehead as she looked at him. Callan figured he made quite the picture. While the ship wasn't exactly cramped, it wasn't super spacious either and he was a large male.

. . .

"Well, yes." Callan showed her the mechanism. Inside, there was a whirring light and then a small ding. He smiled as he pushed the button and waited until something clunked out of the hole at the bottom of the machine. Callan picked up two small cubes and handed one to her. "Each one contains all the nourishment and hydration needed for a life form to sustain itself. The cube only lasts 8-10 hours. Typically, I carry extras with me. Especially in the field as a precaution."

Eva reached out and took it from him. They were small, maybe half the size of one of her fingernails. Callan smiled at her as she pinched the small cube between two fingers with distaste. She raised an eyebrow. Honestly, he didn't blame her. They were odd to her and weren't as interesting as some of the off-planet foods he had seen on his visits.

"You swallow them?" She laughed but looked at him with wide, horrified eyes. Eva looked at the small little square. What a weird thing. She gave it a sniff. It wasn't much bigger than a Tic Tac, but it pulsed slightly with a small glow.

"So, you're giving me alien food?" Eva looked at him dubiously. Callan couldn't help his huge smile as he watched her.

. . .

"Here, watch me, Fated." He popped the little cube in his mouth and swallowed. The cubes were designed to activate with the saliva and then slide down the throat. Honestly, they weren't bad at all. As soon as they entered the body, the cubes began their work, ensuring that nourishment was dispersed. Callan honestly wasn't sure how the technology functioned, but he was super grateful to the scientists who made it work. When he needed hydration, it provided that—when he needed protein—the cubes provided it. It had saved him on more than one occasion.

"I would never hurt you. Or give you anything that would harm you," He took a step forward and was momentarily overwhelmed with the sense of her in his space. That they were alone. "I would die first," he said, his voice low and earnest.

The cube pinched between her fingers, she took in Callan's words, feeling them resonate within her. Ignoring the glow from the ... morsel ... then she placed the cube in her mouth.

He knew the moment it hit her tongue. Her face brightened with delight, the muscles in her throat swallowed. "If I turn green," she narrowed her gaze at him, "I blame you." She gave him a little shove. "I can't believe I just swallowed that." She gave a little laugh, her voice husky.

Callan chuckled. "See, they aren't that bad. You'll start feeling better in a minute. Full and not dehydrated. Pretty soon, you'll wonder how you lived without my magic cubes." He gave her a wicked smile. "Now, let me show you something else magic."

Eva smirked at him. "Really? I think you would have a better pickup line than that. Don't you travel around space ... and stuff?"

She already felt better. How weird. When it hit her mouth, it tasted like the strawberries she had once when traveling along the farmlands of California when she was little with her grandfather. Then, the grass was still green, there were fruit stands dotting the rolling roads. They had stopped at one on a warm July evening. She could still taste the burst of berries on her tongue as she ate them, chasing them with the juice that dripped down her chin. She ran her tongue over her teeth. It almost brought tears to her eyes thinking of it.

. . .

Callan motioned her toward the front of the ship and a corridor that stretched from the cockpit. "Let me show you where you can get cleaned up." Callan led her down the corridor to his quarters. They weren't necessarily spacious, but they were well-appointed with buttery leather, cabinets of the finest IGC metals, a sleeping pod, and his bathing chamber. "Even I think this is pretty neat," he said, leading the way. Eva followed even though she had raised an eyebrow at him. Callan became more aware of her as they entered the tighter quarters, her head turning to see everything. He moved to the side so she could enter the doorway.

"Are there are other people staying here? Or is it just you? This ship is huge."

"My team is with me. You'll meet them later," Callan replied.

"Is this your bedroom?" She ended the question in a low husky voice, wrapping one arm around her middle. "Moving a little fast, cowboy," but she moved into the room. Callan could scent her and had to clench his fists to his sides to keep from reaching out and pulling her to him, bruising her flesh, crushing her mouth to his, tasting her. He closed his eyes to take a breath. He had to control himself. But he couldn't believe how his heart raced. The mark on his wrist pulsed, calling to his Fated. Her scent wrapped around him like a shroud. He took another deep breath to calm himself.

Her eyes scanned the room, taking in the dark, rich leather. The design was modern, sleek. The bed looked enormous. It would have to be to accommodate his large frame. She wondered how he would fit on that bed with her. A shiver went up her spine as she imagined them with the sheets tangled around them.

"You can clean up here." Callan raised his arm, pointing toward the bathing chamber with his chin. He snapped his hand back to his side to keep from reaching for her. He was going to lose his control if he didn't resist. No way did he want that to happen. When he had first scented her, he had felt the blood rush in his ears, his cock twitch in his pants, his muscles tense.

Eva wondered why Callan had stopped. His eyes were closed, his fists and his jaw clenched. She was almost overwhelmed with the desire to kiss him, lean close to him, rub herself against him, and run her fingers through his hair. She took a step toward him and then another.

When he opened his eyes, he found himself staring directly into her grey ones—she was so close he could feel the warm puff of air from her lips, the tremulous sigh escaping her mouth. "I feel like ..." she began. Callan felt it then, the bond reaching between them pulling tight and he decided it wasn't something he could fight or wanted to.

"What do you feel?" Callan lifted a hand to cradle the back of her head, reveling in the delicate feel of the nape. His other hand went to the dip of her waist, kneading her flesh there, exploring the curve with his fingers, running them along her side, ribbons of shadow dripping from his fingers. Eva raised her hand to his chest, raising her face to his, breathless. Callan marveled in the feel of her, warm against his body. The perfection of her features had burrowed into his heart right from the beginning. Looking down at her, the small scar near her right eye, like a small crescent moon, he cataloged it, wanting to ask her about it. He wished to know all about his Fated. Her stories, her scars, her pain, her loves. Callan wanted to hear her whispers in the dark so he could whisper back to her.

. . .

"Like, you're still a prick, but I like you anyway," she said on a whisper, rising onto her tiptoes and brushing her lips to his as they curved into a smile. Callan dipped forward as he took her mouth, slanting over hers. His tongue swept in to meet hers, taking in the inhale of her breath with his own. Incongruously, he thought she tasted of a fruit he once had in the Sigma Pelieus Star System. He ran his hands down the small of her back and squeezed her hips, pulling her forward to cradle against his, the contrast of soft to hard tantalizing.

"Oh?" he answered, smiling. That wasn't exactly what he had hoped she would whisper, but he was still delighted. He deepened the kiss, pushing her back against the cabin wall as she groaned softly. Callan could feel their bond weaving together, the threads almost visible in the surrounding air, glimmering in the ether. He raised one hand, brushing softly against the fullness of her breast, "Eva," he groaned. Callan pulled back slightly from her then... Fates, she looked delicious, her lips full and red from their kisses. Callan slipped his fingers over her nipple and gave it a small pinch through her t-shirt. "You are everything I ever dreamed of," he said huskily.

Eva moaned, her desire spiking, and lifted a leg, hooking it over one of his hips and grinding into him. He had moved onto her neck, sucking, and nipping at her. She could feel how wet she was already. "Oh, God, Callan. I ..." she was breathless. Suddenly she felt wild and out of control, lifting herself into him.

If he had thought she was beautiful before, he realized there was a whole new level of beauty to his Fated now. She responded to him, to his touch, her nipples blooming into hard little nubs under his fingers, her breath coming in short, shallow pants, her body shuddering with need.

Eva was lost in sensation, the feel of his lips and hands on her. She could barely hold herself up and reached out blindly.

"Let me," he looked for her permission. She gave him a nod, her eyes glazed, her hands gripping his shoulders. Callan moved her panties and shorts just to the side and slid one thumb up to her clit. "You are so wet for me, Fated." His voice was husky with pleasure. He moved his thumb and forefinger along her clit, watching her.

Oh, my God. She was going to die. She thrust on his fingers, her leg riding his hip. Eva knew she was soaking wet but couldn't find it in herself to be embarrassed. "Callan, right there ..." He watched her, his gaze intent on hers as he pressed hard on her clit with his thumb. The orgasm burst over her hard and fast, the lights like stars behind her eyes. He wanted to taste her, feel every part of her, and memorize every moment of their coming together.

Callan watched Eva with fierce delight. Giving his Fated pleasure was a joy he thought he'd never have. He withdrew his fingers, rocking against her to let her get every drop out of the moment as he brought his fingers to his mouth to lick them. Her eyes went wide with surprise. "You're as delicious as I thought you'd be."

The orgasm was still rippling through her, but Eva felt mildly embarrassed. She wasn't typically so easy. "I don't know what I'm doing. How I even got here." She shook her head slightly as if trying to clear it. "What is this?"

Callan understood this was a question about the bond she couldn't see, the swirling sense of rightness that was getting stronger the more they were together. He took a step back from her, steadying her on her feet and providing her space. It was hard to think when they were so close.

. . .

"Let's clean up first. I'll get you some clothes. Is that alright? I'll explain what this is. I don't misunderstand you." Callan said, watching her try to rearrange her clothes. She blushed, obviously a little embarrassed, but hopefully, Callan could be clear with her. She had nothing to be embarrassed about and he didn't want to rush her.

"Okay," her voice was small, but she didn't question him. "Show me some more magic, then." She gave him a smile as she injected some of her sass into her comment and Callan felt the full force of her charm.

"Alright then. Bathing," he said, reaching out to the door on one side of the quarters. "When we are off planet, we use this." He opened the door, showing her the small chamber. It contained a bathing tube, a mirror, a small basin, and additional cabinets. "In my dimension, these are more luxurious, but we utilize the bathing tubes on ships like this as they are more practical." He showed her the small glass-like tube off to one corner. It had room for a life form to stand in. For her, it was quite spacious. For him, it was fairly snug. "So, you disrobe," he gave her a speculative look.

. . .

"So, you get naked," she gave him a look. "I'm not getting naked with you in here. Not on our first date." She gave him a wink, and he looked startled.

"Of course, I'll give you your privacy." He hadn't meant that he expected her to disrobe while he was there, although he wouldn't have said no. He gave her an answering smile.

"So, get naked, step in there. Then what happens? Magic? I'm clean?" Eva asked, poking at the glass tube.

"You step inside. There is a panel." He opened the door and showed it to her. "You press these buttons to pick what you'd like, scents, what kind of pressure." He showed her which buttons to push. "Temperatures. It is based on air primarily, no water involved. So, it doesn't waste resources." Callan waved at the tube vaguely. "You'll need to let your hair loose. I think that'd be best."

Eva looked at him and then at the tube. This was another bizarre space-age thing, but she supposed it wasn't unexpected. But really? Did he expect that she'd just get in some air tube? She gave him another glance, shifting on her feet a little nervously. "Can you go first?" she asked. "I just want to see ..."

Callan couldn't help himself, "You want to see?" He gave her a wicked grin. "I'd be happy to give you a demonstration." His eyes were heated honey. "I'll show you everything." Callan saw the pulse point in her throat speed up.

Eva just bet he'd show her everything. She gave a husky laugh. Eva was playing with fire. She was pretty sure she was going to get burned too. However, she couldn't decide if she cared or not. Eva hadn't noticed the small platform set against the wall beside the tube, but Callan stepped up and raised his arms before she could clarify that she didn't really mean that she needed to see E-V-E-R-Y-T-H-I-N-G right that second. As soon as he stepped up, the platform turned blue. "Good afternoon, my lord. We are at your service." Callan kept his gaze locked on Eva as his clothes disintegrated before her eyes and disappeared into the platform. He stood before her completely nude, like nude, birthday suit nude. If Eva had thought he was impressive before, she was not prepared at all. Her breath hitched, and for a moment, it stopped altogether.

Chapter Eleven

Eva gulped. Holy shit-balls. The dude was packing. Seriously, his cock was hard, and he was ready to go. Not surprising based on the previous activities that had just occurred. She had thought he was a big guy, but he was B-I-G. She wasn't quite sure how to respond to a naked Callan. Honestly, she wasn't sure how to respond to any of it. The whole swallowing a blinking cube thing? Now this shower tube that had no water? But for some reason, it was the naked hot-as-fuck Callan that was about to tip her over the edge with his wicked eyes and sweet kisses. He seemed as aware of her sense of panic as she had been in the taking of the things that he was showing her. Now there was this melting clothes situation. It was this that was the most disarming of all.

. . .

The man was aware. He was aware of her as he stood there.

Okay, she could do this. All she had to do was just...stay calm and ignore the part of her that wanted to get into the shower with him. Could she ignore it? Yes, she could ignore it.

His tone was matter of fact as he said, "Okay, Fated, once you've disrobed." He waved a careless hand at the platform as he stepped off and took a few steps toward the bathing tube. He seemed completely oblivious that he was naked (and turned on). Eva felt the heat between her thighs pooling in answer as she imagined what sex with him would be like. The whole against-the-wall action was already a great start. Eva could get used to more orgasms like that. "You step into the tube. You key in your—"

Eva tried to pay attention and ignore the wetness between her thighs, although she had an idea that Callan knew somehow. His eyes were fiery as he watched her. She refocused and thought of something. "Wait, where did they go?" Eva interrupted, totally thrown off by the disappearing clothes. The platform was now empty and quiet. What if it sucked a person in? She eyed it suspiciously.

. . .

Callan was trying to count backwards from one thousand. His cock was pounding, and he could smell her desire from across the chamber, but he needed to explain the mark to her and its significance before they continued.

"The clothes?" he asked, flummoxed. When she nodded, he said, "They are carried back to the mechanisms that generate more at another time. They discard portions that will no longer be useful and then recycle those into other areas of the ship or they utilize the portions that are still viable into others that I will need. Or now that you will also need." As he explained Eva couldn't do more than look at him in open-eyed wonder.

"Are you telling me you have a machine that makes you clothes?" If this was true ... this was some mind-blowing Jetson crap. Daisy would have a cow. Eva stopped mid-thought. Daisy would be worried sick. She needed to get word to her somehow.

"That's.... Amazing." Eva was dumbstruck. She was having a hard time even finding words to describe the idea. Eva had always loved to read about and think about science fiction but seeing it in actual reality was mind-boggling. Eva knew without a doubt that the technology in the ship was far advanced beyond anything that she knew or had read. Honestly, that wasn't a huge surprise if you really thought about it. Imagination could take you to the edge, but sometimes reality really was what kicked your ass.

Callan gave a small chuckle. "Yes. You'll see in a moment." He stepped into the bathing tube and pressed his series of buttons and closed the door. Eva was distracted as she noted he seemed to have quite the collection of scars along his back and torso. It looked like he had some tattoos, too. She liked those, she thought with approval. Yummy. She wondered if she'd could ask him about them. Eva started suddenly as the bathing tube went into action, whirling air whipping around him, as it scrubbed away dirt, blood, sweat. She was fascinated as a scent permeated the chamber. The faint smell of the honey, ocean, and licorice as she remembered it as a child. He pivoted, and she got a nice glimpse of a seriously nice ass. God, she thought to herself, she was disturbed to be in this situation and all she could think about was getting laid. How he could lay her out on the bed, his hands on her thighs. There had been bombs, people had been shot. She was basically stuck here, and she was thinking about getting busy with some guy she just met. Daisy would be so proud of her.

. . .

Just then, the tube shut off, and he stepped out, dry and clean. Eva was floored. "Wow." It was the only thing she could think to say. Callan stepped out of the bathing tube. He glistened as if he'd been wet. It was almost as if he'd showered. How was that possible?

"Magic," he said with a smirk. He strode across the chamber and stepped back up onto the platform. It turned blue again. "Hello, my lord," the disembodied voice spoke again.

Callan said, giving her a wink, and as Eva watched, it seemed as if particles of material appeared from nowhere and wove themselves around each part of Callan's body. She wasn't sure where they came from. The floor itself? Eva waved an arm, wordless in awe. It was like the street clothes he had on earlier, but clean. The platform even provided boots. Eva wondered what the limits were.

"I told you." He winked at her. "Magic."

. . .

Eva couldn't decide what was more incredible. The naked part or the magic clothes part. "So, it'll make me clothes too?"

He nodded, "It will. It has limitations, but the AI will discern what planet we are on. You'll need to direct it with functions. If we are going to a formal function for instance – versus a battle."

Eva nodded. She was uncertain about how she felt about everything, but she was filthy, so she welcomed getting cleaned up and getting some explanations. She moved her hands up to her braids to undo them. Callan watched her hands move over her hair not leaving the chamber. Eva eyed him in the mirror. It wasn't lost on her that the AI had called him my lord again.

"May I?" he asked, moving forward. She nodded and turned her back to him. "Like this?" He began unweaving her long hair and Eva couldn't help but lean into him. She had always enjoyed the feel of someone else doing her hair or undoing it as the case might be. She smiled to herself, even though he couldn't see it.

. . .

"Just like that," Eva said softly in a murmur, tilting her head as his fingers reached into her scalp and finished unbraiding one side of her hair. Her brown hair was thick and long, well past her shoulders. She had taken to braiding it to keep it up and out of the way. She could feel him move to the other side and she couldn't help but fall against his chest, leaning her weight against him as his warm hands moved into her hair, tugging at the knots and tangles, unweaving her braids, loosening it from her scalp, curling and turning it with the movement from his fingers. Her eyelids fluttered shut.

"Like that?" Callan said, his fingers touching the shell of an ear, softly tracing her neck. Eva could feel her whole body come alive as his fingers moved in feathered movements along her collarbone. "If you don't go get cleaned up, we are going to have a hard time leaving this ship." Sliding a hand under her t-shirt against her belly, up along the skin there, back and forth. He was obviously learning what she liked quickly.

"Maybe I want to stay here." Eva managed. "Maybe I want to be bad." She could almost taste his surprise and pleasure as he moved a hand down to her hip, splaying his fingers against her.

. . .

"Oh?" his voice was low, husky now. Eva almost didn't know herself as she pressed her ass back against him. "Does my little Fated want to be bad?"

"Yes, I want ... Callan." She felt like she was still out of her own body, unleashed somehow since he had touched her earlier. Eva would never have described herself as easy. She'd had some lack luster partners. Now though, she almost felt like she was speeding along a road in the middle of summertime, the dips coming along without notice, going over that rise and catching air under the tires. She felt out of control, her desire spiraling.

Eva could feel the wetness between her legs as his hands traced her rib cage underneath her shirt. She wanted his hands everywhere. She could feel him against her, hard, unyielding. He lifted her in his arms and carried her to his sleeping quarters, setting her on the edge of the bed. Eva looked at him in breathless anticipation as he knelt on the floor of the cabin before her. His eyes bright. She felt everything all at once it seemed, the seam of her shorts that was near to driving her insane, the feel of his callused hands on her thighs, and was that her heart or was it his heart that was beating so hard? His eyes were luminous as he took her in and then Eva chilled as his eyes went wide. What was wrong?

. . .

Callan had frozen, raising a hand to the hollow of her throat as he leaned forward, his leathers pressing into the flesh of her thighs. “Was this here before?” There was a faint marking, like a tattoo across the hollow of her throat, a faint tracing line of a moon and stars twining along with it.

“What is it?” She jumped up, evading his hands as she rushed to the mirror in the bathing chamber to look into the mirror. “What the actual fuck? Why didn’t I see it?”

Callan came up behind her anchoring her body to him. Then he held his wrist up to her. She looked at it and then looked at the marking that she could see. A faint crescent moon and tiny stars with a crescent curve. She was baffled by it. While hers was more delicate, feminine, they were a match. The crescent moon and stars were intertwined in the tattoo on his wrist. There was a marking on her neck, how was that even possible? If she turned the right way you could barely even see it. "What is going on?" She backed away from him.

“Is this from your magic cube thingy? Because I did not agree to this?” She waved at the marking. She was mad. This was not cool. She went and picked up her shirt from the bed. If he thought she was engaging in sexy times with him NOW, he had another thing coming. She didn't care if he was fine with a capital F or not. Eva was going back to her previous opinion that he was a prick with a capital P. She cast an accusatory look at him and saw him looking at her with what could only be described as predatory possessiveness. She shoved her arms back into the shirt. Eva knew she looked a mess. She was still filthy and now her hair was a fucking disaster. "WHAT?" she shouted at him. She was confused and more than a little annoyed.

Callan ran his hands through his hair. He was trying to start the conversation just the right way. His Fated was furious. Her eyes were flashing, but Callan just wanted to trace the mark with his fingers. Lick it. He couldn't believe how the Fates had blessed him. She also was marked. He was twice blessed. Callan's hands itched to draw her close.

"I understand that you're upset." Eva wished she had something to throw. At him. He held up a hand placatingly. "It's the mark of the Fated," Callan finally said, opting for simplicity. He had moved to sit on the edge of the sleeping platform. His placed his hands on his knees. "Mine appeared when I took your hand earlier." He waited to see if she absorbed this information. Eva's whole body seemed to come to a full stop. Was he serious? Well, this was some shit wasn't it. She ran a hand through her hair. She studied him.

"So, this just happened. This mark?" Eva pointed at his wrist. She paced a little. Holy shit. She rubbed her throat. "It happens from just a touch?" She turned to look at him, horrified. "Wait, would it have happened with ANY woman? Or person?" The thought that another person could have experienced this mark, connected this way with him, sent a bolt of fury through her that she couldn't even begin to understand. Then she was mad at herself. She *was* mad ... right?

"Of course not." Callan was indignant. "I have touched many women." He immediately backpedaled at the look on Eva's face. "That's *not* what I meant." Eva was still working through the information when he opened his mouth again.

"No. It wouldn't have occurred with anyone but you. It would have never happened with another woman I have touched." His voice was very sure.

. . .

"That better not be what you meant." Eva huffed out as she plopped herself next to him. Her eyes flashed murderously at him. Callan took this as an invitation to continue his explanation. "The fated mark is rare. I have waited long for you. I had almost given up. Although I have read about it in our histories and been told about it."

"It is a story told to younglings for both fated to have one. Eva," he moved to her now, cupping her face in his hands. Stroking her cheeks with his thumbs. "Fated in our race are precious and rare even when they are chosen by each other, but when both are gifted by the fates with a mark, true fated? That is rarer than a star that has fallen into your palm from the night sky. Can you not feel this?" He gazed at her seriously, as if willing her to feel it. He touched his wrist cautiously and Eva felt an answering thrum in her own marking. It was terrifying and ... wonderful.

That was the thing, Eva thought. She *could* feel it. It was insane, wild, crazy. She could almost taste it, sense it, and she could feel it – this bond between them. She had thought that she was losing her mind over him, being irrational. Her eyes locked with hers and then sealed her fate. "Yes." Her voice was quiet, her voice small, but sure.

. . .

Eva crossed her arms and looked at him. "So, this mark," she pointed to him, "shows that you are my soul mate." She waved her hand at her throat. "And that I am your soul mate? That's what you're saying?"

Callan leaned in for a soft touch of his lips, tasting her gently, and then he drew back reluctantly. "Yes. Even more than that. A true Fated is something that is only dreamed of. I am lucky to have found you." He gave her forehead another soft kiss, smoothing her cheeks with his fingers. Eva watched him with solemn eyes, feeling so full of emotion, not knowing exactly how to share it with him, when a ping sounded from the panel near the doorway and then ---.

"My lord," a computerized voice said. "Commander Azer requires you in his office."

Callan turned at the sound, "Thank you Amura." Then he said to Eva, "Well, that's our signal that we need to move, unfortunately," his gaze was serious. "We have much to share together, but I have responsibilities that need to be attended to." Eva knew he was expected back at the outpost. All that had happened rushed forward, the fighting, the bodies, the bombing. They had lingered long enough. She also needed to speak with him about Daisy. She couldn't just not go back. Daisy was counting on her, and she wouldn't just abandon her friend.

"I'll get cleaned up really quick then." Eva said. Then, with solemn eyes she leaned over and gave him a light kiss. "My friend ... Daisy. She will be worried about me."

"I sent a member of my team to inform her you are here safe. So, she didn't worry." Callan smoothed another hand over her hair, unbound it was magnificent. She was a beautiful Queen. "We will speak more of this later," he promised. She nodded and ducked away from him and into the bathing chamber. She was a little afraid of the whole air-tube-thingy, but she was going to go for it. After pulling the two credit fobs out of the pocket of her shorts and setting them safely near the mirror she went ahead and braved the platform, stepping up onto it gingerly with her teeth gritted. Within 15 minutes she wouldn't have believed it, but she had her clothes removed, she was clean, her hair washed (she guessed), and she was decked out in black pants, thigh-high boots and a soft blue top. Kind of badass she thought as she examined herself. She gave herself a little twirl. Nice. She liked this clothes platform – not too shabby.

. . .

Eva moved out into the main cabin area of the ship to find Callan busy with some high-tech gadgets she couldn't quite make out. It seemed that he was inputting some data and was looking over files. There were three-dimensional maps and all sorts of stuff that seemed important. He looked as she came forward, giving her a slow smile. "Ah, Fated come here." He held out a hand for her. Eva stepped forward, looking at all the holograms (that was the word she was looking for) and digital files. He gave them a swipe, and they disappeared. "Put your palm here." He showed her the screen that had the previous files. Eva quirked a brow at him.

Callan had made himself busy while Eva was getting ready. He had answered communiques from off-planet. However, he also had wanted to get Eva logged as his Queen. She needed access to a variety of things and the protection that his name would provide her. Not to mention that she was his now, and he was going to make sure that Eva was forever linked to him in every way possible.

She took his breath away as she came into the main cabin, in Earthling clothes. Those boots. He would make sure she kept those.

. . .

"More magic?" Eva stepped into his space as one of his hands came up into her hair. She had left it down except for the front that she had pulled back into a set of small braids that secured behind her head just so it would help stay out of her face. She placed a palm on the screen as he stroked his fingers through her hair. He typed a series of commands in.

The screen lit up, each point under her finger glowing. Eva turned to Callan, watching him as he typed with one hand. She had taken a moment in the bathroom, or bathing chamber, she corrected herself, to examine the marking (tattoo really) that decorated her throat. Eva still wasn't sure what to think of the crazy-town business. She reached a hand over to touch Callan's face, handsome with his rugged beauty, the need to touch him overwhelming her. He gave her a gentle smile as he completed whatever he was doing.

"What does this do?" Eva asked him.

"Registers you for the ship and everything else. Gives you access." Callan said, absentmindedly, continuing to type. Callan turned to her in a flash, he saw the imprints on her skin. A soft look came over him, his eyes flashing. His hand came up and touched the marking on her throat.

Eva nodded. That was what she had thought. "I like it."

"You do?" Callan looked at her with a knowing smirk.

Ugh. The man was insufferable. Eva thought but conceded that he probably knew how good-looking he was too. Her Fated. Weird. She was trying to reorganize her thought process to allow for this strange new concept.

"Would you stay here? On the ship while I speak with the Commander?" he asked her. It looked like he already knew the answer, but he was asking just to be sure. Eva just gave him a small smile.

"I think you already know the answer. I'm coming with you." She gave him a wink. "And anyway. You have all the magic, so I need to stick with you ... like glue." Callan rewarded her with a laugh. "The shadows too, I saw those." She gave him a little stroke along his wrist.

. . .

"I am not sure what glue is. Unless it's like that weird growth that I found one time on that planet outside of the Eotore Dimension?" He indicated another platform area that was in the main area of the center chamber of the ship. He stepped around her and stepped up onto it.

"Greetings, my lord," the voice began. "What can I do for you today?"

"Hello, Amura." Callan raised his arms. Eva watched him with interest. He had said he was going first, though, so she understood she would be going next. "Full weapons for surface deployment."

"Yes, my lord." Eva could see the air around him shimmer and whirl. She could see a weapons belt materialize strung low on his hips. Yum, Eva thought. Although that was probably inappropriate. He gave her a knowing wink though, as if he knew exactly the direction of her thoughts. A gun of some sort, like those that she had seen the Commander firing earlier was in the belt along with some items that Eva wasn't quite sure what their purposes were for. They looked a lot like the myriad items that police had in their belts to be honest. Although Eva had no clue what those were either. Callan stepped off the platform after a few more moments as the lights dimmed.

"Alright Eva, your turn." He motioned her forward and assisted her as she stepped up. "Hold your arms up," he directed. He gave her a nod.

"Amura." Eva said, softly. The lights from the platform whirred to life, a soft blue. Eva slid her arms up, it was a little cool, she noted with a shiver that had nothing to do with the temperature. She could see the whirl of the energy around her hands and arms. The lights brightened and she could see the same energy whirl around her forearms and lower arms as they traveled to her hands. She could see her head and her neck, the same lights moved around her neck and down to her lower back. She could feel it, it was a little tingly, but not uncomfortable at all.

"Greetings, my lady." The mechanized voice sounded in the surrounding space, and Eva looked at Callan, startled. Callan who leaned against the far wall, arms crossed, watching her with a smile. He gave her a nod. Eva was taken aback. The implications stunned her. Did that mean what she thought it did. She focused on the task at hand though. Callan had told her to watch him, so she assumed he wanted her to follow his lead.

"Weapons, please ... for surface deployment," Eva guessed. She remembered how she had wished for weapons earlier, something, anything to protect herself and Callan. Eva held Callan's eyes as she spoke, and he answered her with a reassuring nod as the process repeated itself.

Eva looked at the platform. "Thank you, Amura." She said with a smile. She stepped off. She looked at Callan and held out her hand. Eva could see a silver belt with some sort of a clip on her hip. She reached down and touched it. She felt the same clip that she had seen Callan use earlier.

Eva took his hand in hers as she stepped down. "So, here in this small pouch." He tugged her close to him as he let her examine another one of the small pockets on the weapons belt. "It holds additional nutrition cubes for emergencies."

"Ok, got it." She gave him a nod as he closed the pouch back up. Even though the little cubes were odd, they weren't bad, and the technology was amazing. She still felt great, full, and totally hydrated. Having extras was smart since you never knew what a day might bring. "There are other items here, none of which you should need." He paused and looked at her seriously. "Have you handled a weapon before?"

Callan hated to consider that his Fated might need to defend herself, but he wanted her to have the option. He needed to train with her when this job was finished.

She nodded, "Yes, we have guns here. I've shot one before." She didn't need to go into details right now, but she had shadow memories of a time in her life that she wasn't so proud of.

Callan didn't press her but continued. "This weapon is registered to you and will only work for you. When you squeeze it, it will fire where you aim. It's set for a kill shot. If you must use it, I don't want you to hesitate." He gazed her. His voice low and harsh, his eyes blazing with intensity. "I have no intention of putting you in any situation where you need to defend yourself, but I won't lie to you and say that I'm sure you won't ever need to use it. I would rather you have an option. If you feel you are in fear of your safety, then I want you to have a choice."

. . .

"Alright. I understand." Eva didn't know how to express to him that she understood. She understood the conflict that he was undergoing. She could feel his worry for her. Somehow it was almost palpable. Eva could also feel the mark warm and sharp against her collarbone. There was an answering tug near her belly button that seemed to reach towards him, almost. She reached out to him. "I'll be okay. I promise." Eva instinctually wanted to comfort him so she did what she could, moved that sense of herself towards him, wrapping it around him in reassurance for an instant. She wasn't sure if he could feel it, but his face cleared.

He held a hand for her and whipped her with him as they ported.

Chapter Twelve

Callan knew they had taken a little too long onboard, way longer than he normally would have taken; however, he couldn't have rushed such a thing. He would have given almost anything to have taken his time in explaining the mark to Eva, how special it was. Having to rush back out and deal with this threat of the Pavo was not how he imagined one of the most special things in his long immortal life. He steeled himself as he led her through the camp, aware of the incredulous looks they were getting.

"Here on Earth my work is through the Inter-Galactic Council. If there is a criminal that they can't handle then they call on my team and ultimately, me." He paused as he watched her absorb this. "They call me their Hunter ... for now."

. . .

"Yes, I heard them call you that. So, you are the good guy," Eva said.

"I don't always do good things," Callan said.

"I don't believe that."

"Their deaths are just, but that is what I am sent for. I am sent to cast judgement. I don't want you to misunderstand." He kept his liquid eyes on hers.

"Are they bad people?" Eva asked stubbornly.

"Yes. I never pursue or kill unless it is justified. I promise." Callan had members of his team to assist with verification, but he had skills of his own too.

"Ok then," Eva said, taking his hand in hers. She knew there was more to Callan. She had heard the AI on board the ship call him *my lord*. Curiosity burned hot in her mind as she turned that piece of information over, but she set it aside for now.

. . .

"These people that attacked," Eva began, "Why would they kill the people on the transport?" Callan didn't have a lot of time to explain the entire situation to her, although he didn't have any issue with telling her about it. He still wished he could prepare her more for what she was about to hear and see. He knew she would be horrified at the reality of it all. At the same time, he knew that she was strong, and she would need to be in order to continue.

"There is flesh trade throughout the galaxy, all species are bought and sold. Some of them are sold to be used as food or as slaves," he swallowed hard.

"The Pavo are known to buy and sell humans," he continued. "They are prolific on and off-planet."

"Food? Are you kidding?" Eva was horrified, her eyes wide.

"No, Fated. I am not. The Pavo are ruthless. This cell on Earth needs to be found quickly. I am guessing this incident is linked. I am hoping, actually. We will first go to see the Commander. Azar and his men have some men that were captured earlier. If they haven't begun questioning them already, I would be surprised." His tone was fierce, and she looked at him with wide eyes, not misunderstanding his intent.

Azer was in the middle of using a small field kit to clean his face and hands as the Hunter and the Earthling female entered. Wiping down some of the battle muck from his face, he stood.

Callan felt somewhat guilty that Azer hadn't had time to go to his quarters yet, but then squashed it. Azer looked up as they came, Callan's hand at the small of Eva's back.

Azer came to his full height behind his desk, his face blank as he came to attention. "Hunter," he gave Callan a nod.

"Commander," he gave a look that brooked no argument. He swept one hand in small circles in a reassuring pattern on Eva's back. To his surprise Eva's voice sounded next to him, sure and steady.

"Good evening, Commander. Were you injured?" Eva said, stepping forward, her dark hair swinging. Callan caught the scent again of fresh flowers from her hair. He wasn't sure what she had chosen, but he loved it. The Commander looked stunned for a moment, unsure of how to respond and then schooled his features again.

"Not anything of note," he paused significantly, eyeing Callan. "Thank you for your concern."

Callan was just about to put him out of his misery when Eva flopped herself into the chair and crossed one of her legs over the other. "So, Callan tells me we are Fated. Look," she pointed to the mark at her throat. Azar's eyes shot from her to Callan.

Callan couldn't help but be delighted. He should be horrified, but her spirit made him want to crow from the rooftops that she was his. She was the total opposite of any female that he'd ever interacted with. Callan's laugh boomed over the space took even him by surprise. "Fated, you are scandalizing the poor Commander." He bent down and gave her a kiss on the top of her head. She looked up at him with a smile.

"I am?" she asked the Commander. "I didn't mean to. This is all new to me so if I'm doing it wrong ..."

she ended on a shoulder shrug and a smirk that showed Callan she was less than sorry. Callan was quite pleased with his little Fated and her sass, even if it was unusual, he wouldn't trade her for all the credits in the star systems.

Talon was having difficulty catching up. He eyed the female draped over one of his chairs. She was beautiful and smelled of flowers. He felt a wave of longing and jealousy but squashed it.

"Of course not, you are not doing anything wrong. Congratulations." He bowed formally to her as was her due. Typically, there was a ceremony; however, if marks had appeared, then it was unnecessary. Her brows rose as she swiveled her head to Callan and her eyes narrowed, but she kept her thoughts to herself.

"Thank you, Commander. We appreciate your congratulations of course." He gave Eva a small nod.

"Yes, certainly." She agreed, giving Callan an evil smirk that would certainly cost him later.

. . .

"Now, we have some business to deal with. Have you started interrogating the prisoners?" Callan asked.

"Yes, we did get started. One died unfortunately. Their wounds were too severe." Azar's brown eyes flicked to Eva and back to Callan. "Are you certain that you want to go over these details," he began.

"I'm certain, proceed." Callan said and seated himself in the other chair, making himself comfortable. Callan kept himself aware of Eva, but he had to take care of this situation and she had said she wished to accompany him. He had to trust her. He had learned long ago (the hard way) that females were not fragile creatures to be coddled.

Azer continued, "We have four captives. Two of them I believe potentially could have further information. The other two." Talon paused, glancing at his hands. "I worked them over pretty well. I don't think they know anything. Hired muscle only." He paused again and looked over to the far wall. "A lot of it doesn't make much sense. "So far, the two that I'm speaking about have been ... uncooperative." Azer finished, giving Callan a significant look.

. . .

Callan nodded in understanding. He knew what the Commander was asking. "What about casualties, losses? Damages?" Callan began to ask.

"No more than expected. We're still looking for a few, but we haven't given up hope." Azar replied.

"We have never held out hope for those taken. The Pavo are not kind masters," Callan said.

"No," Azar agreed. "They are not."

Eva didn't miss the fact that the Commander's voice was low and grim. She had to bite her lip to keep back questions.

"The transport ship was a total loss," Azer said. "I think there were IGC explosives from the outpost involved. It was quick and clean. However, I think it was an error. I don't think they meant it to go off when it did." Azer pondered the information as he spoke, chewing it over.

"I considered that too," Callan admitted. "I saw the color of the flames."

. . .

"Were there people onboard?" Eva asked. Both men looked at her in surprise. They hadn't expected her participation, apparently. She gave them a dirty look. "Well, Commander Azer? How many people died on board?"

"2,321 died. All of them except eight crew were from Earth on the transport." He answered. The enormity of the death toll sinking in. She felt the tiny clenching in her chest, the fear and sorrow of it. She tried to hide it from the other two, but it was hard. She wondered if they could smell the moisture in the air that she felt. She wiped her cheek quickly with the back of her hand. She could feel them noticing her distress, but they didn't comment. She was thankful.

Azar was about to continue when Eva's voice said quietly, "Eight that you know about. If you are thinking that the explosives were stolen. Someone else might have smuggled the explosives onboard. Either a crew member or a warrior from the outpost. It could have been someone from Earth. Is everyone here accounted for? Just a thought," she said carelessly. Both men stopped for a moment and Azar tapped into his communicator quickly and then asked for a count of the warriors on the outpost and a verification of the count.

"Well, that'd be interesting," Callan said. "We are thinking that there is someone here working for the Pavo, so that is in line with something that they would do, have someone here smuggling weapons. The IGC weapons are superior to anything they have."

Azer face was grim, "Maybe the group that was here didn't expect to get caught at all? Maybe they were supposed to be loaded on the transport ship. They were using Earth weapons. So perhaps the fighting ended up being unplanned and was uncoordinated after the transport ship blew up? It would still have to lead to someone coordinating with them to provide access to those weapons though. I don't like to think that one of our warriors is a traitor, but credits seem to be a pretty excellent motivator for many." Then Azer said, hesitantly. "I have also heard that the Pavo trades in secrets and favors sometimes as well." He looked to Callan for confirmation.

"I'm not sure if that's true or not," Callan admitted. "My experience with the group has been one of cat and mouse, mostly. After Janus I have been chasing after the main hub of their group. I have only been able to find satellite groups, smaller versions. It is hard to find information on who is the leader, or the leaders for that matter." Callan wasn't someone who let go of things easily.

He had spent plenty of time on his own, outside of his intermittent work with the IGC, looking for the Pavo in the pools of Fate. He had used immense powers within the Shade searching out pockets of them and then dispatching his court to eliminate them when he could. However, the leader of the group had eluded even him so far, much to his frustration. Callan had constantly been putting out fires across the universe searching for the Pavo,

"So, in total," Eva gave them a sharp look. "Today there were thirteen IGC warriors killed you're saying. Not to mention the two thousand three hundred and thirteen people that were on the transport from Earth that were killed. Dead." Eva looked over at Callan, her look filled with intent.

"Yes, that's the calculations that I have. Then there is a loss of property of course." Azer's fingers typed quickly across the tablet that he held. Swiping across the screen to double check the numbers.

. . .

Callan was just getting angrier as Azer spoke. The causalities today were needless. The individuals that died today trying to secure themselves a future off-planet had put their trust in the IGC, and they had failed. Callan was both saddened and disgusted by the thought.

"Let's go see if I can have a chat with these two gentlemen then." Callan stood up and offered his hand to his Fated. "Seems like we need some answers for the lives lost."

"Indeed." Eva answered. Her hand slipping into his, curling around his, unafraid of what side of him she would see as they walked towards the building that housed the prisoners. Azar, on the other hand wasn't so sure about including Callan's Fated. However, it wasn't his call, so he got to his feet and followed them out, indicating to the warriors on guard to come along.

Chapter Thirteen

"I wish we could smell something beyond the fucking stench of piss, vomit, and trash," Kedron said with revulsion. This planet was terrible. If the money wasn't so damn good, he'd quit this job. Working for the Pavo was its own kind of shit show. Kedron was a lot of things, but he never lied to himself. He wasn't a good man. He had no illusions about it. Infiltrating the IGC base had seemed like a cakewalk at the time. Obviously, that had all gone side-ways. Granted, the Pavo always paid well, but Kedron didn't count on having to scurry off the base like some rat off a sinking ship. He'd say he was lucky to have this dumb ass private to help him. That'd be a total lie. This guy. What a loser.

. . .

"Stop your whining and let's keep moving." Private Hadariel, an IGC warrior, couldn't even believe the disaster this evening had turned into. The Hunter had been in an absolute fury. If he got away from Earth tomorrow, it couldn't be soon enough.

"I never expected them to fight this well," Private Hadariel's voice was low as if he were puzzling out an answer to a riddle he was turning over and over. He was oblivious to the Pavo next to him giving him a glare that could kill.

"Most of the IGC are cowards. This was a total surprise," Kedron scoffed, he sidestepped a suspicious puddle. They couldn't be sure they weren't followed. The IGC Hunter, what a trip.

"I'm glad you're so unconcerned." Private Hadariel answered with a huff. He didn't appreciate the comparison. He certainly wasn't a coward. Well, maybe he was, but he didn't like being called out.

"Didn't even know the Hunter would be here. Wait until the others find out that he's on Earth." Kedron was muttering to himself as they picked their way along the edges of the old airport. Private Hadariel hadn't intended to get this involved at all.

It had not been his fault that he'd gotten so deep at the gambling tables. Before he knew it, he owed way too much money to the wrong people. Suddenly they were calling in favors and asking him for things that he didn't think he'd ever be doing. Hadariel didn't know how he had got to this place in his life where he was answering to the Pavo.

"Wait, who was that girl?" Kedron asked the private. Kedron wasn't a huge fan of Earthlings, but that was an interesting development. The Hunter and the little Earthling girl. Just wait until he passed on *that* information.

"Why the fuck would I know?" Hadariel retorted. Jesus, these Pavo always wanting information. To be honest, he was no longer sure how to get out of it. The stupid bookie he'd borrowed money from would probably kill him if he didn't come up with payment soon. This wasn't working out the way he'd thought it would. He was beginning to wonder if he'd made a mistake there was no coming back from.

"I have no idea who she is." He said this a little more cautiously with just a tinge of respect, side-eyeing Kedron. They all thought they were so much better than everyone else. *Assholes.*

"Find out and watch your tone. Dick." Came the answer as the man escaped into the darkness. The Pavo did not turn back.

Private Hadariel swiped a shaky hand over his face. Fates. He wasn't built for this whole sneaking around business. While he couldn't care less about the Earthlings that the Pavo were shuttling off to whatever end it might be (admittedly an unpleasant one) he did care that his life seemed a lot more stressful than he liked. He thought he'd be getting some perks, or at the very least some sort of extra compensation for his trouble. Instead for his troubles all he was getting was more trouble. Stupid. All this did was solidify in his mind that his mother had been right all along. He really was an idiot.

Chapter Fourteen

Eva wasn't sure what she was feeling. Furious was a word. She moved along beside Callan towards the building where the prisoners were being kept, her mind churning with the events of the day. She attempted to put her feelings in order. Burning rage, that was another. To hear the number of people murdered today that were from her planet. It was horrifying. They were just trying to find something better. It brought back memories for her of trying to find something better, a home, a place, or a sense of belonging. Each time the fragility of it like a gossamer web slipping through her fingers. It wasn't fair. None of it. They would not get away with it. Her hand clenched, her nails cutting into her flesh, hard enough that she was sure she was leaving marks. Callan glanced over at her; his look cautious. This idea of the Pavo here taking slaves from Earth ... Callan didn't give her all the details, but the thought made her want to vomit. For food, slaves? Food? Bile was sharp in the back of her throat.

"Fated, are you alright?" he asked, his voice low, cautious. Callan could feel a sense of sorrow coming from Eva. Poignant and crushing on his tongue, tart and bitter. In the back was a rush of rage to chase that sorrow, but he was new to the fated mark. He knew too little about Eva to be sure of her and of the feel of the mark yet.

"No." She turned to him then her eyes like endless silver pools. Callan reached for her, sliding his hand into hers, squeezing it gently. "I just am sad for the people that wanted to make a new life. They didn't deserve that." He was not much in the way of consoling others. He had never had to be. For all he had done, all that he had accomplished throughout his life, he was uncertain of what to say or do. He was not good at this.

Callan nodded, "Nobody deserves that. They should have been safe to leave and make their way with their families on a new planet. I will put a stop to it," Callan promised. He meant it. The Pavo were barbaric and disgusting – using lifeforms the way they did for food. It made Callan's powers surge to the surface.

Eva squeezed his hand back. She could see that Callan was upset as well. He obviously took his responsibilities seriously. "I know you will." Eva replied, steeling herself for what was to come. She knew she wouldn't be completely comfortable with everything that she'd see and hear Callan do. She wasn't a total idiot (all the time, she amended silently) so she expected he wouldn't be asking very nicely.

The night sky was beautiful, and Eva noted the dusty evening as they stomped along with a small troop of IGC warriors, her and Callan, the Commander and a few others that seemed to collect as they went – a small parade. A tiny breeze had picked up, and she felt it ruffle her hair. The stars shone brightly in the sky and even though the temperature had dropped, she felt oddly warm. She glanced over at Callan; he seemed to be deep in thought, his gaze shifting from one side of terrain to another.

As they neared their destination, Eva's stomach began to flutter nervously. She knew what was coming, what Callan planned to do when they reached their destination. She wanted to help him however she could, but she also wanted to be there for him so he would know that he wasn't alone. He didn't need to face this on his own.

When they finally arrived at their destination, an eerie silence descended upon them all. There were guards stationed both on the outside and the inside of the doors. Inside was a small chamber with more guards standing to attention. While there were a few chairs, they weren't sitting in them. Then there was a long hallway with doors on either side. Eva presumed this was where the prisoners were being, but kept her mouth shut.

"Eva, you'll wait here for me." Callan directed her to a chair. "These warriors will see to your safety while I question the prisoners." Callan's words were distant and his face blank.

"I understand that, but I'm coming in with you." Eva stood her ground and refused to budge. She could see Callan grinding his teeth as she spoke. He obviously didn't want her to be in the room.

. . .

"Are you certain? There are things you cannot unsee." Callan's voice held no judgement. She swallowed, but she nodded in assent. She was sure.

He motioned her to follow. Azar looked at him in horror just as Callan tossed at her, "Just don't blame me if you throw up," which had her questioning her decision.

"You stay near the door." He threw a pointed look at Azer. "Watch her."

"Of course." Talon answered, although he couldn't countenance bringing a female to an interrogation of prisoners, but she wasn't his female, so it wasn't his place to say. His eyes widened when he caught a glimpse of her eyes. They were softened in a way they hadn't been before. She looked oddly beautiful. Pain was a thing that broke things, turned them into different creatures. Some found themselves stronger.

As Callan approached the doors, they swung open. He knew they were waiting on him to walk down the hallway. Callan hoped Eva stayed near the door as he walked down the hallway, flanked on either side by men whose watchful gaze never left him.

Eva followed him and Azar and two guards into Room 1. Just like interrogation rooms crime movies everywhere there were two chairs in the middle of the room. A man was seated in one of the chairs, strapped in with metal bands at his neck, wrists, and ankles. He looked up as they came into the room.

Eva might have called him handsome on another day. She pegged him for a human. He was wearing jeans and a Rolling Stones t-shirt. The gaping lips and tongue faded in black and white. Shockingly, he didn't look like he was beaten at all. She had expected it if she was honest.

Callan took stock of the male as he came into the room. Earthling, mid-20s, he was already nervous. Good. He did not slow his gait as he entered the room but did not hurry. He did however allow his power out, letting it roll from him cresting in black mist along the floor.

"Hello." He could see the man's pulse at his throat. He strode to the chair that was in front of the man and sat down. "I am here as the Hunter for the IGC." Callan could hear the door behind him open again but did not bother to turn as the wheels of a chart were heard. Callan knew what was on the cart and from the frantic look on the man's face he did too. The sound of his breathing became louder in the small room, the clatter of the cart echoing, the soft fall of Eva's gasp as the cart went by like a soft brush of a Tainte on his home dimension.

Eva hadn't realized the reality of what it would be like, her heartbeat faster. When they had brought the instruments in, even though she didn't recognize many of them, she knew that all of them were designed to inflict pain and suffering. She had no doubt of that. She reminded herself of the men, women, and children that had been aboard that transport and found that she had less pity in her heart for the man that trembled in the chair. Eva did hope that he spoke quickly. She watched as Callan selected a tool from the cart with (what looked like to her anyway) total boredom.

Callan was not cruel. He did not enjoy seeing others in pain, even if they did not deserve it. He wasn't heartless, though and he wasn't a cold-blooded killer. Callan would let his actions speak for themselves. It was easier that way.

. . .

"So, let me tell you the rules, shall I?" Callan said to the man. He tested the sharp blade against his thumb. "This is satisfactory Azar. Commendable." He had turned in his chair and gave him a nod. Callan didn't really need the tools of Earth, but he found that depending on the victim, taking the long way was the best path.

"Certainly." Azar answered dutifully at Eva's side. It was outside his realm of expertise to torture prisoners in this way. He was torn between fascination and horror. Callan cut the attacker's t-shirt down the front as he leaned forward. He did it carefully so as not to cut his soft skin. Azar was fairly sure that the man knew something. He had already refused to tell him anything, but then again Azer hadn't taken this particular path. Already he knew the Hunter had gotten further than he had in just a few moments.

"I'm going to ask you some questions. You will answer me – honestly. If you do not give me an answer, then it will be ... painful." He watched as the man's eyes turned impossibly wide and his breathing picked up even more. His skin grew paler. Callan pulled apart the two sides of the shirt exposing the man's white belly. The man quivered in the chair, whimpering nonsensical words, cringing as far away from the blade and the ribbons of shadow as he could get, slowly a wet stain spread in his crotch. Callan tutted as if he could not care less, "Well, now I haven't even asked a question." He pressed the blade right along his breastbone and held it there, pressing it into the flesh.

The man said in a rush, "I know nothing. I promise ... you can ask Felix." A tear leaked from his eye as the stain spread further, his bladder emptying. His shoulders slumped as far as the bands of metal allowed. "Ask Felix." He repeated, defeated.

"What's your name?" Callan began, sitting back up and withdrawing the knife, but allowing the black mist to creep its tendrils farther up the man's torso. His face retreating to the look of boredom. The man looked even more terrified by these than the knife.

Eva was amazed. Within minutes Callan had collected the information that young Mr. Matt Wexton met Felix (no last name) at Hot Lips Pizza in the city just a few weeks ago. He had been paid a whopping sum of 25,000 credits to be here for the job of being hired muscle (Eva scoffed). They were supposed to be getting on the transport with the explosives which were then getting sold to an anonymous buyer at the next station point where they would receive another 25,000 credits.

Callan stood from the chair and returned the blade to the cart. "Well, thank you for your honesty, Mr. Wexton." He nodded to the man, who was now slumped, stained, and had blood trickling from one small slice along the breastbone.

Matt picked up his head and stared at the Hunter. This day was a shit-show from the get-go. He should have known better than to take this job. Fuck Felix. "What happens now?" He was afraid of the answer, but after he had seen the Hunter in action, he was pretty sure what it was going to be.

"I'm sure you know." Callan said, and Matt looked at him in resignation. The misty tendrils tightened around the man's neck with whip-like quickness, a crack sounding in the silence.

Callan turned from the young man then, dismissing him. However, Eva kept her eyes trained on him, watching as the light dimmed from his eyes, his face paling. She felt it was a just judgment so when the door opened; she followed

Callan out, not bothering to look at the young man again.

Callan was careful not to look at his Fated. He didn't feel any judgment from her, but he still felt like it wasn't a side of him that she should have been witness to. He wished she had stayed out in the entry with the other soldiers where she didn't have to see such ugly things.

They moved on to the second room, which Eva supposed was "Felix." The hair on the back of her neck rose, but she wasn't sure why. She figured it would be a repeat performance.

The man might be an alien Eva thought as she came into the room. He was large, bulky, with the height and weight of the warriors that she had seen around the outpost. Certainly, he could be from Earth, but she had the sense that he wasn't for some reason. The restraints that she had seen on the first prisoner were present here as well; however, he didn't seem lessened by them like the first prisoner had. He was blond, his hair long, hanging down to his shoulders obscuring his face. She thought she remembered him from earlier during the fighting. His arms were still streaked with blood and dirt, clothing torn in places. It was obvious that he hadn't been cleaned up. Eva wasn't sure if he had been "questioned" or not since it looked like he had some bruising forming on one cheek and he had shallow cuts in places. She chanced a glance at Azar and noted that he didn't seem particularly bothered by the state of the prisoner. The individual was wearing clothing that Eva would see in any thrift store in Portland, jeans, t-shirt, black boots but he still struck Eva as off, other-worldly. He was obviously expecting them. His head came up as they entered the room, eyes cold and focused. To Eva's surprise, he spoke first.

"Hunter," the prisoner gave him a nod. He seemed to know exactly who he was dealing with, his voice composed and steady.

"Felix." Callan acknowledged, as he sat in the chair opposite him. To Eva he was the picture of calm, but to her surprise the prisoner acted as if he wasn't put out to be a prisoner at all. Callan observed his face carefully, "If that's your name." He tacked the last part on as if it was an afterthought.

The cart made its appearance but didn't faze the prisoner. Not even a flicker. "My name isn't of consequence." He looked over towards the door and then back to Callan. Well, this was some fucked up shit right here, Felix thought. Nobody had told him that the Hunter would be here. Although he wasn't ever surprised at anything, this did surprise him. He couldn't do much but glare up at the King of the Shade Dimension with hate-filled eyes.

The metal was cool against his skin and tightened just enough so there was room to wiggle a tiny bit. He'd fought them, but it was no use. He had no powers on this planet. He was caught and there was nothing he could do about it. He had been hoping that they would listen to reason and let them go. He had hoped they would be able to find a buyer who would pay the 25,000 credits and cut them all in on it, but it would appear that now he had to figure out what to do next because he doubted that there would be any daring rescue now that the Hunter was here.

"Well?" Callan drawled out; the ink streams of dark were dripping already from his fingertips.

"Well, what?" the prisoner asked. He kept his voice as even as he could, but he wouldn't lie and say he wasn't afraid. It was then he spotted the female pressed against the wall. His eyes darted from the King to the female and back. "You've found your Queen." The words were whispered and awed, but audible by both Eva and the Commander.

Callan looked over to Eva for just a moment and then to the man in the chair, recognition dawning. Fuck this. Callan whipped his dagger up into the prisoner's chest cavity with a flash of silver and let his power loose into the prisoner's mind, pillaging and plundering through his memories for every answer he needed. The man screamed, his body arching up off the chair. He couldn't fight, and he couldn't answer their questions. He only screamed, his eyes going wide, muffled by the thick tendrils that crossed his mouth. The thrashing went on for another five minutes until he fell back in the chair, his hands limp on the armrests, his eyes staring at the ceiling.

Eva could see one of Callan's hands on the back of the chair, the knuckles white they were holding it so hard. He whipped his head back to the man and then — he killed him. She wasn't completely sure what he had done, but she had seen the shadows and felt the change in the air. Whatever he had done was *more*. Suddenly, she was hyperaware of the fact that she was trying to hold her breath. Her heart pounding so hard and fast in her chest she thought it might explode. She swallowed past the lump in her throat releasing the breath she was holding.

Talon wasn't even sure of what happened. The prisoner had looked to Eva. Did he somehow know that she was the Hunter's Fated? He shifted his body in front of her, but he knew it was too late. Before he knew what was going on the Hunter was out of the chair, a knife in his hand and he had slammed it straight through the prisoner's chest and wrenched it up and to the side viciously. The man's body jerked with the force of the blow, the light in his eyes dimming. Talon had backed up a step, pushing Eva back further towards the wall, one hand out to keep her from moving forward. He knew he had inhaled a sharp breath, shocked at the Hunter's actions. Didn't they need information? But — those shadows, what the Fates? What was that all about? The Commander knew the Hunter had extra powers. He had always assumed that he had abilities that made him useful to the IGC, but what he just witnessed... Those weren't anything he had ever known about. The teleporting as well. That was something he'd never known about either. Talon's mind spun, recreating everything he had seen. The guards were frozen in place. It was, of course, the Hunter's prerogative to dispense justice. Certainly, they were in no position to question what he did, but the guards were pale, their eyes wide.

. . .

The man had said something about the Hunter finding his Queen. What did that mean?

Callan closed his eyes and took a deep breath. The idea of the Pavo knowing about Eva was unconscionable. He turned towards the doorway. "I got what I needed." Was all that he said. He left the still warm body slumped in the restraints. A pool of blood, faintly green was accumulating under the body.

The thing that Callan appreciated was that Azar didn't ask questions. No recriminations about killing the prisoner. Everyone just filed out of the room. Azar silenced the other guards with a look. He tried not to look at Eva's face as they left, but he saw the fear in it as he swept past. He didn't want to delve deep enough to know what the fear was about. She had every right to be afraid of him, but he was afraid for his Fated's safety in the world he was from.

Eva hadn't missed the whole 'queen' comment. She was terrified that guy was serious. What did she know about being a queen? The whole encounter left her in a stunned silence. She hadn't even noticed the knife in the man's chest until his body jerked. With a quick glance at the Commander's face, Eva could tell he was in shock too, probably not because someone thought he was a queen.

They left the building at a good brisk pace. Eva was quiet, staying close to Azar. Callan walked ahead of them seemingly deep in thought. She was sure that they'd hear the reasons behind Callan's actions as soon as they were in private. Callan was obviously retracing their steps back to Azar's office. Azar threw her a look of concern, but Eva kept her hair covering her face. She was okay. She was more concerned about Callan if she was honest. Eva hadn't missed the weird comment or the look that the prisoner had thrown her. It was chilling, but she wasn't overly concerned since she had nothing really to reference. She'd be scared when she was dead. For now, it was just about surviving today.

Chapter Fifteen

In the Commander's office they reconvened – Earth refreshments were brought in. Azar had sent a communication ahead thinking that this was a good time for them. As they all sat down as Callan cleaned his hands, he pondered his words carefully. Azar produced cans of cold Coca Cola, which Callan eyed with suspicion and Eva snapped up with delight.

"Are you even kidding right now? Gimme." Eva said, with delight grabbing one of the red cans. "I'm dying for a Coke." Callan gave a glimmer of a smile watching the pleasure in his Fated's face.

Callan took a small drink and peered inside the can. Interesting. "My team has a lead. Someone was seen being helped off the outpost. They got away apparently. They're following up." He took another sip, savoring the texture of the carbonation on his tongue. While he felt wasteful that he was using up some of the planet's few resources he couldn't help indulging a little. Overly sweet, but still delicious.

"Really? How do you keep contact with them?" Eva asked, watching him. She had wondered this when he mentioned that he'd sent them to Daisy.

"Telepathic communication. It's one of my gifts," he answered. Her eyes widened. She had SO many questions. His eyes sparkled as he tried to hold back a grin. He could see her mind working and wanted desperately to ask what she was thinking.

"So, are we going to talk about what happened?" Talon asked. He tried to be nonchalant but wasn't sure he was successful.

"He didn't know anything worthwhile," Callan answered, his voice light. "I checked," he added. He wasn't sure if he was doing the right thing - keeping the information from the Commander, but the PAVO hadn't had any details worth noting that would be useful for Azer. The fact that he knew who he was ... that was unacceptable. The Pavo having access to that information was its own set of problems. What really crossed the line was the fact that he understood what Eva was to him. Callan couldn't let him live. Well, if he were honest, he *could* have, but he wasn't going to. A threat to his Fated wouldn't stay breathing.

Talon wasn't completely sure what that meant, but he couldn't really do anything about it. There were only so many things he could control, and the Hunter wasn't one of them.

She picked up a string cheese from the plate of snacks that had been brought in. It was a strange assortment of Earth goodies. Eva picked through it, gummy bears, string cheese, Pringles. Junk food had been a luxury that she and Daisy hadn't been able to afford recently so this was nice. Hard to argue with junk food honestly. After the events of the day, a little indulgence was nice. She captured an end of the cheese with her teeth and tore it down the side, then stopped when she caught Azar watching her in abject fascination.

"Well, a lead would be great," Azar agreed. He wasn't sure what had happened in the basement, but they could use some leads. He leaned over and picked up a snack pack of the chips and then said to Eva. "I have to say I love these. I didn't know you could do that with the cheese," he added.

"It's called string cheese for a reason. I love Pringles too." She gave him a smile. "Give me one."

"We may not have any leads right now. We'll get one though," Callan said. He picked up his own chips and fished one out for Eva.

"Well, that's not exactly true." Talon surprised them all when he spoke. "We have something." He had been tapped into his tablet as they spoke and then said, "When we were talking earlier about the transport and who was supposed to be on it --- that was a good idea, my lady" he began. He wasn't sure what to call Eva now that she was the Hunter's Fated. Honestly, he wasn't sure what to call the Hunter either.

"Please call me Eva," Eva squirmed uncomfortably, fiddling with the empty can.

. . .

Talon immediately straightened in his seat and looked to the Hunter. It was highly irregular and familiar, reserved strictly for close family members and typically even then for members of such a ranking it was only for private settings. He inclined his head, "I am of course honored -" Talon chanced a glance at Callan.

"It is her choice," Callan said in a low voice.

"I am honored then. Please call me Talon." He smiled at her, but he eyed Callan warily.

"Fine," Callan heaved a sigh. "I suppose you should stop calling me 'Hunter' and call me Callan." Talon looked stupefied and then recovered. He wasn't sure what to do with that – it seemed so familiar.

"So," Talon gave him a side eye, "Can I call you King?"

"Fuck right off," Callan gave a half-hearted chuckle. Maybe they had found a new friend or even a new member of the Shade. He eyed Talon speculatively in a way that Talon wasn't sure he liked.

Talon glared back. He wasn't sure to make of this new dynamic, but he was sure he didn't like it. He'd never known where the Hunter was from, Callan he corrected himself. What planet he was from ... but now that he'd spent so much time with him. King? That fit. The guy was arrogant enough to be a king.

"So, I had a sergeant check the records. They also checked who was keyed into the armory, the transport, the records of passengers, and cross-referenced the data of anyone who had been on or off the outpost. I found one person who wasn't supposed to be there. An anomaly. A private who joined this outpost last minute. He was scheduled to be at another outpost but requested this one." Talon gave Callan a pointed look. Callan sat up; they both knew this could be a major break. "He was logged in both times with his communication device. During that time, he was supposed to be at the armory on guard duty."

"He wasn't logged in any other way then. Was he killed in the explosion?" Callan asked. This could be it. The communication device was a default but could be turned off. Typically, it was a function of an IGC uniform to serve as a logging device of your whereabouts. However, they had found that there constantly seemed to be a glitch in the functionality of this when the Pavo were concerned. Somehow, they had figured out a way around the IGC technology.

"No, he wasn't logged in – either in another location or with the metadata from his uniform. That location device was disabled. Although he was logged with his metadata at the armory for guard duty both at the start of guard duty and at the end of guard duty. He just must have forgotten that his communicator also records location data." Talon double checked the tablet, even though he really didn't need to. He had gotten the information sent while they were seeing the prisoners. Thank the Fates this warrior had fucked up.

"And he's still here then – on the outpost? He will have to communicate with the Pavo. If that's what this is." Callan lets his thoughts spool out ... "Then they'll need to figure this situation out. They'll need additional transport. Now they'll know that I'm here. It'll be all-in or they'll move to another outpost to target." Callan let his gaze flicker to Eva's and then to Talon's.

. . .

"Yes, I think so too. If they decide to continue with their plans for this outpost, it might be an opportunity for us. They have already scouted things here and laid the groundwork. However, now that we have been alerted. We should act accordingly, I think." Talon shifted in his chair and ran a hand over his shorn hair. "We need to increase our warrior details like we would after an attack of this magnitude, just not too much." Talon said decisively.

"We don't want to make it too hard for them. We'll need to be careful. I don't want him to know that we're on to – what's the private's name?" Callan asked. His elbows were on his knees, and he leaned forward into his hands, steepling them under his chin.

"Private Hadariel," Talon replied. He looked over the information that he was sent again. "He was originally going to be sent to the Miami outpost, but he put in a request for the Portland. That by itself isn't strange, but his documentation looks ..." Talon paused. "... just too perfect."

"What do you mean?" Eva asked. She had been sitting and listening to their discussion about the asshole who had so casually been arranging all the transports to be stolen and taken from the outposts. This was a big chance for them to trace some of the missing people from Earth and they all seemed to know it. "What do you mean – too perfect?" Eva clarified.

"Just that there is something about the documentation of his academy time that seems a little off the mark for me. He had graduated, but his marks are all exactly average. Exactly." Talon emphasized the word, giving his head a slight shake. "It's like an AI did it, not an actual life form. Then there are recommendations for military service from instructors." Talon gave a weird half-shake. "That NEVER happens."

"So, you can track the path then of the communicator locator data? We can verify if this is the same person who "assisted" someone off base? Our Private Hadariel has been very naughty. Let's find out if he's been getting paid too," Callan said.

Eva pulled a package of gummy bears from the tray and opened it casually. Selecting a green one she examined it first and then delicately ripped off its head with her teeth when she accidentally caught Talon looking at her in rapt fascination.

. . .

"Are you dismembering that bear?" he asked. Rolling the gummy bear around in her mouth and chewing it, she chose to ignore him.

"Maybe?" she shrugged. "I always eat them this way." Then said a little sheepishly, "They last longer this way." Talon kept eyeing her suspiciously though. Eva ignored him and tore off a leg, chewing on it, rolling it around in her mouth a little first. When money had been scarce, she had made a pack of candy last forever this way. (Also, it was kind of entertaining.) She gave him a little smirk.

Callan had found what he was looking for and looked up. "I think we caught an even bigger break than we anticipated. I saw this before and it didn't really strike me then. I thought it was a little odd, but now that I see another –" Callan said, he finished with the tablet and handed it off to Talon, showing him the information, he had pulled up.

The tablet showed information from the IGC warrior that he had discovered on Janus. The anomaly of the data, the mediocrity of the scores down to the physical data and then the recommendations from the instructors was striking.

. . .

"I'm guessing that the instructors rarely take the time to send recommendations usually?" Eva asked.

"Never. Even if it's a top score," Talon answered. He handed the tablet back to Callan. "This is the same 'person'. I'd bet on it."

"That's why I pulled it up when you mentioned what you were experiencing with the data," Callan replied.

Callan smiled. "Now, I think our Private, here, had been on the outpost for more than just the time that he was supposed to be here. I bet he was a Pavo operative."

"The time stamps match up with the logs?" Eva asked.

Callan and Talon both looked at her with raised brows. "They do."

"Then I think you're on to something. Maybe this operative was there to set up? Someone else coming into the mix? I'm not sure how that would work, sending to them a clean one of their own, but it seems like something they would do." Eva said.

"That's an interesting thought," Callan admitted. "We need to think about that. I'm going to put the team on that line of thought."

"So, let's see where our little Pavo operative has been on other days too." Talon said, as he clicked on the link for the location information for that the private's movements, as well as the logs for the transports that had been stolen.

Callan whistled.

"But ..." Talon said, catching on to Callan's train of thought, "... we can use this information to set up a meet with Hadariel if we are really careful." The two men looked at each other.

"It's not likely this is the only location here on Earth though, is it?" Eva said. "I mean, the Pavo. They probably think Earth is like a giant candy store to them." Callan looked at her. Surprised again by his Fated. He felt lucky all over again.

. . .

"No, you're right. However, we go one cell at a time." It was too bad honestly and he could see the disappointment in her face. "We will go ahead and be thorough as we capture any of them to see if we can get a lock on other locations. If I get any sign of another cell, we will move on those also." He made sure to impart to his Fated that he would not let the Pavo steal her people. Eva nodded, the mark at her throat bobbing as she swallowed. "Commander, we will need to leak some kind of information that is plausible." He paused, "About the explosion and losing the transport. I don't want any information given out about the Pavo. Any ideas?"

Eva's eyes brightened, "Actually, I do. All lies are best crafted with parts of the truth." She had learned that lesson well during her life. "They were stealing explosives. So, you could say that it was discovered that explosives were set off on accident, and a transport was destroyed. Mention the number of people that died, the umm, casualties, I guess. Then you can throw in a place that you found out the explosives were supposed to be headed for and that they were then going to be sent somewhere else. You already know where the transport was going, so that's not any secret that you are giving up and then just make up something else. It wouldn't be a reach to think that a prisoner under torture would lie. That way, most of the information is the truth. Only that last piece is stretched. You could say that it was an Earthling. That also wouldn't be a lie."

Talon brightened as she was speaking and looked to Callan. "That's easy, really. It wouldn't be a reach at all. You'd say anything for torture to end. Giving up a location is an easy out. We wouldn't know the difference. The transports were heading to Nemrass in the Aeris Quadrant."

Callan nodded. "Yes, it could work. Simple and effective." He looked at Eva approvingly and she felt a humming answer tugging at her deep in her belly at the look. "We have a plan then?"

"The Pavo have to have a backup." Talon said, "And they are averse to taking out their own." He tapped some more and then said, "Looks like Hadariel was out of the way somehow." He looked over at Eva and Callan and smiled, "We will need to set a meet."

"Yes, I think so." Callan said, scrubbing a hand over his face.

. . .

Talon was exhausted. "You two are going to leave then? Will you go to another outpost?" He wasn't sure what Callan's plans were. He hoped he would stick close by so he could call on him to help if they somehow got a location.

Callan angled a look at Eva, rubbing his wrist with one hand warily. "I will speak to my Fated. We will need to use strictly close coded communication if we go through IGC channels from here on out. Or I will reach out through other means ..." Callan let the sentence dangle.

Eva didn't ask, but she wanted to. Obviously, there was history there. Callan had said that the Pavo were into terrible things. She remembered he had told her some of the things that they had done. Her stomach turned over. This wasn't something that was new to her. The dark side of civilizations everywhere. Slavery of all sorts.

"We will need to talk about my roommate." Eva began, "If we are leaving, then I can't just leave her with no information about me. We have been together for years. She is worried about me already, I'm sure." Eva said morosely. It was late into the night now. Daisy was worried sick about her she had no doubt. Eva chewed on her lip. There was no way that they could go now. The night was already half gone. Saying goodbye to Daisy in the sweltering apartment seemed suddenly like it was weeks ago.

"Well, we can send a detail out into the city to speak with the female. To make sure that she is okay." Talon offered hesitantly.

"No. I'll need to go myself. She won't believe you." Eva said, thinking swiftly. She looked over at Callan. "If we go when the sun rises then I'll go off-planet anywhere you want after that." She meant it too. She'd go with her Fated wherever he wanted it, to whatever far flung planet that he intended to take her. However, she needed to make sure that Daisy was okay, and that Daisy could reach her. Maybe. Maybe, Daisy could join her when things were safer. Callan nodded as she continued, "It's not safe to go now into the city. After I talk to her, I will go anywhere you want."

"My team already spoke with her, but we can speak with her in person when you like," Callan said. If he was alone, he would have been single-minded on the hunt, already porting to his team and tracking their lead. His Fated needed a short rest at least. Centuries he had waited for her, and he would not risk her needlessly.

Callan met Talon's gaze. There were a few hours left until dawn. They'd have a brief rest and then venture out to settle things. "Alright. We will go see the female in a few hours then." He offered his hand to Eva, pulling her to her feet. She gave Talon a smile as they said good night.

Chapter Sixteen

Private Hadariel darted along the edges of the tarmac, skirting the shadows of the control tower like a ghost. It was dark, but the bright moon cast enough light to illuminate his way past the gate and to the far side of the airfield. As he reached the meeting point that had been arranged, he stopped and checked both his comm device and his locator device to make sure that the metadata was disabled and that he was still offline. All seemed in order. He took a deep breath, steeling himself for the encounter, and then stepped into the clearing.

They sent a different Pavo contact every time, supposedly as a security measure, but Hadariel thought it ridiculous. Honestly, he could identify over ten faces involved at this point (not that he would). It was sink or swim now; he thought morosely. He had to pull it off, or he would no longer have a situation to worry about. If this negotiation went well, he'd be in. If not, he'd be lucky to be walking away with his life. What the hell am I doing? He thought for the thousandth time in his life.

He was met by a figure in the shadows, a Pavo contact whose name he had never learned. The figure wordlessly beckoned for him, and he followed. They wound their way through a maze of old buildings until they reached a back alley where the figure stopped abruptly.

"What did you find out then?" a voice sounded in the dark.

"The Hunter killed the two other captives," the private said into the night. When something more seemed to be expected Hadariel added, "Sorry."

"How did you find that out?" the contact asked, looking about nervously.

. . .

"One of the guards down there. He owed me a favor," Hadariel shivered a little. "He said that the Hunter tortured one of them for information."

"This is not good," the Pavo said unnecessarily.

"No, it isn't. It makes the job harder. If he finds out what's going on here, then this outpost is done for. He will be a step ahead of us. We need to be on this now," Private Hadariel glanced around fearfully. He could not afford to fail. He could not afford to be discovered.

"That's not great news. We had a contact there we were hoping to break out once he got picked up." The man spit in a long stream. "Fucking Hunter. The boss isn't going to be pleased." Hadariel looked askance at him. There had been a lot of mention of this boss, but Hadariel hadn't been able to figure out who led the Pavo. That information would be worth A LOT. A LOT. Hadariel turned that idea over in his head and then discarded it reluctantly. It really wouldn't be worth living if he turned on the Pavo. They'd hunt him to the end of the universe if he turned on them.

. . .

"The guard said that when the Hunter went in with the one prisoner, he used shadow magic. She said the guy screamed and screamed."

The Pavo shuddered. "Poor bastard. We'll meet again at the next phase."

"Understood." Private Hadariel turned and started to head into the night when the other man called out.

"The woman. Did the guards say anything about that woman? The boss wants to know."

Hadariel paused, "She was there, I guess. She's still with him. I don't know anything else yet about her. I would have told you."

The Pavo nodded, "We need to know everything you can find out about her." Hadariel gave a jerk of his chin to show he understood.

When the man stepped away, Hadariel turned and walked back towards the gate. He swallowed, trying to dispel the dryness in his throat. The encounter had been on his mind all day. He had to hand it to the Pavo, they sure knew how to create paranoia. He heard someone stumbling in his direction and pressed himself into the corner. He smiled to himself as the figure went past, unaware of him. He shook his head and headed back to his post.

Maybe he could make it through after all. Maybe.

Paron watched the scene unfold from a nearby shadowed rooftop, cloistered in the dark. The Private retreated after getting his new orders from the Pavo. Paron nearly crowed with glee as he began tracking the man. They had found the cell.

The Pavo continued his trek, seemingly oblivious, a ball cap pulled down on his head, covering his face. Paron made sure to stay back, and he continued to taste the air occasionally for any spikes in emotions that the Pavo was alerted.

Chapter Seventeen

Callan ported them to the ship. He thought longingly of Tiebus. While he was tempted to port Eva there so she could bathe properly in the pools, he resisted. He couldn't wait to see her lay in amongst the petals of the Vohemin and wear the crown of the Shade. However, there would be time for that later. Callan ground his teeth.

He resisted.

He wanted his Fated to rest and he needed to speak with her about his home dimension and his role there, and her future role. He had Eva use the bathing chamber first, showing her the settings again just in case she had forgotten. She had poked her head out once to ask him about night clothes and he had said she could experiment with Amura. He usually slept in the nude, so night clothes were not something he had ever asked for.

He programed in nutrition cubes for both of them, then poured a small amount of a specialty liquor from the Shade that he carried on board. It was strong, probably stronger than Eva was used to, but he felt like it had been one of those days. He used his tablet to send his message in the dedicated Inter-Galactic channel chat. This was going to be tricky, but he felt more hopeful than he had for a while about the Pavo situation. Callan rose and made his way back to the bedchamber. He really needed to clean up, he thought.

Eva was just finishing up. It was hard to call it bathing really, but it was quick and convenient. You also couldn't argue that it was more environmentally friendly. Her hair and skin were loving it too. She had to try a few times with the whole "night clothes" command with Amura and had to be very specific, but she was finally wearing a basic earth-like t-shirt and boxers. She really had to do some talking to get panties. As Callan came into the bedroom, she exited the bathing chamber.

. . .

"I brought some nutrition cubes for us and a drink that we have on my planet. It's pretty good – strong though, just a warning." He was setting them down on a small desk in the chamber as he turned to face her, stopping, frozen ... his words coming out slowly as he gestured towards the glasses. "If you want?"

"Hi," she said. She tugged the hem of the t-shirt a little. "I got Amura to get me different clothes. It took a few tries." She could practically feel the heat from Callan as he took her in. She had no bra on, her nipples tightened at his look and his eyes drifted to her breasts. Eva shifted a little, she was instantly wet for him. Eva moved to the bed and sat down.

"Eva." Callan's was low, desperate. He could feel the need curling in his belly. All day he had wanted her, smelling her near him, seeing the curve of her waist and hip, the slope of her neck. His cock hardened. She shifted on the bed, scooting back.

"There is one thing that I want Callan." She had thought it over in the shower. They had started earlier, and she hadn't ever been surer of everything. Her body wanted him, and her heart wanted him.

. . .

"Are you sure? There is no going back," Callan said. His fists were clenched now, barely restraining himself. He could feel his heart nearly beating out of his chest, the mark burning on his wrist.

"I'm sure," she said, almost whispering. He was over her instantly, his face close to her, teeth on the pulse point of her neck scrapping it. Eva widened her legs to accommodate his bulk, pressing her core to him, delighting in the friction it gave her. He drew the shirt over her head. "Beautiful," he murmured, and then bent down to lavish first one breast and then the other, pushing one up with his palm and then the other, cradling each in turn. Callan gave one nipple a pinch, watching her face intently. Eva's inhale of surprise was quickly followed by a whimper.

"You like that little Fated?" Callan said. Ribbons of dark shadows rippled from him, curling over the bed. Callan ground into her, struggling to not hurt her. He'd need to count stars to keep from coming. Leaning in, he nipped her neck, pleased when her eyes darkened, and her lashes fluttered. He pulled her shorts off looking at them as he did so and then her panties, which he looked at askance, but he had more important things to bother with than Earth undergarments.

Eva was scrambling at his clothes. Eva pulled him towards her and pulled his shirt over his head. Callan toed his boots off. Eva swallowed as she scooted further up the bed. He unzipped his pants, his cock springing free as he shucked his pants leaving him completely nude. He slid his hand up his shaft as he watched her, his eyes on hers.

"I've wanted you all day," Eva admitted with a sigh.

"Have you?" He came towards her then, shadow and mist. The thick fog blanketing the bed. "I can make that happen." His eyes narrowed.

He craved her touch and the closeness just as much as her, letting their bodies come together, skin-to-skin. He slid down, paying close attention as he went until he nestled between her thighs. One hand on each thigh he pushed them apart. "Open for me." Eva let them fall apart. His thumbs pressed into to her inner thighs, digging in, just a little, not enough to hurt.

. . .

"Oh God," Eva moaned, arching against the bed. She was going to die. She could feel how wet she was. Her thighs must be dripping. If he didn't touch her, lick her, or fuck her she would murder him. "Please ... Callan ... please."

He looked up her, she was glorious, with her thighs spread like this, a feast. He kept those hands firmly on her thighs as he and leaned forward, licking her from bottom to top, then sucking her clit hard. He rubbed her clit and slid one finger inside her. She was hot and wet, and he groaned at the feeling. Callan stroked her opening and her clit with his thumb, expertly drawing the pleasure out. He slid another finger in, increasing the pressure and the thrust. Her cries were beautiful to Callan, and he could feel himself covered in a sheen of sweat. He wanted her, he wanted her with a passion and ferocity that he had never felt before. She came — hard. White blazing behind her eyes, her hands clutching at his forearms, nails digging in. He continued to flick her clit with his tongue, alternately sucking it while the orgasm flooded through her. Callan pushed his fingers into her wet heat thrusting, his golden eyes shining up at her, letting her ride through the pulsing waves.

Callan gave her pussy another lick and then moved himself back up her body, settling his cock into her core, she moaned as he slid inside. She was magnificent.

"Move damn it." Eva demanded, hooking her legs around his waist, reaching for his thighs.

"Please," she whispered, and his teeth closed on her right ear lobe.

"Please what?" he mumbled against her also nipping at her jaw. She tried to pull back, but he grasped her chin and held her still, keeping her eyes on him. She looked up at him, and he could see the confusion and worry in her eyes, and it made him want her even more. He dropped his forehead to hers, "Say it," he said.

"Please make love to me," she whispered.

"Oh, little Fated," he said, his voice was filled with wonder. "I will." He rocked her against him, his hands cupping her bottom. Her hands splayed out on his chest, and he sat up to watch as he moved inside her. He pushed in to the hilt and then out again. Her hips rose to meet his. He felt her curl her feet around his calves, her hands moving up his arms to his shoulders.

"Demanding little thing, aren't you?" Callan managed to groan. Eva dug her hands into his flesh, urging him on. Callan knew he'd have marks in the morning, but he didn't care. Fates, Callan thought he might die as he thrust forward or embarrass himself - he wasn't sure which.

Eva's breath came in pants, her pussy clenching. He was better than she had imagined. She felt so full, his hands everywhere as he pumped into her, angling to hit just so. Eva's fingers squeezed on his shoulders, she could feel him sliding in and out of her, touching all of her. She had never felt this connected to anyone before.

He slid in again, his head dropping to her shoulder, tasting the smooth skin. He nipped her shoulder with his teeth, and Eva cried out, arching against him, her pussy clenching on his cock. Callan growled, fucking her hard and fast.

"Fated ---" the word came out of his mouth in a growl as he thrust harder. He dipped his fingers to where they were joined, circling her clit. If Eva had thought that she was close before, she was suddenly flying.

"Oh, God," Eva arching into him as she came, spilling over his cock. He thrust once more and then roared out his release, spilling into her. He slumped over her on his elbows, careful not to crush her, his breath coming hard. Dark tendrils tightening over them, blanketing them, pulling them tighter. Eva tipped her head to his, seeing his face as the dark shifted it.

"Fates," Callan murmured. "You killed me." He chuckled and then brushed a hand down her face with a smile. "I'm so blessed." He got up and came back with a warm cloth and cleaned her in gentle strokes. He turned them so they were on their sides, cradling her to his chest. It took only moments before they were asleep.

Eva woke in the morning tangled in a mass of steel and warm skin. One arm was wrapped around her waist, his sleep-roughened cheek pressed to her upper back. His other hand cupped one breast, his thumb stroking over the nipple. She felt a drowsy warmth that had little to do with the sun hitting her in the face.

. . .

Eva had hazy memories filled with love making and one very serious conversation that included things about queens and kings. She wasn't quite sure how that all would work out. Another dimension? Her a queen? She could barely manage her own life. How was she supposed to be a queen. Eva supposed that like anything else in her life she could adapt.

Minutes later, and the ping sounded, "My Lord and Lady Adiim good day. Commander Azar is awaiting your arrival." Eva groaned; she hated mornings. Lord and Lady? Shit. During the night they had gone for rounds two and three. Eva was still tired and still unbelievably turned on. However, Callan was already swinging his feet over the side of the bed and striding towards the bathroom. He had a perfect ass Eva thought to herself.

I'm glad you think so. Came the response. It was so clear and so startling that Eva was glad she was already laying down. What the fuck? She was thrown. She flung an arm over her face.

There was a significant pause. *It's the Fated bond .... They call it mind-speaking.* (Another pause)

Unusual. The mind-speaking. Callan seemed thoughtful and more than a little perplexed.

Eva flopped over. Seriously? She needed a manual, and he needed a warning label. What the fuck. Callan came out of the bathing chamber looking perfectly delicious and it made Eva even grumpier.

"Honestly, you couldn't warn me about the telepathy that came with this?" Eva groused as she got up to get ready. She tried to see if she could read Callan's mind exactly, but it didn't really work. There was almost a sense of him at the edge of her consciousness, a tingle. It made her feel a little better that he wouldn't be traipsing around in her head, but she was still a little grouchy about it. She could feel him there, his eagerness to be about their day, but nothing exactly specific just his contentment, devotion. Eva smiled to herself.

"Well, I read about it a long time ago, to be fair." He looked a little grumpy too, ruffled, but it only made him more handsome. She was highly doubtful that she looked as cute grumpy as he did. "I didn't know it was a possibility. It's a gift from the Fates, really." He didn't sound very sorry. "There is only one Fated pair ever in our history to have this as a recorded effect of their mark. It was an anomaly really." Callan was thoughtful.

"Interesting then. We are weirdos. Figures." Eva said as she ducked into the bathing chamber and closed the door. Geez, she thought to herself this was a lot. It had its advantages to be honest, but it was still a lot to find all this out. Could you read minds while you were touching? There was a lot to consider. This was a lot to handle, and she didn't know anything about Fated.

Hey, when do I get to meet your team? Eva sent him the thought purposefully this time as she got into the bathing tube. Humming to herself as she adjusted the settings. She found it oddly pleasant that she could sort of sense Callan now. Bizarre. Eva didn't say anything but was more than happy to meet Callan's team. She didn't know what they all looked like or if they were male or female. She hoped they liked her.

They will meet us at the kitchen. That is where Daisy is. Callan sent back.

He was interested to meet this friend of hers that meant so much to her. If it were possible, he would get her off-planet right away. However, he knew that wasn't who Eva was. She wouldn't leave without speaking with her friend. He knew that. It was important to her.

Eva exited out into the cabin of the ship where Callan was waiting for her, adjusting the daggers and his weapons. "Really? You're going to be meeting my best friend with weapons?"

"Yes, weapons always. Anyway, after meeting the best friend we have other places to go. We need to make this quick too," Callan said, shooting her a look. He wanted to make his Fated happy, but he didn't want her to forget the seriousness of the situation.

Eva looked somber as she stepped up to get weapons. She had momentarily forgotten in the haze of happiness that there was the entire business of stopping a slaving cell on Earth. She felt a little selfish in her happiness, but Callan sent her a small caress of comfort through their mark.

After Eva had been outfitted, Callan reached for her. Eva could feel his anxiety about her safety pressing against her. She linked her hand with his and squeezed.

"I'll be fine." She brushed another hand over his face and tipped her lips up to his. "I'll be okay." He responded, crushing her to him, curling his arms around her back as he kissed her thoroughly. Eva wished they had time for more than a kiss but knew they didn't.

He groaned, stroking her hair and the pulse of her neck. He felt the mind-touch of her, and looking at her warm face, he found himself smiling. He caressed her cheek.

She gulped and took a step back, her eyes hooded. "Let's go ... so we can come back sooner." She glanced around the cabin and away from Callan so she could compose herself from the kiss. "Are we going to leave from here then? Just poof?" She flashed magic hands at him.

He laughed lightly. "No, we are going to go see Commander Azer. He wants to come along. Which isn't a bad idea." She nodded, finger combing her hair back from her face lightly.

. . .

Within moments they ported. It was easier today for Eva, even though she felt a sharp prick of anxiety running through her regarding how worried Daisy must be. The sun was just rising, so it wasn't too hot yet. There was a sharp acrid smell in the air that Eva was having a hard time ignoring. Most of the clean-up had apparently been done during the night.

We need to keep this between us. This ability. Not because it's wrong, it's special. But (then more haltingly) Eva could sense Callan trying to find the words and the feelings.

She understood and jumped in ... *Because it's an advantage – maybe an unusual advantage, but an advantage. We might need it.* She nodded at him. I agree. She gave him a wink.

Callan gave her a nod as they entered Azer's office. Thank goodness that his little Earthling seemed to be on the same wavelength.

Right, exactly. He gave her an answering wink. *We have discussed little where I'm from, my role there.*

. . .

It doesn't matter to me. Eva reassured him.

It mattered though, Callan thought to himself pensively. He wanted to take her and port her the Shade – to Tiebus where she could see the moons and the flowers. Away from this planet that was dying. All of it made him grumpy.

Chapter Eighteen

Talon glared at the couple as they came into view. It had been a busy night with the explosion and moving all the debris. He had barely gotten in a nap and downed a few nutrition cubes. He was more than a little cranky. They both looked rested he thought snarkily. Damn, he thought, he recognized the feeling that he was having; he was jealous. Talon tried to swallow the feeling down as he looked away into the barely rising sunlight of the single Earthen sun. He shouldn't be jealous of such a Fates blessed union. He was an asshole.

He had told Callan in a communication that he wanted to be included in this foray into the city. Typically, the IGC kept their incursions into the city limited, but this Pavo situation needed to be squashed. To do that, he needed to be with Callan. If he or his warriors ever went into the city, it was in Earthen clothes to blend in with the local population. It was dangerous at the very best of times. While the people of Earth were being cooperative and had not necessarily been dangerous, there was still a certain element of unrest that came about when a landing occurred. It was inevitable on any planet they were on. He shifted on his feet a little. Callan said that they'd port, and he wasn't totally comfortable with that at all, but it couldn't be helped. He adjusted the extra weapons he had strapped on just in case. Being left out of the planning made him itchy.

"Good morning, Azar." Callan said as they strode through the Commander's office door. He could tell that Azar was already high-strung. For some reason this made Callan feel better, so he flashed him a grin.

"Good morning to you too." He looked at them both, he couldn't tell from their faces if they were serious. He narrowed his eyes. "I'm assuming that you've been told how dangerous it is to venture into the city?"

. . .

"Hello, Talon." She paused inside the door, almost running into him.

Callan sent her an indulgent smile. He liked the chaos of his little Fated. Her quick questions and ready smiles that were so unlike the sedate floating strides and demure demeanor of the females that he knew. Eva sent him a blinding smile and Callan bent for to kiss her cheek.

"Yes, of course. My court is there to meet us. We will proceed from there." Callan didn't like leaving things out, but this was something that he'd have to explain later, to everyone.

Before he could continue, Eva spoke. "Alright, are we going then?" Eva asked, looking at them. She was impatient to get on their way. She was positive that Daisy had been sick with worry all night long. Eva had never been gone all night without letting her know where she was, not that it was something she had done a lot.

"Did you make arrangements for your absence with your men?" Callan asked. He had asked the Commander to let his most trusted inner circle know he would be going on a scouting trip today, but to leave the details of the trip completely blank. Callan really didn't trust anyone at this point. While he was beginning to trust the Commander, he wasn't quite sure that he was ready to let anyone else into their plans just yet.

"I did." Talon looked thoughtful as he locked his tablet up in the case behind his desk and some papers he had been working on. Eva had seen him do this yesterday as well, noting that in several buildings palm prints were used for entering or locking things. Probably why yesterday Callan had her palm print coded. Eva sent the question to Callan. There was a quiet chuckle back.

Yes ... that is one reason ... came the reply filled with warmth and humor.

"As you asked, I didn't tell them specifically where we were going or who was going in the party. It will be a good loyalty test. The group is already small, but I'm hoping that they are who I think they are. Loyal." Talon rubbed the back of his neck. Eva could tell that it weighed on him, the secrecy, and the deceit. "They will run interference while we are gone. You said we'd port there?" He looked at Callan with a questioning look and then to Eva.

. . .

Eva was surprised at the anxiety she felt from Talon. It came from him in waves. She would have thought that Talon would have been familiar with transporting, but it seemed as if perhaps he wasn't.

Talon seems super anxious. Is the porting something only you do? She felt Callan's surprise.

Yes. My team and I, but it is a talent of the Shade Dimension where I am from. It is a rather unusual skill. I have rarely seen anyone else with it.

Hmm, I see. Eva sent back.

Callan turned a cool and assessing look to Talon. "Alright then. Do you have everything you need?" Talon gave Callan the assent that he was looking for but couldn't deny that he was still totally either out of his depth or groggy from his lack of sleep so he couldn't figure out the plan quick enough to keep up. "Place one hand on my shoulder Azar. Fated, come here, please." Callan called her forward.

Talon couldn't help himself. "You want me to what?" His eyes darted to the Callan. In all his time in the IGC military no other military personnel had EVER requested that he touch them. Which was an excellent thing, because Talon wouldn't have made it as far as he had if they had. Talon was clenching his fists tightly.

Eva's eyes darted from Callan to Talon trying to assess what was happening. Eva wasn't totally sure what was going on, but as she gauged Talon's face, she was taking a guess.

"It feels weird at first Talon." She gave the Commander a gentle smile and held out her hand. "You can take my hand. It will still work." She wasn't sure how she knew, but she was sure that it would." Callan watched her with his head tipped to the side.

I think it will; he confirmed.

Callan's hawk-like gaze was eyeing Azar now. He placed his hand on Eva's waist. She had used that flower scent again. It wafted from her hair. His balls tightened in response.

. . .

She turned to Talon, "Take my hand." She kept her eyes on him, watching as he gingerly placed his hand in hers.

Eva clasped his hand firmly and suddenly, he felt like he was being turned inside out, winking through a small space and then expanding again until they were in the same position that they had been. He felt like he was going to vomit.

Eva wobbled a bit, as if she were not quite sure her feet were touching the ground. She was probably having the same problem Talon did. He had never ported before and his body was still readjusting to the movement. She removed her hand from his. It was a little unsettling and uncomfortable, but what a neat way to travel.

Eva breathed deeply, filling her lungs with the smell of spices and sharp herbs, fried dough and sugar. Her stomach growled at the scents and her mouth watered as she glanced around. They had ported just inside the door of the commercial kitchen. The sun was just rising now, the golden light shining through the high windows, bouncing off the metal surfaces. It was already hot, but not unbearably so.

. . .

"That was crazy." Talon muttered. He had only heard of a similar type of transportation that could be harnessed by a race of beings in a star system in Baseon. The idea that this was how the Hunter, and his team traveled all the time was chilling. That they popped in and out of spaces. He had to suppress a shiver. There was also this matter of Adiim's Fated touching him like it was of no consequence. He shut those feelings into a box and closed the lid.

Chapter Nineteen

In the back of the space Eva could see a hulking blonde man who was carrying in a load of supplies followed by a bubbling Daisy. She seemed completely unworried and at ease. All of Eva's concerns were apparently unfounded. Eva let out the breath she didn't know she had been holding.

"Callan," the man said merrily, pushing the boxes back onto the steel counter. "Are you here to save me from working? The Pavo might as well capture me at this rate. She is a slave driver." His words didn't quite match the way he smiled with a touch of amusement.

. . .

Daisy let out a loud squeal and came at a run towards Eva, tackling her into a hug. "Bitch. You were gone all night. I was worried about you."

"I'm so sorry Daisy." Eva gave her friend a squeeze surreptitiously checking out the blonde that was lurking nearby.

"What the hell is this?" Daisy yanked on Eva's blouse, spying the faint mark on her throat. Eva didn't begrudge her friend, but Callan hissed in a breath, smoky shadows spilling from him in response.

"Sorry," Daisy mumbled, paling. "You really are King then?"

Callan stiffened and then gave her a curt nod. "Yes, I am the King of the Shade. I'm also Eva's Fated. My name is Callan."

Daisy watched him a moment, maybe deciding whether he was sane and then said with a coy smile, "So, that makes her queen, right?" She quirked an eyebrow at him in question, her eyes twinkling.

. . .

Callan couldn't help laughing, the shadows receding into the corners. He had felt a protective surge at Daisy's violent tug of Eva's shirt without her permission, but he couldn't stay upset at her. "It does," he confirmed. He kept his eyes on Eva's, warm and comforting.

Talon was shell-shocked. The Hunter was King of the Shade Dimension? Holy fuck. It just got crazier – or worse – or made more sense. He wasn't sure which. His entire brain was fuzzy right now after being ported. Honestly, if someone told him that there were three moons instead of seven around Gegawa he'd probably agree. He had thought he'd heard something during the interrogations, but he wasn't sure. Thought the man had called Eva 'queen', but ... honestly, he hadn't anticipated this.

"Eva, this is Brilius." Callan stepped forward and held his hand out, and Daisy pushed back away from him. Eva deposited a shy, nearly imperceptible smile onto her lips as she tucked herself into Callan's side as Brilius approached.

He was blonde and tall, like Callan in this Earthen bound form. Callan had explained that while they were on Earth, they camouflaged themselves as much as possible – not showing their true form. It was best to fit in with whatever populace they were with.

"My Queen." Brilius dropped to both knees at her feet, his head bowed, palms on the floor. Eva felt tears fill her eyes and wasn't sure why. She knew she was meeting Callan's court, but she hadn't known what to expect. It wasn't this though. His blond hair fell over his shoulders, as his shoulders hunched, his fingers tight on the floor. She didn't want him on the floor, or at her feet.

"Brilius," she spoke softly and held a hand to him. His blue eyes raised to her hers, they were glowing, blazing like icy stars. Eva could see the truth in his eyes. He was hers, for eternity.

"My Queen." He placed his hand in hers, rising to his feet fluidly. His voice was low, the cadence harsh in a burn of urgency as he said, "My life for yours." The oath was solemn and the burn along the back of her neck so familiar she knew immediately what it was.

. . .

Callan. She sent out. *Did I just get marked ... again?*

Callan moved to her. He answered her immediately, an edge of puzzlement and concern to his tone. *Brilius made a life oath. However, there usually isn't a marking.*

He moved her hair back, sweeping the strands to one side. Sure enough, there were a series of small marks along her neck in a straight line, delicate, dainty.

"Please, Brilius. Please stand up." She couldn't stand for him to be on the ground. Brilius was still for a moment and then he did as she bade.

"You are marked?" Brilius asked, confused. He peered over the back of Eva's neck. "Do I have them?" Brilius asked, turning around.

"Let me look too," Eva said, moving towards him. She was curious now, not only about what the marks looked like, but if they were the same. What did that mean?

. . .

Callan nodded as they both looked at the markings that were along the back on Brilius' neck. *They are very similar Fated. Slightly more heavy-handed on Brilius than on you. Yours are ... more delicate.*

"They're pretty."

Brilius huffed. "They're manly. Strong. Like me and my oath," he said gruffly. "They're pretty on you, my Queen." He followed up with a wink.

She could sense that Brilius felt off balance about the marking and on-cue ...

"I'm sorry, my Queen that ..." Brilius began.

"Don't be sorry Brilius. I'm honored by your oath." She sent him a smile, and he relaxed. He was thrilled If he was honest.

Callan, she sent out the query to her Fated. *What does it mean?*

. . .

Callan explained that Brilius' marking was an outward symbol of his loyalty towards Eva - something he would never break no matter what happened in this realm or theirs. Callan thought he would save the whole explanation for another time. Brilius had tied his life to Eva's. If she was near death and needed it – she could draw on Brilius' life to sustain hers. Callan glanced sideways at his Fated. It wasn't a development he had seen coming if he was honest with himself. It also wasn't one that he fully understood either. He tried to puzzle it out while he looked at Eva and Brilius', who did his best to go with the flow.

Callan moved forward and waved a hand towards Talon. "Brilius, this is Talon Azer. He is the Commander of the Portland outpost for the IGC," Callan pushed Talon forward. Talon grimaced a little. It gave Eva the opportunity to escape off into the kitchen area to hang out with Daisy as she intended. She wanted to reach back and rub her neck, but she forced herself to leave it alone.

Regardless of her not minding, it was still all a little overwhelming. Eva felt herself relax slightly at Callan's explanation; she hadn't realized how tense she had become in light of this new development. She didn't really understand things like oaths or promises of giving your life for someone else.

. . .

"Okay, Talon let's catch Brilius up on last night's events while Eva has a few minutes with Daisy. Then we will need to get going." Callan let Talon debrief with Brilius as he watched his Fated. He couldn't say he was surprised Brilius gave her the oath. It made their court stronger, gave them extra stability - especially when they were expanding like they were. He was just surprised that his little Earthling could draw forward marks like she could. That was something that they would need to find out about. He wasn't sure how an Earthling was capable of such things.

"This is some crazy shit." Daisy waved a hand towards the trio in the lobby area. Daisy cocked a hand on her hip as Eva joined her. "You best start explaining how this all happened. You were just supposed to go there and sell cookies." Daisy settled a mock scowl on her face.

"Yeah. Honestly – I don't even know where to start." Eva bit her lip in consternation and laughed. "Well, I can definitely start here." She withdrew the credit fobs that she had secured from the paymaster. It had seemed so important then and now Eva could barely believe all that had happened since then.

. . .

"What the fuck are those?" Daisy poked one with a fingertip. "Thumb drives? I haven't seen those in a while."

"No, *not* thumb drives. They're credit fobs. They use them throughout the universe. The order at the outpost? I got paid two grand." Eva handed them over to Daisy, who examined the little bars closely.

"Get the fuck out," Daisy said incredulously. "Two thousand." Her eyes were round in her face and then narrowed. "Jesus. Gary was a total prick."

"Right?" Eva gave a harsh bark of laughter. It seemed like it was weeks ago if she was honest with herself. She gave Daisy a quick re-cap of events, the Pavo, the mark, Callan.

Daisy leaned forward conspiratorially. "So, Earth girls everywhere want to know – how good is alien D?" She gave an exaggerated wink and pursed her lips. "Tell me everything– I mean E.V.E.R.Y.T.H.I.N.G ... don't leave out any of the good stuff either." Daisy clapped her hands as she spoke. "Everything girlie. Everything."

. . .

Eva rolled her eyes back and then leaned on the counter in a dramatic faint. "So good – Bestie..." She gave Daisy an evil smile. "Like, I can't wait for more." Eva batted her eyelashes in an exaggerated fashion. "I know you wish you were having some."

Daisy laughed so hard that Callan looked their way. "Bitch, you know it. Come on girlie. Help me until you have to go." Daisy pushed off from the counter motioning Eva towards the kitchen prep area.

Eva nodded. She knew that the orders were still there even if her own circumstance had changed. She and Daisy fell into an easy rhythm. Eva started whipping the butter for cookies and pulling out the rest of the ingredients for the recipe that they were making. While it had only been a few days, she missed this. She missed the scent of food, the creative process of baking. She wondered then, what it would be like when she went with Callan – if she could find something similar. Baking was a big part of who she was.

Fated? Callan queried. *Are you well?*

. . .

Yes. I was just thinking how much I loved to make things.

She could feel him humming, thinking.

You would want to keep making things? Earth things? Food things?

If I can't – it's alright. As long as I have you. Eva responded.

We can bring you the things you need. Into the Shade. Earth things. There was a pause. *Of course there will be things for you to learn to make if you like there.*

Eva sent him her feelings of pleasure through their mate mark. Callan glanced at her, she could feel it, but she kept her eyes on the butter as she tipped in the sugar.

"What the fuck are you smiling at bitch?" Daisy said in her ear. Eva jumped at least two feet, the sugar spilling onto the counter.

. . .

"Holy shit. Did you have to scare me?" Eva had a hand to her chest as she turned reprovingly to glare at Daisy, but she was laughing just as hard.

Daisy cackled, "Honestly, that was worth it. One hundred percent. By the way, when you leave Earth, you are taking me with you. I'm not getting left behind. I'll be your," Daisy waved a hand around, "handmaiden or whatever." She leaned closer. "Don't tell anyone, but I have my eye on some alien D of my own that I want for myself." She gave Eva another wink. Eva was curious who Daisy had her eye on, but she didn't have time to ask questions since Callan, Brilius, and Talon had wandered closer to them. Instead, they got busy on the batch baking that Daisy had planned for the day's orders.

After about an hour of baking two more ported into the kitchen, now redolent with spices and sugar. Callan was fascinated by the Earthen food that his mate was assembling. The other female teased her a lot, but Callan could see the affection between them.

Snickerdoodles were already laid out on the wire racks. Talon had already had his hand smacked for trying to sneak one while they were cooling. Next up were gingersnaps. Those were Eva's favorites. She had been rolling dough balls in sugar when the two had ported into the kitchen. She'd hurried to wash her hands so she could greet them.

The female was gorgeous. Traditional Earth blonde Marilyn Monroe gorgeous just in jeans and heels. She had red lipstick on, her hair in pin curls and a Hill Billy rock vibe. Eva totally loved it.

"Hi, I'm Eva," she said as she walked over. The woman smiled and bent her head for a small fraction, but there was no dramatic falling on her knees like Brilius had done.

"My Queen, welcome to the Shade Court. I am Sapphrius, the King's second in command." She smiled, her eyes flicking over Eva and settling on her mark. Her smile broadened.

"It is a pleasure to meet you, Sapphrius," Eva said, offering her a hand. Sapphrius took it, her grip cool and strong.

Sapphrius gestured to the man lingering with Callan. "This is Paron." He stepped forward, his movements elegant and powerful. His dark hair, beard, and intense gaze set him apart from the others.

Eva sensed an energy radiating from him, like a low hum, and could feel it reaching out to her, curious and inquisitive. She scrutinized him in response, her head tilted ever so slightly as if she was trying to pinpoint the source of this sensation.

Paron stalked forward to the new Queen. She was stunning. Not as beautiful as the lush temptress over at the stove with her curves, but lovely. What was this though? It seemed like she could sense his power. Was this an Earth thing? Fascinating. He sent out another tentative lick of his power, aware that the King was monitoring him. Overwhelming love, acceptance, and gratitude. Happiness. There were underlying emotions from the past, but the soaring of her emotions was so full that Paron had to shut his power off. It was a rare find, a heart that was a happy one. He didn't need his power to tell him that Sapphrius was surprised when he went to one knee before his Queen.

"My life for yours." He didn't take his eyes from hers, holding his hand out for her to take. He hadn't planned to pledge to Callan's queen, but now, well

– he would take the pledge to her. Not only because of Callan and the Shade Court, but because of what he'd discovered through his power, the nature of her heart.

Eva placed her hand in his. Paron's intake of breath told her he'd also felt it and been marked. She felt a sting along her ribcage. She wondered what it'd be this time. What about when they switched forms? What happened to the marks then?

"My Queen," Paron's voice was somber as they separated. As he rose his hand went to his side – touching it gingerly.

Paron lifted his shirt showing a complex and very large design of vines, thorns and what looked like animals running up his chest and across his abdomen. Eva went to raise her shirt but was interrupted. Paron stepped closer he could feel the connection between them through their markings, like a low current beneath their skin.

Don't you dare. Callan said through the mark.

Fine. She shot him a grumpy stare.

. . .

"I'll be right back. Apparently, my skin isn't to be shown." Eva gave an eye roll.

"I'll come with you." Callan followed her to the storeroom. "Let's see then Fated." He raised the edge of her shirt, uncovering a tiny intricate floral pattern that ran up her side. If she looked closely, there were small animals with fangs, fur and eyes peeking out of brambles here and there.

"Hmmm ...interesting," Eva said, trying to crane to look at it. It wasn't what she would pick, but she wasn't hating it. There were ravens and what looked like a cat's paw or a tiger maybe and huge thorns.

"Yes, interesting," Callan agreed.

"So, Sapphrius is your second?" Eva asked, as he leaned into her, pressing her against the back counter. Eva wound her hands up her chest.

"Yes, you will learn that many of our residents of the Shade come from other areas of the universe. They seek our protection, or they seek to give it to others."

. . .

"Hmm." Eva's voice was husky as she let him place her on the counter. "As long as they all know that you're mine."

"That's right, Fated. I'm yours. Are you mine?" She nodded as he ran his hands up her rib cage and cupped each breast gently. He pulled down the neckline of her blouse, leaning back to admire her demi cup bra. "These Earth contraptions. I like them." He said, as if to himself. He lifted her breasts from the cups and thumbed her nipples. "I want to bite these little Fated. Do you think you could cum just from that?" His eyes were hot on hers as he bent down and kissed her gently, sucking her lower lip in his mouth, nipping at it.

"No," she barely breathed the word out as he drew back.

"No?" he questioned. "What about if I did this?"

She could see the shadows slink up her body towards her breasts, replacing his hands, balancing them, thumbing the nipples, sucking on them. She gasped at the sensation, her eyes flying to his.

. . .

"Do you like that, Eva?" His amber eyes glowed wickedly. Eva squirmed on the counter, but other shadow ribbons held her firm. She knew she should probably say no, but she didn't.

Yes.

I knew you would. Came his response in the dark.

Her core was drenched, contracting almost in time with the pull on her nipples. Eva felt his thigh between hers, hard – the pressure against her clit almost enough that she could cum. Her hips surged forward against his thigh, seeking the friction.

Later Fated, I will fuck you like that, tied down. Would you like that?

Eva's sex gave a corresponding flutter. She wasn't even close to satisfied. Callan chuckled.

. . .

Eva glared at him. *Later Fated, I will ride you while YOU are tied up. Would you like that?* Callan moaned in her ear and bit her lobe hard.

I would like that so much, my Queen.

Eva lost herself in the feel of Callan's tongue stroking hers, diving into her mouth in time to his fingers flicking her nipples. Maddeningly he wouldn't slide those wicked fingers down to her clit, but she edged herself forward onto his thigh, rubbing her clit in just the right spot as suction increased a nearly painful amount on her breasts. She came in a gush and knew without a doubt, shuddering, that her panties were soaked.

Callan stroked her back. "Such a beautiful Queen," he murmured and helped her compose herself before they went into the kitchen. He gave her neck another little lick. He purred a little into the hollow of her neck, nipping there, licking the salt of her sweat, tasting her mark.

Callan. She moaned, drawing his mouth to hers, his lower lip into her mouth, pulling on it with her teeth. Eva couldn't help but bite down a little. She slid her hands around to cup his ass and pull his cock against her. She felt wild, like they wouldn't ever have enough of each other.

Soon Fated. We will have more time. Soon. His voice was a promise.

She forced herself to pull away from him, adjusting her clothes and stepping back into the kitchen with the others. It took everything she had.

Daisy had put Brilius and Paron to work, and Eva was so thankful that her bestie was there. Talon was being awkward trying to make small talk with Sapphrius when they exited the storeroom.

"Cool mark, huh?" Eva said to Paron.

"You have it too then?" Paron kept his voice level, trying not to sound too disconcerted. It wasn't possible for anyone to discern the meaning behind the marking. It was pretty private information specific to just him.

"I do. It's similar, but mine is much smaller and feminine." Eva said with a bright smile.

. . .

"I've never heard of such a thing happening." It was Talon who had spoken. He sounded confused. "Has this happened in other courts? Or is this just in the Shade Dimension?" Talon was still reeling from the information that had been revealed since they had arrived. Now with the Hunter, he corrected himself, the King's court pledging themselves. His mind stutter-stepped and blanked. Honestly, he couldn't even find an anchor. He genuinely like them both. Callan and Eva. While Adiim was ruthless (and more than a little frightening) - he seemed genuine. He'd always heard of the Shade Dimension as more of a cautionary tale. Someplace you'd never want to go to. Now, perhaps he wasn't so sure. Maybe those tales were exaggerated ...

"We are a different court. The Shade Dimension operates under its own oaths and rules," Sapphrius answered with a small shrug.

"Our King follows the Fates." She sounded bored as she answered, but Talon fell silent. "Anyway, we need to get going. We have a package to collect." She gave a wicked grin.

. . .

Talon noted that Sapphrius didn't give a concrete answer either. "What is the package?" he demanded, but Sapphrius ignored him, turning and walking out of the kitchen.

Callan shrugged, "It is a surprise."

Talon had no fucking clue what was going on. He wasn't even sure if he liked any of this. But every part of him told him that if he did not like it, he'd better get the fuck out now.

"Paron followed a Pavo last night. We are just going to collect him and then ask some questions." Callan smiled at Eva.

"Let's get going then." Eva moved towards the door.

"Are you sure? You could stay here with Daisy. I'll have Paron or Brilius stay with you." Callan wasn't sure about putting his Fated in harm's way all the time. This would be the last job he'd take as a Hunter for the IGC. It was time to return to the Shade Dimension and his court. Not to mention, with a Queen at his side. While the Shade Dimension wasn't exactly a safe place, he felt like it was safer than other areas of the universe. He had much more control there.

"I'm sure." She gave him a soft smile. He nodded at her.

Eva and Daisy said their goodbyes. Daisy would manage deliveries for the day, but she made Eva promise that she'd keep her posted and absolutely no leaving the planet without her.

They materialized in a dank apartment block that had seen better days. The sound of their steps was muted by the worn carpet and their feet padded softly. Sticking to the shadows they let themselves in.

It hadn't taken long to find and secure the Pavo that Paron had found. He'd been asleep when they'd crept in.

Chapter Twenty

Eva took a step into the abandoned warehouse, her feet crunching over bits of broken glass and scattered plastic. The air smelled stale and dusty and she noted the thick layer of grime covering the walls. The only light filtering in came from the dim lanterns behind her and the dirty windows above, hazy streams of grey light illuminating the room's edges. She wondered how Paron or Brilius had tracked down this forgotten place.

They had secured their prisoner well on a chair against one of the few sturdy pillars. Callan had already asked her to step out, but Eva had insisted that she was fine. Paron and Brilius both had peered owlishly at her but said nothing.

. . .

Sagan couldn't believe this. This was a mess. His ribs were killing him too, although that hardly mattered now. He was totally fucked.

He looked around at the two men. One of them had pulled out a wicked-looking knife. He was the one to watch out for. He ground out, "I know nothing. They'll be after you – for taking me." He flexed his fingers in the restraints a little.

"Really?" Callan stepped forward, caressing the knife's edge along Sagan's pants, along his thigh.

Duuuddde. Sagan thought, eyeing the knife. What a fucker. His balls flinched, trying to withdraw into his body. "I'm an errand runner." The man crouched on his heels right next to the chair. The slice of the knife was so smooth that Sagan almost didn't realize it at first, the separation of fabric. So precise it didn't even graze his skin. "Look ... man ... I told you ... I don't know anything." The last came out as a whisper, his eyes looking over at the man with the dark hair crouched next to him.

Callan allowed his power to come forth, pulling the inky black shards sharp along the captive's soft belly. The monster in him loved this part of the job. The captive whimpered.

"What do you want to know?" Snot dribbled, mixing with spit. Brilius stepped forward.

"We want the location of the others. Where are they?"

"What do you think, Brilius?" Callan asked, his voice sounding almost thoughtful, but not quite reaching his eyes. Part of him worried about the extra eyes he knew were trained on them and the aftermath of the prisoner's inevitable death.

Sagan's eyes darted between the two men, alarmed. The man next to him looked up. "I don't know what you want." Sagan's eyes closed in horror as the man behind him leaned forward, whispering in his ear. "Everything." Sagan's eyes flashed open, but he kept his mouth shut. Sagan swallowed, dry. The man at his side must have caught his eye. There was something on his face. It was a look of pure, animal pleasure.

. . .

Eva couldn't look away. She wasn't sure if she was scared, but Paron reached a hand to her. As soon as she took it, she was flooded with peace, white and calming. He pulled her close so she could only see parts of the room, edges of Brilius' arm shifting, claws slicing, flesh tearing, screaming – and through it all there was a backdrop of calm. She saw nothing in Paron's eyes, but sadness. Her lashes fluttered to her cheeks, and she sent back to him feelings of love connected to the kitchen with Daisy, cookies they had just made, gingersnaps dimples with sugar crystals, the sweet smell of vanilla, and her favorite scents of cinnamon. Her eyes opened to find Paron staring at her in curiosity.

The Pavo was slumped in the chair, a bloody corpse. Callan and Brilius conferred with Talon and Sapphrius.

"What did they find out?" Eva asked in a hushed voice. It was as if they were in their own pocket of the universe.

"A location. Hopefully that will do it and we can get them all. Shut it down. The Pavo are all sick, twisted. Their emotions are all wrong." Paron's forehead wrinkled. "We have to handle the Private at the outpost too. The Commander can take care of him I suppose."

Eva looked over at him curiously. "Thank you, for what you did."

Paron didn't think she needed to thank him. If anything, he should thank her. He'd lived a very long time and he'd not experienced anything like that before.

"Are you well Fated?" Callan asked. His eyes flicked over her, the flush on her cheeks, but she still seemed pale.

Eva didn't hesitate as she slipped in beside him as they left the bloody room. "Yes, Paron took excellent care of me," Eva assured.

Callan nodded. "Good. Let's go hunting then."

Chapter Twenty-One

Callan transported them directly to the building location that the captive had given them. The old laundromat was squat against the street, its white brick cracked, and windows blacked out. The side street was eerily deserted, which was quite surprising for this time of day, although if it was a place where evil happenings were occurring, then it was probably not too surprising that people were staying away. They weren't totally stupid.

Callan scanned the area, looking for any signs of life. He didn't see any, but he could feel that something wasn't quite right. He had a feeling that they were getting closer to the truth and whatever it was, it wasn't going to be pleasant. He turned to his companions, who all wore the same expression on their faces. Grim determination.

It was time to find out where the Pavo were hiding.

"Eva, tuck in tight directly behind me. I want you behind me at all times." Callan stood and drew the daggers that he preferred to fight with. "Eva, weapons," he motioned to her.

Eva nodded and stood, pulling her gun from the holster and holding it low against the side of her leg. She latched onto Callan's shirt at the back of waist, sliding her hand across his skin and under his waistband.

Female ... the sound was a growl or a groan in her ear it was hard to tell.

Focus. She laughed through the link.

Stay close to me at all times, Fated. Do not take off looking for yourself. Promise me.

. . .

I promise. She meant it. Now. She bit her lip. She would try to continue to mean it.

"Slowly and carefully," Talon said, as Callan eased the door open.

"Look for any wires." He held a pair of scissors in his hand. Talon had briefed them on the Earth explosives that the Pavo cell here favored. Callan admitted that Talon had come in handy.

Inside it was just as black as the windows outside. Callan immediately started to scan the room. There was a very faint trickle of light coming through the boarded-up windows. Each of them had a heavy metal grate covering them and the metal was thick and gleamed slightly in the faint light. There was a long low counter shadowed in the dark in front of them.

"There." Talon pointed. Down at the bottom was a thin wire stretched across the frame of the door. He bent down and cut it quickly. "Go." Callan stepped through into the black. He kept his footfalls light and purposeful, setting each down into the dusty ground gently. The concrete floor was littered with debris. It was impossible to not hear the small crunching sounds that their feet made as they shuffled into the inky black space. Eva did as she was directed and hovered behind Callan's broad back, touching his shoulder lightly.

The gun sat in her palm easily. Eva took a breath. She didn't mention to Callan that she had a few years she didn't like to mention. Years lost not having a place to live. Being too young and drifting on the streets. Getting caught up with all the wrong sorts of people. It wasn't her favorite era of her life. Eva tried to shake off the memories. Instead, she focused on the beautiful strong body in front of her. He swung around suddenly and looked down at her. Right into her eyes.

I'm okay.

We protect each other Fated. He could feel her fear, but he could also feel a sort of sureness. He was going to kiss her senseless when they got out of here.

Callan moved forward across the lobby, careful to sight the entire area. There was nothing there before going behind the low counter. Talon met his eyes and signaled to him. Callan gave a nod. While Callan didn't like it, Talon seemed to have the knowledge needed for the current situation. Brilius and Talon moved forward, eyeing the space for booby traps.

Behind the counter, the air was thick with the rustling of plastic sleeves gently swaying back and forth, suspended from a network of rails in the ceiling. Hundreds of articles of clothing hung in neat rows, their fabric shimmering in the artificial light. The others seemed unperturbed, but the effect was eerie. Callan didn't like it, the hair on the back of his neck prickled.

He could sense the others moving behind him, Eva's hand lightly on his shoulder and Paron and Sapphrius to the left and right of her. They began to move through, cleaning and looking as they went. There was a small office towards the back, so they moved towards it. Sapphrius was a wraith, moving along the edges as Callan called forth his power, dark mist flowing forward.

The building wasn't small from the outside, so Callan knew that they still had ground to cover.

The trip wires also showed that there was something here. This wasn't some fantasy that Sagan had concocted. Perhaps they had moved on, but someone had been here, so that meant that if they still weren't using this place, there was something to find. They found several more trip wires and Callan easily spotted an off-planet pressure plate bomb that was barely covered by a piece of cloth out in the middle of the floor. Obviously, it had been laid there for the more casual encroaching civilian than Callan's party. The office was also empty. Stark and completely clean, void of the debris that they had seen in the outer lobby area.

Eva's nerves were on edge as they had swept through the building. She had watched as Callan and the others had found the devices that she had only really seen before in movies. Crazy. She paid attention though. This was an unfamiliar world and if she was with Callan, she wanted to be a useful partner. Talon was cautious as he cut the wires with a handy little pair of snips, barely touching it. She marked how he was careful not to shake or hesitate. On every turn, though Eva hoped they would sight something. Anything. It was all leading somewhere. She knew it, felt it in her heart. Callan shifted suddenly and Eva had to catch herself from touching him too hard. She didn't want to startle him.

. . .

They searched again through every corner of the building, carefully and methodically. It was Paron who called out in a harsh whisper,

"Here."

Paron indicated an area of the floor that was covered with a carpet. This was tricky, could be a pressure plate underneath really, he thought to himself. He didn't see any wires, but that didn't mean it wasn't another sort of trap. It could very well be hiding some kind of door to a basement though. "Do we risk it?" He asked in a low voice.

"Step back. You too, Fated." Callan said, "Step back with the others. We need to check." Eva nodded, while she didn't want Callan injured there was no sense in arguing. They needed to check, and he certainly wasn't the type to allow anyone else to do the job, least of all her. She moved back to Sapphrius and the others.

Callan got his fingertips under an edge of the rug, feeling for anything alarming as he lifted the carpet carefully. He looked around the edges methodically checking for any hidden connections that might potentially be signals or booby traps. He didn't see any, not that it meant there weren't any, but he couldn't see any at least. Callan shrugged, to himself mainly and then rolled the rug over to the side, cringing a little on the inside as he did so, but nothing happened. He could hear the audible intake of breath Eva made from behind him. There was a trapdoor in the floor - the metal door unmistakable against the concrete of the floor.

“Interesting.” Talon said from where he was standing behind Eva.

"Step back. We need to make sure this is safe. First step is to make sure it isn't booby-trapped." Talon said, “We need to clear everything around it.” Callan nodded. He could see the logic in that, but part of him was eager to get under that floor and get to the bottom of this. He didn't like waiting.

"Makes sense," Brilius said.

Sapphrius moved up next to him and the two set about clearing the immediate surrounding area. Slow, careful, and methodical. They moved around the trap door, carefully cutting the wires that they found, before moving back up to the trap door.

Talon on the other hand continued scanning the floor before he looked up to Callan and giving the assent.

Callan steeled himself. He had seen the Pavo's work before, and it wasn't a pleasant sight.

Chapter Twenty-Two

Eva could feel her own heart racing in her chest as they slid the latch open. It seemed to take forever to her. They were silent as they opened the door. Eva knew it was possible that there were bad things down there, but potentially there could be clues or ...

A steep staircase greeted them, leading down into an old basement. Talon had long since produced a small flashlight as they moved through the dark building, and he kept its circle concentrated as they moved into the space. The stairs went down a long way, to the hard concrete floor.

"Fated. I always want you behind me." Callan didn't bother speaking through the Fated bond, but his voice was kept low. She kept her weapon drawn and ready. Just like the others she could smell the copper-tinged air and a heavy smell of decay. The damp air that came from the basement and the smell of mold and death rose. This was not a good place.

Little bits of trash were scattered around the floor, as if rats had been eating from the discarded items there. There was also rustling and what sounded like movement.

"Shit." Talon was the first one to speak up. "There are people down here."

"Yes," Callan replied in a whisper.

Brilius and Callan went first, the light dim as they went down the stairs. The sweeping patterns of Talon's flashlight beam flickering slightly on the walls against the stairs was decorated with a rusty red in places. Brilius paused a few times, examining pebbles, groupings of debris, but apparently there was nothing of note. Each of their steps sounded in the silence, scraping, and scuffing along the roughened cement. The rubber soles pulling the pebbles and rocks and rubbing them against each other. Eva could barely stand the noise. The light flickered around the stairwell and Eva struggled to clamp her mouth shut, her jaw working, her saliva activating in the back of her throat.

The basement reached far into the dark, the full length of the building that they had cleared above and as far as Eva could see there were rows upon rows of cages.

Stacked and stacked.

"Oh my God." Eva's hand rose to her mouth. They were full of people. Talon moved closer to one of the cages, the light bobbed into the cage and captured the shackles around the wrists, the neck ... it was a woman, her face slack. Eva let a sound that was half a sob, a gasp.

"Fuck," Paron ground out. This was more than they expected to find. But it was what they thought was going on though. These people had been here for weeks. It was definitely the Pavo. This was their preferred way to deal with on-planet cargo. They worked with populations like they were cattle, not like they were actual life-forms. Never in any of their encounters or in any of their information about the group had there been any inkling that they worked in any other capacity. Callan motioned them forward, sending his power forward. Paron held his back, he knew better than to loosen his power here, it was more of a liability around this kind of pain.

Watch yourselves. Callan sent out telepathically to the group. Talon startled, barely catching the flash-light. Eva tried to ignore the burn of bile in the back of her throat and the pain in her chest as she moved up to Callan's side. She grasped onto the link with her Fated by the small filament that wove between her and Callan, holding onto the goodness and the love that already had strengthened between them, allowing it to comfort her. She could feel him beside her as they made their way down the aisles, solid and real, but also, she could feel him along the link, allowing her to access his thoughts and the promises of vengeance. The others stalked beside them, vigilant, sure-footed, and sorrowful. Eva made sure to look at the faces in the cages as she went. She didn't see any signs of life in them.

Why did they let them die?

. . .

They aren't dead. Callan answered. *They are in stasis. The Pavo make use of it so that they don't have to deal with unruly prisoners. Unfortunately, it isn't very kind to the minds of most life-forms. The Pavo don't need their minds though. That isn't what they are selling. They are flesh-peddlers.*

Callan could hardly contain the storm of rage that was building, but he swallowed it and pushed it deep within. There were so many prisoners here. These people were obviously suffering. He could sense his Fated's distress. Ultimately, it was the Pavo that committed these acts of violence, but Callan knew that there was a market for slaves throughout the universe and that made him angry as well. The council pretended they cared, but he knew better.

He smoothed out his thoughts, cleared his mind, and prepared himself for battle. He felt a warmth on his mark and looked to see Eva, her eyes a bright and shining gold. He grabbed her hand and held it for a moment. He could feel the warmth of her love and the power that radiated from her. It poured through him.

Talon and Brilius moved in concert looking closely at all the cages and the shackles. "This is some dark shit," Brilius said in a low voice as he moved along. The Pavo were masters at making money at the expense of others, but this wasn't even about that. They were playing a longer game. It didn't matter how many of the poor people died as long as there were enough left alive to make it worth it to the buyers.

"Touch nothing," Talon said. "There could still be hidden wires and shit." It didn't seem right to speak in this space, the bodies curled in on themselves in the small kennels. It was obvious that they were suffering, even if it was in silence.

"There are a few up ahead further in the back. Five probably. They transport lifeforms like this — in stasis." Callan replied keeping his voice low and suppressed by his power, so they weren't heard.

"They don't seem to be using any energy sources. How do they keep them alive?" Talon asked.

"They don't. This is just to keep them from dying, to keep the flesh available." Callan's voice was grim. "We aren't going to do anything to them."

. . .

"I like that idea a lot. We move them and we leave," Talon said, moving ahead of them. "We need to move them all quickly, or people will come looking for them."

Talon moved ahead of them, and Brilius went back to Paron. "You good?" He asked the other man.

"No," Paron replied. His gaze was steady as he surveyed the room. Paron was pale, but his power was locked down tight.

"We aren't leaving these people here," Eva whispered fiercely. "Even if they aren't as alive as we think they might be. No one can do this to another person."

"I agree, Fated," Callan said, his arm tightening around her. His power was unshakable. "We'll leave the basement. We need to find some way to transport them all." He glanced at Eva, who nodded. Her eyes glowed amber now, and he could see that power radiated from her. It seemed as though his Fated had garnered additional powers with the mark. Good. The idea brought him a deep sense of satisfaction.

. . .

They moved along, finding more cages with additional bodies. Eva tried to hold herself together, she tried to push the thoughts and the feelings away. She was supposed to be in control, not like this. But she found herself holding Callan's hand and squeezing it tightly.

Callan felt a momentary burst of pride at Eva, his Fated's sense of justice and her capacity to care. This wasn't what they had expected.

They reached a corner pillar. Callan sent directions to the team as they prepped. He could kill them with his power, but there was no fun in that.

Will you stay in this spot? For me? Callan knew she wanted to be part of things, but he didn't think she had the training to participate in what was about to occur. When he finally took her to the Shade, he would train her properly in combat. The idea gave him satisfaction.

Yes. I promise. She didn't hesitate to agree.

. . .

The team moved forward into the space, black mist rolling as Callan moved forward. Eva didn't move as Callan allowed his power to subside enough for the Pavo to sense their presence.

"What the hell? Allan, didn't you lock up?" The in-fighting was predictable.

"Of course, I did asshole." The five individuals that were there had been gathered around a meager heating element. Apparently, they had no qualms about seeking their comforts while their captives suffered in cages. Callan didn't think it was worth explaining to them it was just a shifting perspective. Sometimes you were the captor and sometimes you could be the slave. Holding someone else against their will – there was no honor in that – no amount of money worth it.

“Well, it wouldn't have mattered if he locked up.” Callan stepped forward from the shadows.

“What the fuck? How did you get here?”

Callan loved the useless questions that they asked. If urgent medical help wasn't needed, he'd take his time. Callan wondered why the off-planet Pavo hadn't bothered to better equip this cell. They had seen them use Earth weapons on the attack on the Portland cell as well. What a waste of his time.

"Can we get this over with?" Sapphrius asked. She was vicious in her fighting, preferring to use blades to gut and slice spilling innards and letting people die slowly. Nobody had time for that.

“Information Sapphrius,” Callan commanded, making sure that his intent was clear. She rolled her eyes at him, but indicated she understood.

Sapphrius grabbed the closest one, lifting him off the ground with one hand and reaching quickly into the man's mind, searching for the knowledge they needed.

"How many more?" Sapphrius asked. The Pavo was screaming and flailing, but Sapphrius grasped his mind in an iron fist. "How many more?" she repeated.

The man's big eyes were wide and terrified, just like the others, he was shaking with terror.

Sapphrius brought his face close to the man. "How many more?" she demanded, the threat in her voice low and clear. The man looked down, and then up into Sapphrius' eyes.

"Where are you taking them?"

She dropped the man unceremoniously to the floor. "They are being shipped off-world and sold, from what I can tell. They don't know anything." Sapphrius gave the Pavo's body a disgusted kick. "Literally nothing."

"Paron?" Callan called, his voice barely above a whisper. Sapphrius went from man to man, pausing for a few moments in front of each one, as Paron placed a hand on each of their heads. Eva wasn't sure what was happening, but she snuck a glance at Paron and saw his eyes glowing faintly. It must have something to do with the powers that the men had, and she knew that Paron's power was aligned with thoughts and emotions. Or at least she thought it was.

After what seemed like an eternity of silence, she watched in horror as each of the men slumped to the floor in succession, not making a sound. Eva couldn't tell if they were unconscious, dead, or worse.

"Anything?" Brilius asked. He was unperturbed by the display walking restlessly around the fallen Pavo.

"The same," Paron's voice was bleak. "This group was in the dark. They didn't have any information beyond their orders. Secure Earthlings. Deliver the packages. Time, dates, places. We have those." Paron shrugged.

Callan sighed in frustration. "Fine." He pulled his power back towards him, the black mist and tendrils edging around the bodies. The smell was acrid and sooty as it covered their mouths. The bodies disintegrated with a sigh and a puff as if someone had blown a breath over it, the bodies were gone.

"You should have let them suffer," Sapphrius muttered.

"I agree, but we have people to see to, so your bloodthirsty streak will have to wait," Paron said.

. . .

You can come out now Fated. Eva stepped forward, minding the patches of charcoal dust. She wondered at herself a little — at her ability to feel satisfaction that these men were dead. She agreed with Sapphrius. They hadn't suffered enough.

"We will need to work with the outpost to get medical here Commander. Can you make that happen?" Talon nodded and moved off to climb the stairs and get a group from the outpost to assist.

As soon as he was out of earshot and up the stairs Brilius shot a look to Callan. "Do we trust him?" Callan shrugged.

"We'll see, I guess. If we can't then we will find more Pavo. I won't lie and say I wouldn't be disappointed." Callan was a little depressed to think about it though. He liked the commander, and he knew Eva did too. He wouldn't be terribly surprised though.

"Do you think this was the whole cell?" Sapphrius asked. Her eyes slid over the basement contents. The Pavo was a dark business. Certainly, the Shade dimension had their own issues, but it was one of the reasons that she had joined Callan. The Shade took care of their own. The sense of right and wrong was clear. With the IGC they were willing to bend their morality if the price was right. Callan wasn't like that.

"I doubt it," Callan murmured as he settled his hand into Eva's as they moved out of the basement. Callan knew that was what they were all thinking. The information they had gotten wasn't very good or very clear. Obviously, none of these individuals had been leading the cell. The only data that stuck out was that they knew there was a leader. Someone off-planet that placed the order. Someone in the IGC. That was valuable information.

Chapter Twenty-Three

Talon's feet echoed as he climbed the stairs up through the basement to the top building. He was cautious as he pulled himself through the trapdoor, rough brick prickling his palms, worn, and pitted.

He crouched on the wooden floor as he looked around, hidden in shadow. He didn't need to stick his foot into a booby trap.

Talon had been in enough combat situations that he knew not to poke his head out of some hole and get a knife to the eye. He pulled his gear vest down as he stood to full height, constantly scanning the darkened interior. It was still silent and dark, foreboding. Talon suppressed a shiver. He had been sweating since they came into the place, and it was colder in the building than outside. He took a breath and got out his tablet and communicator, walking carefully a little further from the trapdoor, mindful that he didn't step on anything untoward. His nerves were still heightened by the events in the basement. He didn't need to stick his foot into a booby trap.

Talon wasn't looking forward to making the link to his second in command. There had been some discussion with them regarding the fact that he had come on his own with "the Hunter" earlier. Most were still terrified of Callan. The powers that he held were viewed as unnatural by most, of course they didn't know the half of it. Talon barely held in a chuckle. He was shocked to find that his feelings about the matter were firmly in the pro-Callan camp. Huh. He was surprised at himself.

Certainly, there were many races throughout the galaxies and the universe that held their own share of powers, but Callan's abilities were in a league of their own. Now that Talon was a little better acquainted with Callan, he understood why that was the case. He'd been careful not to slip up using Callan's given name or any other details that he didn't think were common knowledge. He had the sense that he was now part of a small group of people that was privy to some things that Callan didn't allow many to see.

To some that might be something that they squandered, or they might be more accustomed to that sort of thing. They might have family secrets, friends that they held confidences with – but to Talon, this was never a position he'd held, a keeper of secrets. It made him feel part of their circle. At any rate, his mission was to get IGC sources here to help those poor Earthlings trapped down there, locked in stasis, suffering Fates only knew what.

Talon had keyed into the communications line with the outpost. He grimaced and waited, counting off seconds in his head while he could hear his team members clicking into the communications.

"Commander." His Second, Subul Razok picked up quickly, his voice eager. The younger lieutenant had been well-qualified for the position. He was often over-zealous, but Talon couldn't fault his work ethic.

. . .

Talon kept his voice as careful as possible. "Lieutenant, we have finished our sweeps of the location that I spoke of."

"Did you find them?" Razok's question came across the line just as Talon imagined it, the man leaning forward with his coal eyes bright, his breath exhaling in a rush. Talon could hear his breathing on the communication line.

"Yes," Talon paused – collecting himself, smoothing out his voice and the furrows in his brow. "We found some." Talon was more cautious about the amount of Pavo found. He wasn't so sure that they had found the entirety of the cell.

"Really?" Razok gushed. "Amazing."

Talon could barely restrain the snort. "Well, the Earthlings in stasis don't think it's amazing. We need medical."

There was a distinct silence.

. . .

"Look Razok," Talon tried for patience, again scanning his surroundings, stretching his eyes into the darkened space. "The Hunter and his team found them. The victims are in stasis. We need medical teams deployed. That's really all you need to know."

"How did they find them?" Razok spluttered on the line of the communicator. His voice cracked and broke, even though the line was clear as a bell. "They're just in cages? What the hell? How are we supposed to get them out of there?"

There was another long pause. Talon bit back his impatience. He couldn't afford to infuriate his Second. He clenched his jaw.

"We have the necessary equipment to deal with this type of retrieval. We're dealing with a lot of Earthlings..." He paused. "Quite a lot."

"How many?" Razok asked.

"A lot," Talon repeated. He couldn't answer it. "The Hunter and his team were tracking Pavo slavers here on Earth. That was the mission. You need at least two dozen warriors to come. Bring transports and medical to bring them to the outpost. They'll need IGC technology to bring them out of stasis properly. There is a loading bay on the side of the building that we can use. We will bring each – person there and then load them."

Razok made to speak again, and Talon cut in, "NOW. *Hurry up.*" Geez, Talon thought, he didn't really need an argument, he needed the asshole moving and on his way.

"Of course. Yes, Commander." The answer was reluctant. Obviously, he'd have to talk to Razok. He had forgotten himself. They had socialized while on base and apparently that had gone to his head. He thought maybe that he could balk at his Commander's orders because they were drinking an occasional glass of Goblin Tears.

Talon wasn't sure how deep the Pavo was entrenched here, but he didn't want to risk it. They needed to act quickly.

"I will have the Medics standing by." Razok assured him.

. . .

"Very good," Talon ended the call and set the communicator on the floor.

There was something that circled in his mind, a question that he couldn't shake. He pulled the tablet back up and tapped the keypad, opening an active communication line. He wasn't sure quite what was stopping him from calling. He hovered over the link. Talon stood there, perched over the tablet. Something was stopping him from calling.

The Pavo were smart enough to know that if they were causing disturbances here, they could get caught. That was why they had kept their activities confined, or so he thought. But there was also the fact that they had established a presence on Earth, even though they were aliens. They had been caused enough of a disruption that they forced the council's hand. Enough that the council voted to hunt them down, their operations here would be stopped. Talon wasn't sure that the Pavo were going to take kindly to that. Talon tapped the communicator on his chin. This was a much bigger operation ... he just couldn't grasp how. Every time that he felt he could almost figure it out the pieces floated away from him.

. . .

He'd done as was asked. The outpost personnel were on their way to handle the poor souls trapped in stasis. Getting them out of the cages and out of the basement without causing alarm – well, that would be a task. He wasn't really looking forward to it if he were being honest.

He peered around the hanging sheets of plastic that wafted in the darkened expanse of the laundromat. Eva had explained that the Earthlings would bring their clothing here to be cleaned. This location apparently had been closed years ago. Now the dust had settled in a thin coat on the floor in a light powder, gentle and soft, indiscriminate. Noise came from down below and voices. Talon heard the scraping of feet along the staircase and then saw shadows creep forward, the forerunners of the King of the Shade's power. They were on their way up.

King of the Shade. That was some shit right there. For almost the entire universe the Shade Dimension was off-limits. Nobody sane went into the Shade. The planets there were unknown and the dimension itself was spoken of in whispers. Ships that wandered into the Shade didn't do so of their own volition. If they went in it was for nefarious reasons. They were trying to escape the IGC perhaps, or they were thinking it'd be a quadrant shortcut; however, that was never the case. Those ships weren't known to return and were thought to be swallowed whole.

The actual Shade stretched between three of the four quadrants, intersecting them like someone had spilled a tub of oil across the sky, thick, viscous, and iridescent. While everyone knew of the Shade Dimension, Talon would bet all his credits that there were very few that knew that there was a King or that Callan was that King.

He was having a hard time processing what he'd seen down in the sub-level of the Earthling building. He scuffed his boots into the dust and debris of the floor as he waited for the ascent of the King and his court. He had fought in many places throughout his career with the IGC and he didn't think he was prepared for what he had witnessed.

"Did you call for assistance then?" Callan asked, as he climbed up, holding his hand for Eva. The tendrils of shadows swept ahead of them, spreading into the blackness of the building, searching for anyone that was hiding. Talon was pretty sure nobody was lurking, but he wouldn't say no to extra verification. After being creeped out in the basement he had no desire to end up like those poor bastards in the cages. Being a slave on some distant planet was not in his life plan.

"Yes. I spoke to my second. I've asked them to pull up to the loading bay doors there." Talon nodded toward the big doors that were in the back of the building. The doors were a good seventy-five feet high and thirty feet wide. Hinges as wide as a truck, covered with rust and grime, paint flaking off. They would definitely be the best chance of loading Earthlings from the building without them being seen.

"We'll just need to get them opened up."

"Sapphrius," Callan nodded at his second. She had just come up from down below and immediately stepped towards the area indicated with Brilius to see about getting the door unlocked. Eva could hear the crunch of their footsteps.

"I figure we can bring up everyone on a gurney and move them into a transport. If we go through the loading bay, then we run less risk of them being seen." Talon thought for a minute. The idea of the populace seeing the bodies in stasis. That would not be a good thing. Mass panic. Earth was already barely holding it together with the concept of aliens from other planets. The IGC had been clear in their command that they needed to move population off this planet. There were resources here, but people weren't considered one of them. Earthlings were to be distributed off planet. Talon had his orders, but he wasn't too sure anymore if he wanted to be part of the IGC. The thought was startling.

"Very well." Callan assessed the Commander. It appeared he'd be surprised, pleasantly. "There's still the matter of Private Hadariel."

"Yes, I have an idea about him," Talon replied. They'd made their way forward towards the doorway and the long countertop. Eva was shuffling around the hanging plastic sheets, running a hand through them, the shadow tendrils racing around her feet, her eyes still shimmering with gold. Talon leaned forward against the counter.

"Let's hear it then," Callan said. He was gazing back at Eva, distracted.

. . .

"I thought I could arrange a meeting with him – in a separate location on the outpost and then offer him additional credits. Pretend to be part of the network."

Callan snapped his attention back to the commander. He was impressed. It was a solid idea. "That's a good idea. He might let something slip. I'm not sure that this is all of them. Maybe he can give us something else."

"Maybe nothing, maybe something," Talon said. "Either way though, we need to tie up that loose end. We know that he's part of this." Talon's mouth compressed into a hard line as he looked towards the basement.

"We need to have Paron there, watching," Eva said, coming to Callan's side. She had been listening as she looked around a little more. She couldn't put her finger exactly on what was bothering her, but something was.

Callan cocked his head at his Fated. "Certainly. He typically has that duty. Perhaps the Private will decline the Commander's bribe and run off and try to connect with someone else. Maybe the Private has known more all along." Callan agreed that having all the meeting surveilled was a good idea.

"I'll set it up when I get back to the outpost," Talon replied, shifting a glance to Eva in interest. The Earthling was very interesting. This whole business of the fate marking was one thing, but the oath markings were a separate issue, one that Talon had never heard of before. He didn't know exactly what the implications were, but surely there would be some.

"Commander, the doors are unlocked and ready." Sapphrius and Brilius joined them at the countertop. "Do we think this is all of them?" Sapphrius asked the question nobody wanted the answer to.

"I doubt it," Paron answered. "Let's not borrow trouble. I'll listen in on the meeting with the Private. If he knows nothing ..." Paron shrugged as he let the sentence trail. "I'll kill him." Paron intended to drag him off and question him a little. Not so gently of course. He met his King's golden eyes with his own.

. . .

"Sapphrius." Callan didn't give further instructions.

"Of course." Her reply was instant.

What is she doing? Eva asked Callan privately. She didn't want to question him in front of his team, or court, she supposed was the actual term.

She is going to stay hidden here. Outside. To keep watch. Just in case there are Pavo that return. It just seems a little too neat and tidy. Callan could feel her agreement through the mark.

What about us?

We will return to the ship Fated. We need to get ready to depart.

Daisy. Eva threw desperately at him. *Daisy must come too. I promised.*

Of course. We will get Daisy. He felt her settle, curling into him.

. . .

"Brilius. You'll go to Daisy. Bring her to the ship," Callan said. "We will play out the hand we have been dealt and see where the chips fall. After that," he threw a glance at his Fated, "After that, we will be returning home." His lips curved into a gentle smile.

Paron eyed the picture they made. Beautiful and whole despite the horrors from the basement. King and Queen.

Talon was envious as the Shade Court members ported to their assignments, or in the case of Eva and Callan, back to their ship. He wasn't sure how he'd feel once they were gone. Would he feel sad? Yes, he felt as if he'd made friends. His people, the Jurox, were shifters on their home planets and tended to live in packs. The idea of a nuclear family was one he'd grown up with as a cub. He'd always thought that he would find that same sense of family in the IGC. Certainly, he had, to some extent, but it wasn't the same. There were elements of it to be sure, but ... Talon sighed ... it wasn't what Callan had.

. . .

“You look like you’re having a distant thought,” Sapphrius’ voice intruded. “We appreciate you working with us on this project," she said politely. "I’m sure you have someone waiting at home for you?" The last a query that Talon wasn't sure that she wanted an answer to. The commander was handsome and would be a nice diversion. She would be amiable to having him join them if Callan decided that he should.

“I like your court,” Talon said, dodging her question. “It's unique.” He tucked his hands into his pockets with a rueful smile. Sapphrius felt another little spark of something else as she looked at the commander with fresh eyes. She realized his smile was a little dazzling.

"Will you stay here then? On Earth?" Sapphrius drew a shallow breath. She was calmer now that she was out of the basement. Despite what her team thought - she hated blood. "Or will you leave the IGC?"

Talon turned to her. Stunned.

. . .

He looked around the room, not really seeing it. Sapphrius could tell he wasn't really seeing the here and now. He took a deep breath and exhaled.

"I'm not sure," Talon replied thoughtfully. "At this point, it would make things messy." He'd have to find another IGC outpost. He wasn't sure if that was even a viable option. Could he just leave. "It would be hard for Callan if he didn't have a contact here." Talon swallowed. "Until this is finished."

"It might be interesting. If you joined us." Sapphrius looked at him consideringly -- as if she was imagining it. She was a bloodthirsty one, so Talon wasn't sure how he felt about it.

"I'm not sure what my options are... besides the IGC. It's all I've ever known." Talon said. He'd become attached to Callan, his Fated, and his court. She was different. He suspected she was somehow more than just a human. Something about her was different. He felt it. She was more than one thing. He was pretty sure she wasn't human, but he wasn't sure what she was.

"Things change, Talon," Sapphrius said. In the end, she thought, everything changed. The only questions were how and what would form in the spaces between. "We have some interesting possibilities for a newcomer to the Shade," Sapphrius murmured, her eyes traveling over his perfectly formed body. "Perhaps we will talk later."

He sighed softly. "I'll think about it." He reached out and took her hand. She was a little shorter than him, but he felt a little awkward doing so. He could sense the spark of interest once more, though.

Chapter Twenty-Four

As Brilius stepped into the apartment, he was both disgusted and relieved by the sweet scents of cinnamon and sugary icing that Daisy used to create her Earthling treats. He had grown to savor the taste of death and destruction in his line of work, but there was something alluring about this sense of peace that he had never expected to find. He was tempted to remain here and enjoy the stillness. For a moment, he savored it, even as his mind churned with uncertainty about what tomorrow might bring.

He called out to her as he walked into the flavor-filled kitchen. "Hello?" he asked.

. . .

She was bent over the oven, her eyes focused on the task at hand. She slowly shoved the tray into the oven, the edges of her lips twitching with a contented hum. As she closed the door, she pulled the hot pads from her hands, a thin film of sweat glistening on her forehead.

She really was quite pretty, with her lush curves and her long charcoal lashes fanning over her cheeks. He was distracted by a shriek as she turned and caught a glimpse of him stalking forward. "Jesus Christ!" A hand flew to her chest as if to keep her heart there.

"No," Brilius was confused. "Who's that?"

"Idiot." Daisy didn't even want to explain to him the whole concept of Earthling religion to him. She shrugged her hands out of the hot pads, flinging them onto the counter, and set her timer. "Why are you here? Tell me what happened."

She was excited to hear about the mission, Brilius wanted to smile despite the grimness of the situation. There was something in her voice that soothed him.

. . .

"It was pretty awful," he grimaced. "Eva told you about the slavers that we were looking for?"

"Yeah, a little." Daisy nodded, her eyes shifting back and forth as he spoke.

"Well, he paused, unsure of what to say next, "We found them." He wanted to let her know that it had gone well, but he didn't feel like he was in the position to reassure her of anything. It had seemed a little too easy. He wouldn't be surprised if there were more of those little hidey-holes of Pavo scum lurking about.

Brilius moved across the kitchen to one of the chairs, sitting down and resting his long arm on the back of it. His eyes blazed into her as he crossed his ankle on his knee, and Daisy felt her breath catch as she took in the expanse of male.

"I'm here to get you and bring you to the ship." Brilius peered forward to the cooling rack. The smell was tempting. "Can I have one?" He'd learned the hard way that she didn't take kindly to taking without asking.

. . .

"Sure, go ahead." The corner of her mouth tipped up with a teasing quirk. Brilius gingerly picked up one of the cookies. (He had learned that all round sort of treats were called cookies on Earth. It was a fun word to say.) He took a bite, enjoying the small bits of brown goo that were sprinkled inside.

"They're good." He tasted the sweet and the salty, delectable. He took another bite, and a wide smile split his face. He shut his eyes to the Earthling delights.

Brilius was a goner. His eyes glowed as he devoured another one, and then another.

He moaned with ecstasy and held out a hand. Daisy slowly put the plate into them, looking at him with wariness.

"Thanks." Daisy was a little nonplussed. "Did you say that you came to get me?"

"Yep." Brilius tucked the rest of the cookie into mouth as he allowed her time to adjust to the information. He could practically see the gears in her head going.

. . .

"How long do we have before we have to go?" Daisy was no nonsense in life. She had packed and moved more times than she could count. She had no plans to be left behind. Wherever they were going, she was going with them.

Brilius shot her a smile. "How long do you need? And can we bring these?"

Daisy chuckled and went to pack a bag after double checking the timer one more time. "We will certainly bring those with us. I don't need very much time at all." She cleared her throat as if she had something to say and then shook her head. "But if we are bringing snacks, there are a few other things that I will need to bring."

In the end it did take Daisy longer than she had expected. The thought of leaving her planet behind started to weigh her down a little as she looked over their small apartment. They'd had good times here. Well, bad times too, but they had been together. She sighed as she brought her duffle and a rolling suitcase towards the center of the room. Daisy thought of Eva too. Eva was starting a new life in a new place and, as she looked around the apartment, she knew there were things Eva wouldn't want to leave behind. Eva didn't have a lot of memorabilia or things like that, but she had a few. There were only one or two photos she had from before they had met, but Eva had them tucked in a book on her bedside table. Daisy could possibly leave either of those.

How could she need so many things? Brilius wondered. He'd told her that she'd be provided for. He'd been honest with her. What she would do with the things she was taking he had no idea. At the palace she'd have everything she'd need. Honestly that puffy overcoat? It was warm on Tiebus - what would she wear that for? Brilius thought about saying something but decided to let her go ahead and take what she wanted. It was driving him crazy, but he had other things to worry about. Things like slavers.

"It's going to take me a little longer to pack than I expected big guy." Daisy admitted sheepishly. "Maybe come back in a little while?" Daisy could tell that Brilius was annoyed, and she felt a little bad about it. She knew he was in a hurry, but she wanted to bring a few things that were important to her. Daisy knew Eva would understand. They both had rough upbringings - she wasn't going to let go of her memories of her old life so quickly.

. . .

"Alright. I'll give you an hour of your Earth time. Then I'll be back for you. We need to get back to the ship." Brilius nodded at her seriously before slipping out.

Brilius had left on another errand, he'd taken two more cookies and disappeared. She had gone through Eva's room and just added in another hoodie to her bag when her door opened again. Daisy was turning to chastise Brilius for being so impatient – it had taken her forever to pack all the cookies properly and to pack up ingredients for two more batches.

Daisy hummed as she worked, stacking a duffle for Eva and one for herself. She eyed the stack thoughtfully. Certainly, Brilius wouldn't mind - it wasn't like he was carrying them to the car. She chewed her lip consideringly. On the other hand, she was going to be going to outer space, so she was allowed to want to bring some stuff. She was lost in her thoughts when her eyes swung to the front door.

Daisy froze as the imposing figure filled the doorway. His face was hardened, a livid scar running through one of his menacing, green eyes. He had a thick neck, wide shoulders, and tattoos like a winding ivy of black ink around his knuckles and wrists. She knew instinctively that this was no friendly visit. There would be no quips or witticisms to give this man. He was here to hurt her. When he stepped into the room, Daisy spun on her heel and flew towards the kitchen, searching frantically through drawers for a weapon to defend herself. The air was thick with dread and Daisy's heart thrummed with terror.

"Come here girlie." His meaty hands were claw-like as they knocked into items on the counter that she had out, scattering jars, boxes, and bags. Daisy tried to move out of the way, pulling drawers out haphazardly, gasping as she tried to draw enough air into her lungs to scream. The lack of air in her lungs made her feel lightheaded. She was desperate for Brilius to return – all she could think of was, PLEASE, come back!

He grabbed a handful of her hair, yanking her back. Just that small tug made her scalp burn like he'd set her hair on fire, it burned her eyes as she struggled against the grip. The man banded his arms around her as she bolted, his forearms meaty around her neck, his sweaty palm over her mouth.

Her legs flailed, her teeth bit, but it was no use. She could see the man's teeth flash in a wicked smile.

"Nighty-night," his voice said, rough in her ear.

The man drug Daisy's unconscious form down into the street, satisfied with the Private's information that he provided. Combined with his other source – things might just turn out okay after all. Granted, his main contact off-planet wouldn't be happy at all that they'd lost the entire shipment from the basement. He paused as he slung the Earthling over his shoulder. Yeah, he'd be answering for *that* and not in a way that would be pleasant. The IGC was a right nightmare of a contractor. He'd be in favor of never working with them again, but he wasn't in charge either.

He secured his cargo and headed towards the ship that would take him off-planet. The King of the Shade generally didn't negotiate, but according to the contact now ... he'd change his mind. With this sort of collateral, the Pavo would have a serious leg up finally and might be able to get some routes straight through the Shade. He grinned to himself and prodded the little morsel. She did look tasty.

Chapter Twenty-Five

Eva ventured into the main cabin after getting freshened up. She felt a hundred times better, but also a little bad that they had left their friends with so many chores to do. Callan assured her that occasional delegating was something that came with the territory. It wasn't like they should be there when the IGC came, anyway.

"What has you in such a fine mood?" Callan smiled at his Fated as she appeared. She looked more beautiful every time he saw her.

"I can't wait to show Daisy how the bathing chamber works. And clothes." Eva's eyes twinkled.

"She is going to *lose* her mind." This wasn't an exaggeration. Daisy loved clothes and the idea of some AI that made whatever clothes you wanted – well, suffice it to say that Daisy would go crazy. "Speaking of Daisy ..." Eva's voice trailed off.

"Brilius went to get her, but she needed a little packing time apparently." Callan gave a little laugh. "Brilius said she was amassing a lot of *things* to bring. She was also baking, so she wanted to finish. He went to help Paron and then they were both going back to bring her and her things." Callan had gotten an earful from Brilius about Daisy and her piles of stuff that she wanted to bring.

Eva had to laugh a little. Well, hopefully they told her she didn't really need clothes, so she didn't waste time packing things she didn't need, but Eva sympathized. The idea of moving and leaving all your things behind was daunting. Eva didn't mind so much because she had Callan though. Not to mention, she knew Daisy would make sure all her favorite items would make it on the trip. There was no remaking your favorite pair of shorts. It just wasn't the same. "So, do all the cabins have the same bathing arrangements and the Amura thing?" Eva waved a hand in the air.

. . .

"Yes, Fated. The Amura is standard." He sent her an indulgent smile. He leaned away from his work as she came to him, standing between his thighs. Callan wrapped his arms around her and pulled her close. Eva arched her neck for a kiss. The way his hands moved over her made her want ... so many things. Smooth and warm - they sent shivers down her spine.

"Remember what I said?" His eyes darkened; they were almost black as he leaned into the crook of her neck, setting his mouth against it. She could feel his tongue reaching out to her skin, tasting her, biting, marking her. Eva's breath quickened, and goose bumps sprang up on her skin. Her panties dampened.

"No," she lied. She did remember what he'd said in the storeroom. She hoped he did.

"I can't do everything that I want to do to you here." His eyes roved the ship, "But we can make a good start." Eva's heart pounded as Callan's power seemed to beat in time to it. Her pulled her close, setting her down to nestle into his rock-hard length. He cupped her ass, lifting her and hooking her legs over his lap so that she fit against him. Eva groaned, reveling in the sensation and the pressure, rocking against his cock.

"Do you feel how much I want you?" Callan whispered. His fingers reached into her hair, combing the strands back from her face idly. "Are you wet, my Queen?" The shadows moved up her belly, tightening and loosening as they went. Callan's mouth was desperate on hers, his tongue diving into the recesses, his hands gripping the back of her skull.

Eva pushed away from him, suddenly feeling desperate as she stood, her chest heaving. "I want to know if you're wet for me." Her eyes were narrowed, but her pupils were dilated with want as she reached for his zipper. "Hold still," she commanded. "I can't tie you up the way I wanted." She sent him a cheeky grin. "If you move, I'll stop."

Callan put his hands up on the sides of the table, palm side down in mock surrender. He liked this side of his little Earthling, well – not so much an Earthling anymore. The side that fought him for control. The side that was willing to play games.

. . .

She eased his zipper down and freed his hard cock. Eva's mouth watered as she sank to her knees before him. A pearl of moisture at the tip. Her eyes met his.

"You are wet," she teased. Her hands fluttered around his cock, small and warm. She traced up his length and down to his balls, weighing them in her palm, squeezing, before she brought up her other hand and grasped his length firmly. Callan couldn't help but let out a moan, his hips rolling up with the slightest movement.

"No moving," she warned as she leaned forward, her hair falling in a curtain as she licked the pre-cum from the tip lazily. Callan grit his teeth and gripped the edge of the table as her mouth dipped down over the tip, her tongue running along the slit of his cock.

Eva reached one hand to a hip bone and kept one hand on his cock as she increased suction, leaning into her task. She wanted to slide a hand into her panties, rub her clit, but contented herself with tightening her fist. Eva stilled anytime that Callan jerked his hips, decreasing her suction. She knew that there'd be hell to pay later, but she would be no passive partner to her Fated. Not when it came to this. Eva's mouth slipped down his length again, but only because she had lowered her mouth to lightly bite his balls.

Callan bit his lip to keep himself from moving his hips, or groaning too loud, he leaned forward to reach her, but one look into her eyes and he knew that he wouldn't be able to resist. He groaned.

She drew his cock in until her eyes burned, and it hit the back of her throat. The skin pulled tight over the tip of his cock, and thick, hot cum spilled into her mouth. She swallowed as he came in a rush and then collapsed back on the counter. Her mouth watered with desire as she thought of his cock deep inside of her. The taste was still in her mouth and on her lips, wrapped around his cock.

"You were a good boy," she said silkily, rising to her feet. He pulled her forward for a kiss.

"I'll bet you're ready now." He slid a hand to her crotch, rubbing there and Eva's eyes almost rolled back into her head. Callan didn't even bother to hide the fact that he was already hard again as he stood and positioned her at the tabletop, pulling her pants down to her ankles.

Eva's face pressed into the table as he exposed her backside, but her checks were flushed, her sex pounding as he positioned himself.

Callan slid his fingers into her pussy, driving into her. "You're a mess Fated, so wet." Eva groaned, gripping the table. She was soaked, her body vibrating with need. Eva wanted him to take her hard, to devour her, to make her cum.

"Please, Callan." She could feel his shadows smoothing over her, sliding over the small of her back and she had wicked thoughts about possibilities. Now though, she wanted her Fated. Callan's cock slid into her, one hand on her hip as he pumped into her. "Oh, God," she moaned.

It felt like heaven, full, as he pounded stroke after stroke. Callan didn't compromise or think of her as breakable either. He fucked her hard, settling a hand into the small curve of her back.

. . .

"Do you need more my Queen? Tell me," he said, his voice husky.

"Yes." She was almost there, reaching. Suddenly she felt the press against her clit, rubbing there in time with the pounding, she realized Callan was using his shadows and the thought made her cum hard, screaming open mouthed against the table as the black shadows rubbed against her clit as Callan's cock plunged into her pussy.

Eva felt limp as Callan turned her over, lifted her leg over his shoulder. "Scream for me again, my Queen." He slid deeper into, suddenly, not giving her any time to recover. Her eyes closed as her hands gripped his shoulders. Her body sizzled with need as she squeezed him deeper. He continued to thrust as she came down, and the pleasure took on a distinct character. "Oh, god," she gasped, her hips lifting to meet him.

"Callan, harder. Deeper, please, fuck me harder." He obliged, calling his shadows to him, and wrapping them around their bodies, fucking her fast and hard. Her body responded, her moisture coating his cock, he groaned at the sensation.

. . .

“I'll - I'm not sure ..." she whispered and then moaned as he hit that spot inside her. Her head felt fuzzy, her body hummed as he took her. Callan's eyes fluttered closed, and he groaned. He pulled her to him and sank deeper in, his grip on her hips tightening as he pressed into her.

"I want as much as I can get from you." His eyes glowed. “Then I want more. I want it all.”

It was all she could do to keep from coming again herself, but she willed herself to wait for him. She wanted to watch him cum. She wanted to see his dark eyes go wide and his mouth open as he came inside her.

“Cum, Callan.”

She stroked his long hair back from his face, eyes locked on his.

He gave a strangled moan as he came, his hips slamming into hers as he spent himself inside her, and she watched his face, saw the pleasure and release there, and felt the hot splash of his cum filling her.

. . .

He continued to thrust into her for a moment and then he slowed, sagged against her, pressing a kiss to her shoulder. She felt his cum trickle from her body and pool onto the table. "I didn't want to hurt you. I'm sorry."

She laughed, running her hands over his shoulders, delighting in the play of muscle and sinew. "I'm not made of glass."

"Damn, I don't know if we are going to survive each other," he said with a laugh. He helped her stand up, giving her a gentle kiss, he drew her into his arms and carried her back to their chambers.

"We might as well do a reset and a clean-up," he said with a laugh. He looked askance at the table. "That too," he said with a laugh.

Eva didn't disagree. After a quick turn with the bathing chamber and another whirl with Amura and a change of clothes she felt much more presentable. Eva made sure to tidy up in cabin too.

. . .

He'd just given her a smile when it suddenly fell away from his face, and he paled. Eva knew even without him saying anything that something was profoundly wrong.

"What is it?" She could feel his dread as his eyes turned to her - dimmed.

Chapter Twenty-Six

Once Brilius felt he'd given Daisy enough time he'd prodded Paron to come with him to pick Daisy up. Seriously - how much stuff could the little Earthling bring? He and Paron ported outside of Daisy and Eva's apartment. The decision to knock on the door, like Earthlings, was out of consideration. Paron really liked to see Daisy jump and give that breathy little gasp (which Brilius totally understood). Earthlings were quite interesting if he was honest with himself. Brilius was in fine spirits as he'd filled his belly with Earth treats, teased Sapphrius a little bit, and they'd been able to scout the location for the meeting between the Private and the Commander. The meeting spot was going to be decent as far as those things went. The Commander originally had wanted to meet the Private in a different spot, closer to the outpost, but it wouldn't have afforded any sort of spot for Paron to look (or to listen). Eventually they'd found a much better spot that gave them both what they needed.

The apartment block had a stillness to it. The street was unusually empty and only a few of the windows in the other units glowed with light. Earlier when Brilius had been there the hum of Earth noise had been in the background - ambient and soft.

They stomped up the stairs, their boots making clomping sounds as they moved up the floors. Certainly, they could move more quietly, but Daisy had complained loudly that they startled her. They had just reached the doorway when they both stiffened. It was open, the lock splintered, the wood ragged.

"Daisy?" Brilius called. "Daisy!" Brilius pushed his way into the unit followed closely by Paron.

Paron sent his power surging forward, afraid of what he'd find. It lurched into the space only finding remnants of fear, surprise, and anger from Daisy. Just whispers of emotions, stale, at least an hour old. Behind that were the emotions of someone else, a stranger, not an Earthling. Paron stretched himself, stretched his power ... moving it into the cracks as he and Brilius hurtled through the door.

The apartment space was in shambles, furniture tossed on its side. Brilius crouched to the floor, sniffing. Paron moved through the space, into the kitchen, where drawers were pulled out, kitchen implements scattered onto the floor.

Daisy's happy space was now encroached upon by a heavy presence. Brilius took it in and felt his body still. He looked at Paron and they nodded at each other. Brilius moved silently, assessing, waiting until they had checked the entire scene. Paron had already come to his own conclusions – they weren't good.

"I guess we both know what happened then," Brilius said. His voice was heavy with self-recrimination. Paron shut down his power. He didn't need it to know what Brilius was feeling. They had obviously failed to keep Daisy safe (as they should have). They should have expected that someone would come after her.

. . .

"Yes. I think it's safe to say that there was a Pavo that wasn't in the basement," Paron said. He paused, thinking it through. "Perhaps the Private provided information about Callan and our Queen? Perhaps it led someone here?"

Paron tasted Brilius' guilt and sadness, even without spooling his power out. "It's not your fault Brilius." He laid his hand on his shoulder in consolation. "We all accept responsibility."

Brilius understood Paron was trying to make him feel better, but Brilius was the one who was supposed to collect her. It had solely been his decision to leave. He had been impatient. The evidence was all around them that she had been taken. He crushed his fingers into the edge of the cheap Formica, crumbling it to dust. It was he who had failed.

Brilius felt a crushing sense of despair. He'd had a responsibility to Daisy to keep her safe. He had failed. It wasn't just that. He was in service to Callan and to his new Queen. He'd sworn an oath. The smell of the dust that had once been cheap furniture mingled with the odor of Brilius' distress. Paron steadied himself, settling his mind, his power.

. . .

Paron stared hard at his back as he stood, muscles, sinew, and bone shifting in his back. Paron knew better than to say anything to him right at this moment. They both knew that Daisy had been taken.

"I'll need to go see Callan." Brilius' throat bobbed. "I'll have to tell Eva that her friend is gone. We will need to track this fucker." The counter crumbled some more. Paron nodded.

"I've got the meeting with the Commander. That Private." Paron was thoughtful. "I will grab him, regardless." He was resolute. "He will give us every ounce of information that he has." There was a heavy weight as he sent the information out through his link to the king.

Chapter Twenty-Seven

Brilius ported into the ship, swaying slightly on his knees. He had parted with Paron at the apartment in the city, bringing himself directly to his King and Queen. He barely knew what to say. Brilius hung back near the entrance to the ship; leaning his palm on the smooth metal of the interior, trying to compose himself and get his emotions under control.

The King would be furious and the Queen ... Brilius swallowed heavily. The Queen. Brilius couldn't even swallow his mouth was so dry. How could he even face them?

Brilius had been with Callan for nearly one hundred Earth years. He had joined him initially through the IGC as a mercenary. His interest had purely been in Callan's role as the Hunter, not as the King of the Shade. Callan was protective of his kingdom and his title. The Shade was a fascinating place, but secretive. Its politics were not complicated – the planets all worked together symbiotically.

For years, Callan had met with Brilius and Sapphrius outside of the Shade Dimension. He had kept that persona of the Hunter separate. Brilius had understood his reasons. It wasn't until many years had passed, and Brilius had shaved off some of his anger at his own planet and circumstances that Callan felt comfortable letting him know he wasn't just the IGC's Hunter. Brilius still remembered his disbelief the moment he found out.

Many had distrust of monarchies. Within the universe there were many planets that were rife with corruption, which was to be expected. Most planets had political structures that had old rules, or old blood, or old debts. They ran by greed, power, or both. Brilius disliked anything to do with people in power for these reasons.

. . .

Brilius came from such a planet. The distaste that he had for royalty ran deep. The whole dynamic of being subject to a king was hard for some to take. Brilius was one of those who didn't exactly have a lot of respect for politics or titles. For many decades he made his own power, his own way. Like Serix, their missing team member, he liked to go his own way much of the time. However, once Brilius trusted – he gave everything.

He paused in the entrance of the ship, his fingernails cutting his palms. Callan walked towards him, his expression betraying nothing. Brilius took a deep breath, "I have something to tell you." He paused, his eyes looking off to the side, "It's not good." Brilius swallowed and gulped. Callan stopped before, his arm reaching out, a small squeeze to his shoulder.

"Come."

Callan's tone was steady. Brilius stepped through the doorway allowing Callan to follow behind him. Eva's eyes, wide and tear-stained, glancing between him and Callan.

"There was an incident," Brilius began.

. . .

"Daisy?" Eva's voice was wooden. Her throat was tight, her eyes taking in Callan and Brilius' haunted eyes.

"She's gone. Brilius and Paron went to pick her up, and the place was trashed. There was ... a struggle." Callan's hands clenched as he came to her. "I'll find her. I promise."

Eva couldn't even find words as she gripped Callan's hand tightly. "Is it the Pavo? Did we miss one?"

"Yes, we think so," Callan answered.

Eva closed her eyes and leaned into him, her heart aching for Daisy. She could still see the cages in her mind, and the frightened faces that had been inside them. She desperately tried to push away the horror, but it seemed to linger in the air around her. Daisy must be so scared.

"The Commander has already sent a message to the Private. We moved it up." Callan only felt anger at this point. Eva wasn't wrong. They had been too cocky in their assumption that their party was safe. Daisy should have been more protected. Callan hadn't been thinking that their enemies could reach them or didn't have information that they were party to.

"I'll get her back. Then they'll pay the price of the Shade." When Eva looked to him this time, she saw only glimpses of her Fated in the lines of his face. Mixed in between now was the King of the Shade, giant curling horns, dripping shadows, glowing golden eyes, and claws in place of fingers. Eva's heart skipped a beat in her chest, but she leaned into him. She was not afraid. THEY should be afraid.

Brilius trudged forward, his steps heavy and slow. The Queen had a ghostly pallor, her dark hair, nearly black against the paleness of her skin, looked like raven's feathers as she leaned against the King.

"Are *you* alright?" Eva asked, coming forward to take his hand. Brilius felt his shame bright and hot. Words stuck in his throat.

. . .

"Yes, my Queen. I ... failed you." He could barely get out the words even though she looked at him in confusion, her grey eyes shooting to Callan quickly as Brilius averted his eyes from hers.

He considers it his fault Fated. On his planet, the burden is his. Callan explained to her through the link.

"You didn't fail Brilius." Her eyes became stone. "This is *their* fault. The Pavo." Eva stepped forward into Brilius' arms, hugging him fiercely. "I need you now. We need you." She murmured against his chest.

He let his arm reach around her and cradle his Queen, taking comfort in her softness. "They will pay." He couldn't help but respond. She was right. She needed him and they would pay accordingly. They would not only pay the price of the Shade, but they would pay HIS price. They would pay for taking from his Queen.

Chapter Twenty-Eight

Paron stretched himself out on the rooftop, stilling his breathing. His hand smoothed the pebble rough feel of the paper, curling the edges back and forth while he waited for the Commander and the Private to enter the alleyway. He had spoken to Brilius already after going to the apartment. They needed this to work. Needed information from this contact. Paron sent a prayer to the Fates that they'd get some.

Brilius was off looking for clues, desperate. He felt responsible. It had been his job to secure Daisy, and he knew it. Paron didn't need to spell it out for him. He had failed. And Azer was right, this contact was their best chance at another crack at the Pavo (and now to find out where Daisy was). Giving up wasn't an option.

. . .

As Private Hadariel entered the alley, he froze. He was from Ghetea originally if Paron wasn't mistaken. He was slight in his Earth form, but Paron knew the Gheteans were giants on their own planets. It must be strange to Hadariel to be so small here on Earth.

The seconds ticked by until finally a figure appeared in the mouth of the alley, cloaked in darkness. As the figure drew closer Paron could make out the brown eyes peering out from beneath a hood, surrounded by shadows, barely visible from the light of the street lamps flicking beyond.

The Private stepped lightly, his breath held tight, his eyes darting from one dark corner of the alley to the other. He stayed close to the sides of the buildings, his hands clenched nervously as he crept forward, cautious in his steps.

Paron let his power unravel, letting it creep into the night towards the target. He could taste the fear quivering in the darkness in Hadariel's consciousness ... watery, flawed.

. . .

He watched as the Private walked along the dirty cement, between the flickering lights, and then stopped in a spot that was hidden partially by one of the trash receptacles that were used on the planet. Paron knew this was within sight of the designated spot that had been set by Azer.

Paron kept his power seeking, moving forward into the atmosphere as he waited. Eventually, he picked up the signature that he recognized. Once Paron was familiar with someone, it was easy to pick them up again. Paron could sense the moment that the Private saw Azer – his emotions spiked, the fear sharp and acrid tasting. Paron pulled himself forward on the rooftop, his belly scraping. He remained still and silent, his power like a blanket around them, listening and studying their every move.

His heightened hearing made eavesdropping no problem. Azer knew they'd be watching, but he wasn't sure if he knew they could listen. Paron smiled to himself. It was unlikely. He could hear the slight change in speech, the increased hesitance, the way Azer's voice sounded in the gloom.

"Private," Azer said coolly. He gave a nod. The breeze that slipped over Paron's cheek carried movement. Voices, there was sound coming from the next building over. Paron could just make the words out. He moved closer.

"Commander," the answer was practiced as the Private stepped forward into the light. Paron almost groaned. What an idiot. If he was looking to take the Private out, this is where he would have done it. The Private made the perfect target there in the light. He could have shot him with ease, even with one of those crappy Earthen weapons. Paron remained still, his power pulling on the darkness, blending into the surrounding night. He waited. He'd been trained well. He had to trust that Azer would ask the right questions. They needed this contact - every lead at this point was critical.

There was a long moment of silence. Paron shifted his feet with the need to move. To act. To advance. To find Daisy. When they had told Azer about her being taken, Paron had been surprised by the emotion in his face. Interesting.

"You've made a pretty big mess for our friends." Azer's voice was stern and his face no nonsense. Okay, thought Paron. This was a good way to go. He could sense Hadariel's confusion and doubt.

. . .

"A mess?" The Private scrambled. The Private's eyes darted to the alleyways, intimidated. Paron could tell that Hadariel knew what Azer meant without a doubt, he was just looking for damage control.

"If you'd come to me and been straight with me instead of sneaking around." The derision on Azer's face. Perfection. Paron wished Callan were here to see it. "I could have diverted the Hunter." Azer looked at the Private like he was an idiot and Paron knew then that he had sealed the deal.

"Sir. I ..." Hadariel stumbled. "I didn't realize ..."

"We need to clean this shit up," Azer's voice was low, rough, and rushed as he leaned into the Private's space and grabbed his collar suddenly, yanking him towards him. "I'm not getting killed over your crap. You haven't seen the Hunter in action ..." Azer let the sentence dangle and shoved the Private away.

Paron waited. He had to be sure. He let his power float out of the shadows in the alley. There was a hint of a different taste -- The Private's emotions swung to glee, gloating. Totally contrary to any that he'd ever felt from him before.

"I fixed that." Hadariel's face was flush under the lights, his eyes wide. The golden glow from the street lamps bounced off the white cheeks of Hadariel's form, giving him a youthful appearance. Paron wasn't fooled.

"You fixed it?" Azer repeated it. It wasn't even a question. Paron could taste Talon's absolute confusion, but he had been careful to keep his voice flat and even. They seemed to both be holding their breath while they waited for Hadariel's response.

"Yeah, I fixed it." Hadariel's voice had dropped an octave. Paron couldn't help but smile. He continued to watch the exchange unfold, his own body tingling with anticipation. "My contact kept asking about the girl. The girl from Earth that was here with the Hunter." Hadariel's face was practically manic now. "*The Hunter*," Paron could tell now that he was just bragging. "Nobody had anything on him, but he's going to come begging now. That girl – she's important. I got her address. She has a friend and ..." he paused for effect ... turning in a circle, his arms spread like he was unveiling a secret. "Guess what."

. . .

"What?" Azer's voice was devoid of emotion, Paron knew he already guessed. There was a sense of dread pervading the air from the Commander.

Hadariel paused for effect, leaning in, eyes bright. "I helped." He seemed so proud of himself. His mouth grinning. Azer's face, for the first time that night, seemed to relax. He set his shoulders and seemed to breathe for the first time all evening.

"I see." He took a step back. "So, you took her." He repeated. Paron could taste the anger coming off him.

"We took her." The breath hadn't even finished from his throat before Paron had ported behind the Private. His body heavy in the atmosphere, solid. Paron could hardly contain his own rage, but he'd master it. He could taste the glee that Hadariel felt when he spoke of giving Daisy to the Pavo. His Queen's only friend in this world.

"Did you now?" The words were silky soft – deadly with promise, a cynical twisted smile on Paron's lips. Hadariel was turning and twisting, trying to see who the newcomer was. Confusion colored the air, tangy and sweet.

Somewhere in the distance, a cough, the sibilant hiss of a snake, a whisper from somewhere.

Rats scurried along the walls, fighting over scraps of stale bread, the scrabbling of claws and chewing of rodent teeth ringing out in the night.

Hadariel had obviously thought they were alone. He struck his elbows out wildly, but it was useless. Paron banded his arms tightly around him, trapping them against his own body. Hadariel tried to strike his head back, to ram it against the head of the individual he knew was holding him fast. It was no use.

Paron chuckled darkly. "Honestly, I have to say that I like that you are struggling. Weakly though you are. I'll bet you wish you were on your home planet." Paron breathed the words against the side of Hadariel's ear. He heard the gasp of breath and felt the flinch of Hadariel's uncertainty. "The things that I will do to you now." Paron's words were filled with dark promise.

. . .

Hadariel stilled. This was bad. He had thought he had been smart, but he was obviously so wrong. Hadariel's eyes swept to the Commander.

"You were never going to get away with it," Azer said, his voice rife with disgust. There was a pause as he stared at the Private. "You were an idiot to get involved with the Pavo. And an amoral one at that."

Azer's eyes shone angrily now, stony. Hadariel realized he had misjudged the situation entirely. He thought he'd found a comrade, a friend, an ally. He couldn't have been more wrong.

Paron wrapped an arm around the Private and ported, leaving Azer standing still in the same spot, his hands at his side, his back straight.

Fates help the Private and the Pavo now. Well, they probably wouldn't. There would be no place to hide now that they took Daisy.

Chapter Twenty-Nine

It was cold. Daisy totally didn't wear an outfit to be kidnapped in. That wasn't on her agenda. Already her jeans that she was wearing were torn at her knees. She'd also somehow lost her black hoodie that she'd been holding, which was a shame because it was absolutely freezing. Someone had brought her some water and something that might be food, but she wasn't totally sure. The small tray held a tiny cube.

Eva had explained the odd nutrition cubes, so Daisy thought that was what this little grey thing was – perhaps? Daisy licked her finger and reached out to touch the little grey cube with it. She pinched it between her finger and thumb, just to see, and brought it to her mouth. She was hungry, and she didn't know how long she'd been here.

Daisy popped the cube into her mouth and chewed. It was like a tiny piece of gum, and it was soft, but not the worst. She swallowed the little cube whole, and for the first time in what felt like days, she wasn't hungry.

She wasn't sure if it was good or bad, but she didn't think it was what she was craving. Well, if they were going to drug her, they wouldn't have left it up to her now would they, Daisy reasoned. It had tasted like nothing, and she was instantly disappointed and relieved. Relieved that it didn't taste bad, but disappointed because Eva had told her that the cubes tasted like your favorite flavors. She was hoping for some kind of baked treat. Although, it really wouldn't be the same. No chewy center, she thought mournfully.

Daisy had tried to talk to a man that had come in, but he didn't have any answers to give her or any he was willing to give her. He'd only affixed a metal band to her wrist and shackled her to the floor of the ship.

Now she was shackled on some thin mattress and was obviously flying somewhere. Daisy huffed and examined the metal bands again. Her fingers pulled futilely at them. Geez. This sucked.

. . .

She was going to be damn well taking home the prize at this rate.

Unexpectedly, her stomach grumbled, and Daisy shook her head in dismay. Then she kicked herself – she hadn't even checked the cube before eating it! What if it was rat poison? It wouldn't be the first time she'd done something stupid like that. But why would her kidnapper want her dead? They had to have some use for her alive.

Her thoughts were interrupted by a loud bang, and Daisy looked around in confusion. It sounded like something had broken, and a moment later the airlock door opened.

"Not dead yet?" the man asked her, cocking a brow.

"What's that supposed to mean?" Daisy frowned at him. She wrinkled her nose in confusion.

He was tall, the top of his head brushed the ceiling. Broad shoulders and wide arms ended at long, well-manicured hands. His hair was a dark shade of red, his eyes a bright green. Icy and calculating as he looked at her.

"Well, you ate it. That could have been a bad decision on your part." The man shrugged and cracked a small grin. "Seems to be working well enough, though, so I guess you're fine."

Daisy tilted her head at him curiously. "Thanks, I guess for your concern." She was having a tough time figuring out what was happening here. Was she captive by the Pavo right now? Eva had told her about them. Or was this something else entirely?

The man laughed; a pleasant sound that made Daisy's heart skip a beat. "You're welcome," he said kindly, his green eyes twinkling.

Daisy felt her cheeks flush with embarrassment. What was this guy thinking? She didn't like the idea of being kidnapped and used for something unknown, especially when she had no clue what it was. She looked away from him, insulted. Maybe.

Daisy felt her indignation begin to subside as she looked into his face. Maybe he wasn't so bad after all. She gave a mental eye roll. Wait - she was shackled and a prisoner. She cleared her throat. "So ... you're taking me with you? Where are we going? What do you want with me?"

He smiled reassuringly at her. "We are headed to meet someone. Yes, you're coming with us."

"No, I'm not." She paused and then looked back at him. "Us?"

The man looked down at her and then chuckled. "I think you are." He touched the shackle. "Yes, us." He didn't elaborate.

"I think you should let me go," Daisy told him, irritated. She tried to ignore the fact that she was obviously chained up and didn't really have a choice at this point.

"Well, it's a little too late for that now," the man told her. "We're almost there."

. . .

"Where?" Daisy wrinkled her brow, staring at the shackle with concern. None of this boded well. "I don't want to go anywhere. I want to go home, and I want to sleep," Daisy said, dropping her head against the mattress with a huff.

He chuckled. Earthlings. They were simple creatures. "Apparently you are quite the prize."

"Ugh." Daisy hated being out of control. This feeling was something that she'd felt in the past and she didn't like it.

"Well, you're a valuable commodity. So, we're going to stash you somewhere for a little while. If your friends come through, then they'll come and get you." He winked at her, but Daisy didn't feel any sort of relief.

Daisy thought through what she'd learned. Friends? They must be talking about Eva and Callan. So, was this about the Shade? Interesting. She'd never ever thought of herself as a bargaining chip. She looked at the man again and tried to ignore how attractive he was.

. . .

“Stash me somewhere? What does that mean exactly? Are you just going to keep me locked up here?” Daisy was thoroughly exasperated.

“At least until we get to where we're going.” He smiled at her. "You’ll be safe and sound."

"And who, exactly," Daisy said, propping herself up on her elbows and looking at him, "is it that you think is coming for me?" She was curious.

He shrugged noncommittally. He looked her over in obvious appraisal, and Daisy felt color burn in her cheeks. "We'll see I guess." He gave her a wink before closing the airlock door behind him.

Chapter Thirty

Governor Faneh tipped her screen towards her; the link was still difficult from Baseon to Earth, but her contact with the Pavo had been reliable enough. She'd been pleased that they had kept up their end of the bargain with shipments. Baseon's mines might not be sanctioned by the IGC, but she had responsibilities to fulfill, and she would make sure she kept her promises as Governor to her people. She didn't care what it took. There were no lines she wouldn't cross.

She still sure that her involvement with the Pavo was undetected by the rest of the council. However, she wasn't totally positive that she could stay clear of the Hunter. He had always been a bit of an interest for her. He'd never been willing to play along. Faneh always thought he was a little too proud for his own good, too aggressive. However, she wouldn't have minded having him in her bed either.

Now that she knew he'd picked up an Earthling she was extra interested in him. No telling what weakness she could exploit now. She tipped herself back a little in her chair to stare at the Baseon skyline. It spread before her, like the sea and salt, with the tiniest little torches of flickering light dotting the surface.

The salty stink of a saltwater fish market wafted up Governor Faneh's nose as she inhaled, taking in the stench of decaying fish caught in the sun. She loved it here. She loved the way the ships would come to the docks to unload the goods the people needed. She was the only one who had any real power here, and she liked that. This was *her* city.

The skyline of Baseon was as imposing as it was beautiful. The buildings, though constructed to obscure, still let the natural daylight fill the city. Looking at it, the buildings seemed to almost be rolling off the hilltops, falling onto the walkways, streets, and little bodies of water below.

. . .

Yes, she thought ... she might be able to get the Hunter to be on her side finally. He would see reason that the connections to the Pavo, the market and trade — the trafficking — it was all beneficial. She knew that the 'Hunter' was really Adiim. The Shade could benefit if only Adiim would bend just a fraction. Faneh swayed in her chair. Her pale blue flesh glowing with her thoughts. Adiim and his foolish games. Playing his anonymous role as Hunter. It had taken her decades to learn who he really was.

She'd like to think she would have figured it out on her own eventually. It was one of Adiim's own court who had slipped. Sapphrius, his most loyal second. Faneh smiled and lowered her hand to her lap and rested it on her thigh.

Even the IGC were fools. They had no idea the lengths she and the Pavo were willing to go to stay in power. No one in the council even knew anything happened on Baseon. They only saw the reports she chose to give them. They could only see what she wanted them to see. There were other worlds, and other opportunities, but Baseon was her world. Her home. She was going to stay on top no matter what it took. If she needed to bring the Shade Dimension to heel to do it. She would.

. . .

It was going to be a lot of trouble to go through to collar the King of the Shade, but now that he had found his Fated. Faneh smirked to herself. Now - she had hope.

She'd think about that after she got rid of some of the loose ends. The Hunter had no history on Earth. When she'd found out that he'd made connections while he was there, she could have been knocked over by a feather. He wasn't one to make such foolish mistakes. The Pavo had a contact on the outpost, and she thought it was the perfect time to get her hooks into the enigmatic King.

The IGC had contracted with the mercenary and his band many centuries ago. He'd been careful – so careful Faneh had trouble finding any holes in his story. She was patient though.

She looked back to her screen when she heard a knock on the door. Governor Faneh looked up. "Come in," she said softer than she truly felt.

Jameson Brock looked over at her, his long blond hair pulled back in complex braids along the length of his scalp. "Governor," he said, his eyes flicking to the open screens on her desk.

. . .

"Yes, take a seat," she said, waving towards the chair opposite her. Brock was a fine specimen. She wouldn't mind collecting him too. For that matter, she thought idly – Adiim had a few of his court she wouldn't mind having. She wondered if they could come to an arrangement. They would be *delicious*.

"It's unnecessary." Jameson had some distaste for Faneh. However, he wasn't that picky. He was more than aware of the Governor's work with the Pavo and her obsession with Adiim. He wanted no fucking part of it. Not to mention he knew all about her type of poison. Hard pass.

"Oh, I think it is necessary. I need to speak with you," Governor Faneh said.

"Have you found out where the Hunter is?" Jameson drawled, his face looking hard and shadowed.

She frowned, her second eyelid catching on her lashes. "Not exactly. But he was on Earth. I want a team dispatched there to immediately speak with the outpost personnel," she cooed. "They might know something. There is a Private there who should be able to provide information."

"Very well." Jameson could do that. He did already have a brief on Hadariel. Although, Jameson was pretty sure that he was dead (or would soon be dead). He'd double check, but it'd only take a moment.

"I will send a team to the planet tomorrow," she smiled. "And I need you to make a pickup."

"A pickup?" Jameson queried, raising an eyebrow.

"Yes. There is a ship on its way in that is carrying important cargo." Faneh looked down at her nails, trailing a hand over her thigh, exposing the expanse of flesh. She looked coyly up at Jameson. "I want you to pick it up."

Jameson was nonplussed. Cargo. Well, with this cold-hearted bitch, it could be anything. "No problem. Send me the coordinates," he paused on his heel. "Is that all?" It was merely out of politeness that he asked.

. . .

"Yes, but it is precious cargo. No deviations." The warning was clear.

"I got it. No deviations." Jameson said that with a tinge of sarcasm. He only half understood the game Faneh was playing here. It didn't matter he told himself. All he cared about was his pay.

"Good. I'll inform you of where it's landing." Faneh glanced at the screen again, her eyes narrowing as her lips turned up in a sinister smile. "You'll be paid handsomely."

"Of course." He turned on his heel and stalked from the office and away from her. He looked down at the intel and then the coordinates. They matched up. He sighed.

Chapter Thirty-One

Paron stalked around Private Hadariel, but he wasn't the only one. Brilius could barely manage to hold himself back as his hands clenched and unclenched. His Earth form strained against the unnatural force pushing him to transform, as his claws pushed through the thin layer of skin of his fingertips.

Hadariel was secured to the chair with bands of iron in the center of the room, a drain below his feet, a table directly in front of him. Paron didn't have to let his power free to know that Hadariel was scared, but he was putting on a good show, keeping his face as free from emotion as he could.

. . .

"Your time is almost up, Hadariel." Paron's voice echoed through the room.

Paron walked around the table, reading Hadariel's face. He was afraid, but he would not show it. Hadariel's chin lifted defiantly, and Paron could feel the man's anxiety radiating.

"You may as well tell us everything. I'm not going to let you escape."

"Fuck you," Hadariel's words were defiant, but there was a pleading note in them.

"That's just too bad." Paron held out his hand, and Brilius gave him what he wanted.

Paron went to the wall and opened a cabinet full of implements. He passed his hand over the contents, and a scalpel. Perfect.

"I'll give you one last chance to answer my questions. You really don't want things to end like this, do you?" Paron asked, nonchalantly. Paron would prefer him suffer if he was honest with himself.

"You're a fool. You're all fools. They'd kill me." Hadariel's voice was desperate, his brown hair matted together with perspiration.

Paron smiled. This was going to be fun. It was hard to keep the glee from his face, but honestly, he was still so afraid for Daisy and so angry about their failure that he needed this and he knew Hadariel would give them everything. He'd rather it be the hard way.

"You will answer the questions, Hadariel. It's only a matter of how long the process takes." Paron sat on the table and sliced Hadariel's cheek open without warning.

Hadariel had no way to brace himself against the pain. He screamed, and blood ran down his face.

"How does it feel? Trapped here in this delicate Earthen body? Weak." Paron's voice was considering. He looked over at Brilius' heaving chest. "So," he began conversationally. "When was your first contact with the enemy?"

"I don't know what you're talking about, please." Hadariel's voice was a whimper.

Paron cut again.

Hadariel screamed again.

"When was your first contact with the Pavo?"

"You're crazy! She'd kill me, you know. If they find out I told you ..."

Paron smiled. He was tiring of this game. He leaned forward; the blade hovering over Hadariel's face, close enough to cut.

"I'll start with your genitals. I wonder how long you'll last then." Paron could taste the spike of fear.

. . .

"Brilius," Paron called. Brilius didn't hesitate to come forward. His breath came in short pants as he tried to control his human form.

"Fuck you." Hadariel's voice came out in a whine, spittle dragging from his mouth.

Maybe he needed a little added motivation.

Paron placed his hand over Hadariel's head, and he said, "Don't move."

Hadariel's eyes went wide as he felt the power flow.

Paron pushed his power into Hadariel's mind, Hadariel whimpered, and his eyes rolled back in his head.

The man was terrified. Paron held his power over the man for a few more moments.

"I'm not going to kill you," Paron said, taking his hand away, and he let the power go.

. . .

Hadariel slumped in his chair.

"Should we try some of these?" Paron asked, showing Brilius the implements on the table. “They’re kind of interesting.”

Brilius thought for a moment. "No. I want him to feel it."

"We want to know where Daisy is." Paron leaned against the table casually while Brilius combed over the implements, practically foaming at the mouth.

"The girl?" Hadariel's eyes were rolling in his sockets, wild with pain. Brilius moved forward — one hand shifted, the claws cold to the touch, biting into Hadariel's skin with each squeeze.

"Yes, the girl. Where is the girl?" There was a deeper note in Brilius' voice, an edge. He slid a hand between Hadariel's legs.

Hadariel screamed in pain.

. . .

"The Pavo took her. Off-planet. I ... I .... I don't know where." His voice ended on a whine, spittle hanging from his mouth.

"Where did they take her?" Paron asked, but Hadariel's mind was gone.

"I don't think I can get anything else from him." Paron said in frustration.

"The Pavo took her. That's all we needed to know. We have to find her now." Brilius growled and squeezed both his hands simultaneously. Blood dripped into the drain.

"I don't know," the Private strangled out a moan. "They moved.... transport ships. Docks."

"Where did they move to?"

"I don't know," Hadariel groaned.

Paron had had enough. He moved his hand over Hadariel's eyes, pushing his power into the man's mind. He felt the presence of the Pavo, closer than they'd thought. He could see a trail, see where they had been. He moved the energy through Hadariel's mind, looking for danger, looking for anything he could use. He rarely used his power like this since the mind was destroyed, but he somehow didn't get the impression that Hadariel was going to make it.

Paron jerked his hand back.

"*Let's go.*" Brilius urged Paron, he wanted to get on the trail. They needed to get in contact with Callan and Eva too. Brilius didn't want to waste any extra time on the private.

"I've gotten everything I can." Paron said simply. "Let's get out of here."

"I'm not leaving him alive," Brilius said, in a dangerous voice. Paron didn't bother mentioning that there wouldn't be a chance of that. Once Paron entered someone's mind like that — there was no return.

Brilius lunged forward, his talons slashing through the shirt and skin of man. He watched as the blood escaped from the fresh wound, pooling on the ground beneath him. He brought his hand to his mouth and tasted the hot liquid, savoring its salty taste as it burst on his tongue.

Brilius stood transfixed over the body, his face twisted in rage and his hands shaking as he dug back into the body, ripping the heart from the man's chest. Paron looked on with a mixture of horror and fascination. He took a few hesitant steps forward to whisper, "We should destroy the body."

"Yes, we should," Brilius said with a smile. "Too bad we don't have time for that," Brilius said, sounding bored with the topic. Brilius tossed the heart to his side casually. “Let the bastard rot for all I care.”

Chapter Thirty-Two

Callan and Eva ported to the public docks along what used to be a major navigation channel into the Pacific Ocean from the city of Portland. The docks still were filled with ships that were heaved up from the water, their hulls streaked with rust and thick, clumpy layers of dried moss and sea life.

Light from the half-moon shined down onto the oily water, casting long shadows from the docks. The water glistening. In the distance, the lights from the city twinkled like diamonds in the night sky.

. . .

The docks were spacious, as they had been built to accommodate large ships. The wood carved, planed, and weathered by salt.

This was the location that Private Hadariel had given, according to what Callan was told. Brilius and Paron materialized next to them. Eva could hardly hold back the gasp that tore from her throat. Brilius and Paron stood stained with blood, their eyes wild.

"Brilius, Paron are you okay?" Eva asked as she took a step forward. Callan put his hand on her shoulder, but she shook it off. They seemed out of place, like two predators that had just returned from the hunt. Both were breathing heavily, coming down from the adrenaline.

"I'm fine," Brilius said with a grimace.

"You look like shit my friend," Callan said as he looked him over.

"Hey," Brilius snapped.

. . .

Paron looked around and then at the docks. "We need to move fast."

"Are you okay Paron?" she asked, trying not to lose composure.

She pushed a tendril of thought through the link to Callan. *Fated?*

They're alright. Brilius' eyes were bright, animal like behind the glassy texture of the humanoid orbs. She could tell that he was holding on to the Earth form with gossamer threads.

Sapphrius ported in. Her blond hair neat as a pin. Her eyes darted to each of them. Eva knew Callan had given him the information that he had, which wasn't much. Eva could see her draw herself up, straightening her spine, nodding to Callan.

"My King, my Queen." Sapphrius inclined her head.

"What happened?" she asked, once again trying to keep the panic at bay.

. . .

"Hadariel didn't make it." Paron's voice held no remorse. Brilius gave a rough, guttural snort.

"I hope you got everything you could out of him first," Callan clucked his tongue at them, but he couldn't help but send a concerned look at Brilius. He was a wreck. Brilius' hair was standing on end, the blond ends crimson. There was spatter on every piece of clothing that he was wearing. His fingers were bloody to his wrists. He looked as if he had ripped the Private apart. Certainly, it wouldn't have surprised Callan at all.

"Well, what do we have to go on then?" Eva asked, matter of fact. She shot a glance at Brilius. "I'd offer you a wet nap, but one isn't going to do you any good." She moved towards him, leaning forward and kissed his cheeks, leaning into him.

Paron and Callan stilled. Brilius sighed as Eva's warmth met his own, she seemed unperturbed by the blood.

"We don't have much to go on, do we?" she said, allowing Brilius to wrap one of his hands up and softly squeeze her neck. She gave a small smile to Callan and Paron. "You got something though, right?"

"What did Hadariel give us?" Callan asked.

"Just that he was instructed to get information about Eva." Paron looked apologetically to Callan. "It was all Pavo's schemes. Someone thought if they got information, they could use it against you. With it then they'd be able to manipulate you. Negotiate with the Shade. Hadariel mentioned a female."

Eva pulled back from Brilius. Her mind spinning. So, Daisy had gotten picked up instead of her. They had thought they could use Callan's Fated against him. Or did they even know about that? Likely not.

"Hadariel said that they transported Daisy from here. From the docks. We are hoping there is something to find here. It's not much of a lead," Brilius said, sheepishly.

"At least you got something out of him." Eva said.

. . .

"Not enough." Brilius' eyes fell to the ground.

Callan looked to Paron. He had known him for centuries. "What else?"

Paron looked to his King.

"I saw in his memories a transaction taking place. An argument between Hadariel and a Pavo. It didn't look like a standard buy. Hadariel was giving information out, but he didn't know if they had already gotten her, or if they had found her." Paron's eyes were downcast. "But there were clear details, fragments, that suggested ..." Paron hesitated.

"Suggested?" Eva encouraged him.

"It's hard for me to articulate exactly my Queen," Paron tried. "I'll need to let my power loose for a moment." He hesitated to do so. It was hard to explain to others, but the emotions were so high right now. However, he saw immediately that Eva understood.

. . .

She set her hand over his. "Go ahead." He gave her a nod and let his power free, letting it wash over him. Eva wasn't sure if she was helping, but she tried to somehow buffer the others' emotions. While he could still sense Brilius' rage and despair, it was not as sharp. Callan's emotions were banked, careful.

"There were moments that he was present for. Meetings that he was there for." Paron closed his eyes, feeling the grip of Eva's fingers over his wrist, concentrating. "Hadariel was afraid. It was bigger than the Pavo. He hadn't realized. That the fish were so big. A Governor." Paron's eyes opened.

Eva smiled at him. "Well done." She was sure that would help.

"Holy shit." Brilius heaved a breath. "This is bad if there are IGC Governors involved. This is all intentional." Brilius looked to the others.

"Yes. This is bad." Callan's mind was already thinking through an action plan. "Well, let's look and see if we can find anything here first. Just to be sure. I doubt it." Callan swept a hand through his hair in frustration. Well, if this was the play then they'd need to be faster, better, more devious. "We need to be quick." Callan looked into the darkness. "I'm not feeling positive about it."

Paron frowned, thinking. "The information that they were getting from Hadariel was mainly about Eva. He didn't know anything about Daisy specifically. He thought he had leverage before. He was trying to get information on Eva. He was trying to get out of a deal."

"That's true." Eva let out a heavy breath. "I hope they don't realize that Daisy isn't me. Or think that she's expendable."

They were starting to walk down the dock toward the water.

"Let's see if we can find anything that will give us a clue where they took her." Brilius said.

They followed Brilius down the dock, the wooden planks creaking beneath their feet.

. . .

They were silent as they went along. Eva could sense the doubt in their thoughts. The worry that there would be nothing. The fear that they wouldn't be able to find Daisy. A few times she felt Brilius' rage, she looked to him. He would look back, straightening his posture. He was trying to stop. She smiled at him.

"If you were going to take someone from here, where would you take someone?" Eva asked the group.

Angry as she was about being a pawn, she knew Daisy was probably scared and confused. She couldn't imagine how frightening it would be.

"There are lots of options. Too many," Brilius said. "They'd only meet here for a transaction potentially. If they took a transport from here. With connections??" Brilius looked over to Callan. "They could be anywhere in the universe."

Callan had been thinking as they walked. "Well, I had planned to set aside my role with the IGC that we have been taking on. It has been time to go back to the Shade for a while now." He chewed his lip pensively.

. . .

Sapphrius nodded. She'd been porting around the docks and had rejoined the group. "There isn't anything here. If there was a transport ship here it's gone," her words were quiet, somber.

"What's next then? If they took Daisy, it was for a reason. Ransom?" Eva's mind spun. Holy shit. Her best friend was just gone. She glanced over at Callan, Brilius, Paron, Sapphrius. Well, she would burn the fucking universe down for Daisy. No way would the Pavo get to keep her.

Sapphrius sent her a glance. "We could recall Serix and take the court back to the Shade." Eva narrowed her eyes at Sapphrius. She wasn't sure what her game was.

"Or?" It was Paron who spoke up. "We could stop fucking playing fucking games."

Sapphrius didn't take offense but stopped where she was. "*Or*, we can stop fucking around. They took someone because they wanted the Shade. They want the resources of the Shade – what the Shade offers." Her eyes gleamed.

. . .

“I agree,” Callan said, coming closer to Eva, stroking up her arm. Eva slowly turned as he spoke. “I think it’s time they meet the Shade.” Callan held his hand out to his Fated, his eyes glowing in the darkness.

"Let's introduce them then." Eva's voice was sure as she set her hand in his. "And get Daisy back."

To Be Continued ... follow my Author Page to be alerted for Book 2

Afterword

Thank you for reading my book! Every page read makes me so happy.

If you enjoyed this book please consider leaving a review on Amazon, Goodreads etc. Even a few sentences means so much to authors who publish on their own.

Follow my author page on Amazon to get automatically updated for new titles.

Made in the USA
Las Vegas, NV
19 May 2023